Nicole Locke discovered her first romance novels in her grandmother's closet, where they were secretly hidden. Convinced that books that were hidden must be better than those that weren't, Nicole greedily read them. It was only natural for her to start writing them—but now not so secretly!

Discover more at millsandboon.co.uk.

HER DARK KNIGHT'S REDEMPTION

Nicole Locke

MILLS & BOON

First published in Great Britain 2019
by Mills & Boon, an imprint of HarperCollins*Publishers*
1 London Bridge Street, London, SE1 9GF

Large Print edition 2020

© 2019 Nicole Locke

ISBN: 978-0-263-08628-7

MIX
Paper from
responsible sources
FSC™ C007454

This book is produced from independently certified
FSC™ paper to ensure responsible forest management. For
more information visit www.harpercollins.co.uk/green.

Printed and bound in Great Britain
by CPI Group (UK) Ltd, Croydon, CR0 4YY

There are some readers
who just keep you going. And I owe
two such readers my great thanks
for cheering me on through this book.

Diane, our chats have been such a joy
when I was writing the darkest parts
of this story. Especially special?
Your messages of 'How's it going?'
I must admit those kept me writing
on days I feared the keyboard!

Karine, it has been a
serendipitous gift meeting
you through your wonderful blog
https://songedunenuitdete.com. Those
pictures you sent me of beautiful
Troyes were a brilliant inspiration!
Thank you!

Chapter One

France—1297

'I can assure you, *monsieur*, the child is yours.'

Reynold didn't bother to turn for the woman who was standing behind him. He rarely acknowledged anyone unless it suited him. The woman's guttural accent and well-aged sweat stench ensured that she was most definitely beneath him in every way.

In truth, almost everyone was. If Reynold was forced to entertain among the parasites who clung to the teat of court, he would say, but for the King of England, he was beneath no man.

In the privacy of his own home, he barely acknowledged he was beneath God.

He was a knight, highly skilled and deadly with almost every sword and blade man had ever made. Yet what no one knew was the fact that he was deadlier with the games he played. Those who did discover this hidden talent didn't survive to spread the tale.

He was also fortunate enough to possess wealth

that rivalled King Edward's. Some of it was amply displayed in his private chambers, where he and the peasant behind him stood. Cascading silks, intricate gold-threaded embroidery in colours resembling precious gemstones and volumes of books. He owned many homes and travelled more than any man he knew, and the books always travelled with him.

The only matter that irked him was his wealth didn't rival the church's. But he consoled himself that they had had a thousand years in their plundering and he had years ahead of him to bridge the difference.

He was all of this, yet what set him above others was his family name: Warstone. Through that title, he gained unimaginable power and unparalleled fear. Though he wanted only to obliterate every last relation, tear down every monument and shred all scrolls bearing the name he was born into, for now, he used it for his purposes. In the end, it suited the games he played. And he looked forward to the time when the name wouldn't matter anymore. Then he wouldn't acknowledge the Warstone legacy just as he didn't acknowledge the commoner shifting warily behind him.

Commoners always shifted when in his presence, often readied their little feet to make a dash for safety. It never did them any good. They could run to beyond the edge of existence and, if he desired, they'd be dead. Nobles were too stupid or lazy to realise they should be warier in his presence. Instead, they often shared their pitiful lives or confessed…as if he'd have pity.

Wondering if the wench behind him needed to die, he shifted his gaze from the sights beyond his window, to the reflection in the glass which revealed a distorted reflection of her…and a child she held.

Distorted, but enough to know from her dark hair to her tattered clothing that the babe in her arms couldn't be his…if that was to be her claim. It was visual information that didn't surprise or please him and he waited for what her fear should be telling her. *Run.*

Perhaps she had some noble blood and didn't know her life was about to end. Not here, in this particular undisclosed home in the heart of Paris, however. He wouldn't sully this sanctuary with her spilled blood.

But die she must. He didn't abide by liars or cheats and, by her clothes and the colour of her hair, she displayed both these traits.

For now, he waited. The night sky was black, but not still. All around were the twinkling of candles among the haphazard elegant buildings. If he strained his hearing, he could discern sounds of laughter and shouts. Paris never slept. It was one of the reasons he enjoyed coming here. There was a certain acceptance of all walks of life, both human and animal. And since the city housed everyone and everything, he enjoyed his anonymity. Because until his game was done, he didn't want to be found.

'*Monsieur?*'

'Are you still there?' he replied.

The woman's small gasp reminded him why he allowed her access to his home in the first place. Vermin often provided distraction from the long winter nights. This was her sole purpose when his guards notified him that a woman requested to see him. The only difference between her and all the others insisting on his presence was that this one carried a child.

When he granted her access, he hadn't exactly felt curiosity. That would have implied some emotion and, as usual, he felt absolutely nothing. After all, she wouldn't be the only woman to claim a child was his. There had been many such claims since he was old enough to procreate. So many false claims carved out his longing for a child and buried it along with his heart somewhere along the darkened paths he had been forced to take. Still, he craved what he read in a book: about a home and hearth after a long journey. What he had never experienced in life—a family, a *true* family—and so he granted her access.

But now that he saw her reflection, he regretted his impromptu decision.

Now he had to suffer through her denials, perhaps pay her some coin. Most likely he'd order her killed. Disappointing.

Returning his gaze to her reflection, he continued, 'The child isn't mine, but the coin you'll receive when you leave could be yours.' Temporarily. 'But only if you leave now without another word.'

He prayed she'd keep quiet, even though he knew she wouldn't. A waste of a life and his time. He had never lain with this woman. It wasn't her poverty giving her away, it was the colour of her hair.

He never laid with a dark-haired woman when his own was as black as his soul. He wanted no babe to be called his. Oh, he knew it held no certainty—however, he was a master at bending the odds in his favour.

Thus, he never lay with the same woman twice, never left a trace of him in her bed or semen in her body. Never lay with a dark-haired, or a grey-eyed, woman. If she had a babe, then the babe had a possibility to be fair like the mother and he could deny his responsibility.

'The child's yours, if you'd only look.' The woman took a step forward, her foot soft on the wood planking. She wasn't properly shod for winter. Another desperate wench trying to survive the last months of winter. Too bad she spoke and ensured she wouldn't survive this evening.

'Words you give me,' he said. 'It appears you don't want the coin. I'd have my guards take you from this room, but I'm aware of the child in your arms. For its sake, I will give you until the count of three to leave. After that, whatever harm comes your—'

A coarse laugh erupted from the woman. 'I knew you'd be like this. Cold and unforgiving. But I don't care, it suits my purposes, it does.'

This woman had…purposes. Intriguing. If this commoner had purposes, she knew something about him. If so, his need for anonymity had been compromised, which didn't suit his games at all.

His survival depended on his obscurity. This woman would die, but he had questions first. Deliberately, Reynold turned and swept his eyes from her feet to her features.

The woman was far coarser than her reflection revealed. From the roughness of her skin to the mud staining the bottom of her gown, the very air she held was one of servitude, and something else he recognised...greed.

Avarice. It was that emotion prompting him to look at the babe in her arms. If she had financial purposes, they weren't well planned. The child was small and he hadn't been in Paris for almost two years. This one looked puny and, despite the icy winter wind, the babe was scarcely covered. The cheeks and hands red though they'd waited inside his heated home.

The head, however, was completely exposed, revealing a shocking amount of black hair. Black hair similar to that of the woman in front of him. But she wasn't claiming the child was hers...only his.

With hair that dark, he could not immediately dismiss it. 'Who is your mistress?'

'Not my mistress, though I pretend she is. Paid me nicely to keep quiet, but I knew you'd return so I waited. I waited, because as much money as she had, you have more.'

The woman shrewdly perused the room, her eyes resting on a gold enamelled box. 'I'd say you have plenty more.'

'You say the babe is mine and the mother paid you to keep quiet about me? You're quite the confidante.'

'I'm no confidant or friend. I hate her. She believes I am only fit to empty her chamber pot. No one looks at the servant cleaning their piss. But I was there the night she left to visit you and I was there the months after you left. When the time came, I let her know I was noticing.'

The woman smirked. 'Thought she was the clever widow, passing off the child as another gentleman's. So when I said I knew it wasn't his, she paid me exactly what I asked her to. She begged me not to tell her current lover because he paid her more because of it.

'But I got wise, 'cause she loves this child, and she paid me quick. This woman is cold, like you. She wasn't afraid I'd tell that listless braggart who moaned between her spread legs. Oh, no, she was scared I would tell the true father.

'That's when I knew you were important. That's when I knew you'd have the hefty coin. Something to set me up real nice.'

His memory flashed of a wealthy blonde widow who took coin for her favours. Though he couldn't remember her name or exactly what she looked like, there was such a widow here and he had lain with her a year ago.

An emotion scraped across his heart. One he hadn't felt since he overheard his parents' machinations to break him. It was now slinking across his insides as if it had merely been waiting. It was faint, but even so, familiar.

Fear.

Because though there was enough evidence before him to question this commoner's truth, there was enough plausibility for it to be true. A greedy servant, a black-haired child and a wealthy mistress, who loved her child enough to protect it against him. The widow he thought of had been a courtier, but had fallen on hard times, thus, an exception to his rules. She was a noble who knew how to run.

But on the heels of that fear was something bright and piercing. If this child was his...he couldn't think that way. Mustn't despite everything, but already he could feel the need to hold her in his arms, to see for himself. As he had done so many times before. Would the need never stop haunting him?

And how could a true mother let this child into the arms of the vile creature before him? 'What did you do to her?'

'I've done nothing to the mother.' The woman shifted the child in her arms. 'She's at her home, she is.'

'You'd have me believe you stole a child from its mother? It's more likely the child's yours.'

'It has black hair.'

'You have dark hair.'

The woman made an impatient sound. More warnings went off in his head.

'She won't want to see you. Why don't you pay me and I'll hand it over? Don't you want your own child?'

She held it like an offering and the child opened its eyes. He couldn't see their colour, but he could see this child was a plausible age. Small, under-fed, but old enough to be his.

He risked all, listening to this woman. He risked more if he didn't. He could kill this wench and the babe, but a mother with a missing child would put more players in his game than he was willing to manoeuvre. His board was already full.

Unfortunately, he didn't know where the mother lived for they had met at another location. A flaw in his clever plan for anonymity.

So his only option was to follow this wench and step outside. He might as well be stepping into a trap. Now this was a distraction worthy of his attention. 'Prove to me you're not the mother and you'll get what you came for.'

The woman's eyes narrowed. 'I take you and you'll pay me?'

If this mother wasn't the woman he lain with, he'd give one clean swipe of his blade across her neck to silence her for ever. Then he'd stab and twist the knife into the heart of this traitor, so she'd feel it. Liars every one.

If the child was his, it had no place in his life. His brothers would kill it, but only after torture. If the child was truly his, and he cared at all, he'd turn around and abandon it all over again.

He had enough players on the board and more moves to make. He might not have started this particular game, but he was determined to finish it. A child had no place in his life. As for the servant, she'd be lucky to survive his blade.

He kept his gaze on the wretched woman before him. 'If this child is mine, I'll reward you amply.'

Chapter Two

'You could not have possibly done what I think you have done.' Aliette pinched the bridge of her nose and clenched her eyes. A temporary solution to the very visible evidence she returned to after the morning's work.

'I didn't,' Gabriel said readily.

Ten years of age, his tuft of brown hair sticking up, his light brown eyes framed by eyelashes wasted on a boy. He looked innocent, but everything he said was a lie.

A good lie. She suspected he said it to ease her worries, but it was all too apparent he had indeed gone out and stolen four loaves of bread. She didn't want it to be true.

It needed to not be true.

But it was. Just as it was true she was responsible for a ten-year-old boy whose parents have been sent to the gallows and an elderly couple, Vernon and Helewise, who were ripping into their bread as though they hadn't eaten properly in a sennight...which they hadn't.

She was failing them. At least Vernon and Helewise were used to it, they had been with her the longest. Before her, they had survived on their own. Aliette discovered them over a year ago, in another part of Paris, sitting on the ground in the filth of the streets. Helewise, whose bones were crooked from her ears to her toes, and Vernon, whose eyes were so clouded he couldn't see more than shadows. They were too frail to move when slop was thrown on them.

Over the years since she'd been abandoned in Paris, she'd seen hundreds of street beggars. The old or frail were usually dead within a week either by starvation, assault or reckless carriages.

But not these two and they fascinated her. Over many weeks, she'd watched as Helewise, too crippled to walk, told Vernon where to find food. They made terrible thieves. Vernon, almost blind, was slow and Helewise's loud verbal commands let any nimble, listening child to reach the prize first. There were no fresh loaves for them or animal-trough remains. In truth, what they scavenged was dropped by others or given by charity.

Filthy, starving, but nothing hardened their souls as it did the others, as it had done to her. They were kind to each other and shared food if they were fortuitous that day or the warmth of their bodies if they weren't.

But her observing ended the day Vernon made

Helewise laugh. It wasn't the laugh of the privileged, full of conquering lightness. Nor was it the laughing sneer of the street. Her laugh was full of…she didn't know. It lit up both of them and did something to her heart as well. Like warmth, only so much better.

That was the day she gave them every scrap of food she'd scavenged and they welcomed her to sit with them. Then they gave her stories. Of who they were and where they came from. Stories about legends and brave heroines and love. That was the word they used. Love.

Was love what kept their souls intact? Whatever it had been, something began that day she gave them food. At first, she thought the tightening in her chest was something foul she ate, but the feeling grew and wouldn't let up. It was like that warmth which spread with Helewise's laugh, but it had an achy longing about it as well.

A longing for something she knew she'd never possess. Her parents had abandoned her. No matter how much she wished for someone to love her, it wouldn't happen. If she was capable of giving or receiving it, she certainly would have found someone in all the years since. Still, seeing love between Vernon and Helewise, she wouldn't let it go either. Even if at times her longing filled her with sorrow and not just warmth.

She blamed that longing for moving them to where she had been living: under a small bridge. It was in an industrial area of Paris, with no private homes or residences where respectable people could potentially force them to leave because it was too near the tanners and stank.

When shelter and safety were tantamount, scents that made your eyes water mattered little. She couldn't count the times she'd been accosted or had a weapon pointed at her. Sometimes it was to take something away from her like food or clothing. Most times, they looked at her as a threat and used a dagger, or a large blunt stick to ward her away.

Paris was a jumble of wealth and poverty and she'd learned to take advantage of the good within the bad. And there were drawbacks with the bridge, the lack of walls not much of one. The true drawback was it was far from any food and much too far for Helewise and Vernon to scavenge on their own. It was up to Aliette to feed them.

On one of these travels, she'd spotted Gabriel outside the gaol making sounds she'd never heard in her life. On the streets, there was abuse and maiming. There were harsh words and harsher fists, but the street's survivors were bitter or angry.

Gabriel's helpless sobs were as if his heart was cracking. As though he only just realised life contained cruelty. He cried as an innocent would cry. A word Aliette knew, but had never truly understood. She tried to be good, but she stole and lied. Her life couldn't afford anything pure. Gabriel's clothes, though worn, were newish and clean. And he looked soft despite the bloodied mutilated mess where his right ear used to be. He had never been born and raised on the streets as she had.

As the guards had. Guards who chatted because the sounds of a weeping child near their feet was meaningless to them. For Aliette, Gabriel's defenceless whimpers called to her.

A few gentle questions his way and he told her of his parents' imprisonment and their hanging scheduled the next day. How he had no one and no home. He could tell her nothing of why they chopped his ear and not given him a simple flogging. Such an extreme punishment for one so young.

His eyes were so full of grief, so full of fear. Half-starved despite the cleanliness of his clothes. Despite his ear, his hands told her he wasn't raised on the streets like her. She knew what happened to soft children. To thieve or be used. By the carving of his ear, he had failed at thieving. She refused for anything else to happen to him.

Slowly, coaxingly, she led him to their home under the bridge. His feet were laden down with exhaustion, hunger and loss. His eyes darting from her to every corner, looking for traps.

No matter her soft words, he remained wary until Vernon greeted him and Helewise opened her arms and, crumpling at Helewise's feet, Gabriel laid his head on her knees and promptly fell asleep.

The longing to belong grew fiercely inside Aliette. The life she led with Helewise and Vernon wasn't good enough for Gabriel. She could no longer steal a few turnips or potatoes. She needed proper food. They needed more than huddling under a bridge with one blanket. To achieve that she couldn't only steal, she needed work.

Which wasn't easy. Everyone needed to work. For an unskilled woman, no one was willing to pay her actual coin, but after a while of going from market stall to shop to farmer, she found people who paid her for work with extra food, day old bread, more threadbare blankets.

So much work, but eventually their supplies were noticed. Gabriel had gained strength, but not enough to defend against thieves or those with weapons. She needed to protect her acquired family.

She had searched abandoned homes, but more

than once she returned to the bridge with bruises and cuts made by residents who guarded their territory. It forced her to venture into finer neighbourhoods, until she discovered one that had been once grand, but now lay neglected. Many of the homes were boarded, the owners waiting for years until the area became suitable again.

The house she found was boarded tightly up, secure against those too lazy or desperate to break in.

Over a period of weeks, she watched the property and worked the back boards on the servants' entrance loose. When she walked through the dank rooms, she knew she'd found what they needed. The roof didn't leak much, there was a space for a small fire and there was furniture for comfort. Chairs and tables. *Beds.*

They couldn't have asked for a better home. With such fine furnishings, she suspected the owners might have left Paris for the winter and she didn't imagine that they could live here indefinitely. Spring would soon be here, though there was no sign of it. And a few extra months until warmer weather would give them much reprieve and allow Gabriel to gain better health.

But Gabriel had stolen and jeopardised everything.

Without unclenching her eyes, she said, 'At

least tell me you didn't steal them all from the same baker.'

'Not at all,' the boy quipped, not an ounce of guile in his words. To him, the words he said were the honest truth. Yet it was another lie since the remaining untouched loaves bore the same mark from the same bakery. He said the words to make her feel better.

Nothing about this could make her feel better. She had two options. She'd need to return the loaves or pay for them. Neither scenario would end well for them. If she returned the loaves, it was likely he wouldn't accept them and she had no money to pay.

Easing her hand away from her stinging nose, she let out a breath and opened her eyes. Gabriel's large brown eyes were more enormous than ever and sheened with tears.

His gangly body shuddered when she embraced him. He did not put his arms around her, but she did not expect him to. Almost three months with him and he was still unused to a kind touch. Who had he been before his parents were sent to the gallows?

'I was only trying to help.' Gabriel wiped his nose with his sleeve. 'Helewise and Vernon's stomachs are growling and the potatoes are rotten.'

That was because she pinched them out of a hog's trough and counted herself fortunate that she grabbed them before anyone else since they were only half-rotten. She was working, but it only accounted for some of their needs. More often, she depended on what she could scavenge.

All of them thieves, none of them good. Her, least of all. That was the reason her family left her in Paris when she was five. Fifteen years didn't make a difference. She was still appalling at it.

Now this. Four loaves from the same baker meant they'd be noticed. She'd take back two of the loaves immediately while they were still fresh.

First though, she'd observe the baker interact with his customers. If he wasn't kind or reasonable when she returned them, they'd be hunted the next time they walked the market. It was a risk she wasn't willing to take. This was the best home they'd had and she knew they wouldn't find another before the winter ended.

'I need to go.'

'Don't,' Gabriel begged. 'Let me do it. I did the wrong.'

Was this how he had lost his parents? They went out, committed some crime and couldn't return? These questions would never be answered, though she'd tried that first day and the next to see them privately. To this day, Gabriel said nothing of what he was stealing for the punishment of losing his ear. In fact, he didn't talk about his childhood, ever.

She bent to bring her eyes level with his. 'You did nothing wrong. Please don't think that. But I need you to stay with Vernon and Helewise to keep them safe or help them escape. You know this.'

Gabriel clenched his jaw and she glimpsed the man he'd be. One didn't stay a child long on the streets.

'I'll be back for you.'

Gabriel shook, sneezed and shook some more.

She wouldn't be his parents. She wouldn't leave any of them. They were a family now. One she'd found, one she protected, one she was giving her life for.

'No matter what it takes, Gabriel. No matter what, I'll return.'

Chapter Three

Down the winding pathways Reynold followed the woman carrying the child. She made one more offer for him to hold it, but he refused and she didn't ask again.

Another turn in the muddied, roughly cobbled streets. This area had once been grand, but now held the musk of ages, the patina brushed away to show instead the mortar underneath.

He had picked this part of neglected Paris to reside in because it contained no lavish homes. No grand balls or people with influence. In every city he stayed in he avoided those parts of town.

It didn't suit his games to be noticed and ostentatious wealth was always noticed. He made only one exception to the rule of absolute anonymity: his books. He had too many to hide and they were far too precious for him to leave behind. They travelled with him to every home. So, despite the many pains he took to blend into the fabric of every city he visited, his books were always seen. Only an individual with an obscene amount of wealth could own such luxury. But what could he do? They were his family, his sole comfort. At least they were quiet and could be kept at home.

As he should be doing now. Another turn and the woman stopped in front of a door.

This home was more derelict than the rest. Windows were cracked and curtains were scorched from the sun; from this distance, it was clear the silk was thin and frayed. Even the daub was crumbling into the street, forcing the wattle to look more like a skeleton than a house. He glanced down the street. Most of the other houses in this area were boarded up. This was the only one occupied.

If it was occupied.

'She's in there,' the woman said, shifting the child again. It was awake and the angle she held it, with its head on her shoulder, showed the full length. Yes, this was a child who could be his.

His. A burgeoning warmth, hope, bloomed inside his chest and he crushed it. Cursed ever reading Odysseus's tale and giving him ideas that there could be more for him. Nothing and no one ever was.

There would be no hearth and home at the end of his journey. There would be only death. His only hope was that he took his family down with him.

'Let's go in.'

She looked to the child, then him.

He had no intention of taking that child now or later. He was free to block attacks and to make one of his own. Unburdened, he was free to leave and continue his games.

The woman eyed him, surprised he refused the child. 'One look and you'll know it's her you spilled your seed in,' she said. 'You'll know this burden's yours.'

Even if it was…it didn't matter. He was too close to what he'd been born to do: to take down his family.

'Then we shouldn't tarry much more,' he said, fully intending for her to enter first. 'One more look and you'll be a rich woman. What's keeping you?'

The indecision in her eyes turned to greed again, to cruelty. Ah, yes, he was familiar with people like her. They were easy to manipulate.

She pushed open the door. The sounds and the smells accosted him immediately.

Sobbing. A woman's cries as if everything in her world was gone and missing. Deep racks of grief interrupted by coughs and wheezes. By wet gurgles, like a clogged brook.

Like blood that didn't stay within the body, but

came up through the lungs and out of mouths and noses, forced through tiny pores in the skin.

Which explained the smells. The dank smell of mould, a leaking roof allowing mildew to move along the walls. That smell fought for dominance over the acrid smell of piss and human waste.

But it was a deep cloying scent that permeated the entire house and settled against his very soul. Death. Human decay, as if they walked straight into a desecrated tomb of newly buried bodies.

It stopped him in his tracks.

'Told you to stay at your fancy home, didn't I?' the woman sneered at his side. 'I told you to stay and take the babe, but you had to come. Suits me fine, but I was only trying to be nice, to do you a favour. Had to make it difficult for me. Wasn't as though I wanted to come back to this either. I've had to suffer enough these last months, waiting for you to return. Should make you pay me more for coming back when I thought I didn't have to.'

What was wrong with him this evening? Why did he stop? He didn't let boredom overcome his safety and allow strangers in his home, especially those he was soon to kill.

'Cilla? Cilla, is that you?' A woman's thinned voice wafted from another room. Cultured and reedy with sickness. 'Do you have her, Cilla? Did you bring her back to me?'

The wretch, Cilla, glanced his way, her eyes narrowing. He shook his head once which was enough for her to understand she needed to stay quiet about his presence. It didn't hurt that it suited her purposes as well.

With a shrug, she swept into the other room. 'I'm here with your bastard, my lady.'

'Oh!' Fresh tears, the sound of joy and gratefulness. 'I thought you'd left. I thought you took her.'

Reynold held back. He needed a bit more exchange between these two to satisfy his purposes.

'I merely took her for a walk,' Cilla said. 'She needed a bit of air.'

'What would I do without you, Cilla? You're so…good for her and me. Staying with me when everyone else left. Keeping her well, keeping her away from the sickness. Of course, she needed air. But…she needs me more. Bring her here, please.'

The tone of her voice, a cadence broken by hacking coughs, he did not recognise, and Reynold waited longer in the shadows. He liked waiting in the shadows.

A snapping of blankets, grunts from Cilla and wheezes from her mistress. Reynold envisioned Cilla giving the child back to its mother.

'But you were wrong to take her without letting me know,' the woman's thin voice now containing some superiority. 'You made me worry. You know how I cannot have any worry in my condition. Once I recover, your deeds will have to have some consequences.'

'Of course, mistress,' Cilla said. No doubting she had heard this argument before. The words held no threat. The woman in the other room was dying.

Dying, but cultured with a ring of privilege. Perhaps she was the noblewoman he had lain with those many months ago. There was only one way to discover that, by stepping into the other room.

Silently, a few paltry steps and everything was revealed to him. The room held scant pieces of furniture, no tables or niceties. The wooden floors highly polished where a rug once had been. The colours of rose and yellow in the broken bench hinting at what the room once must have been. A grand parlour.

Now it was a sick bed with a full chamber pot underneath, and various small linens flung around it like bloodied halos.

A few more moments lost as the woman spoke to Cilla, but kept her eyes on the child like a lifeline. The sickness had made harsh lines fan from her eyes, but as she gazed at the child, they softened.

Privileged. Entitled. But that gaze was of a

mother to her child. Whether she was a fallen noble or whore, she loved the child who was trying to sit in her arms.

'Did you bring any...?' The woman's voice drifted as her travelling gaze fell on Reynold and held there.

He didn't recognise the house or the room because he had never been here before. But he did recognise the woman lying on the bench with blankets draped over her thin frame. The sickness had ravaged that frame and sucked the glow from her cheeks.

He didn't remember her name, her station, or the night he found temporary relief within her body.

He didn't remember the thick gold of her hair because every woman he'd lain with had a similar colour. However, he did remember the colour of her eyes. He remembered that all too well, for when he first saw her he calculated that colour against his own dark grey and wondered whether the dark blue was too close to his own. That if there was a babe, it would be mistaken for his.

No woman was worth any unnecessary risk. But he remembered her false haughtiness and her weakness. Traits that suited his purpose as well as the feminine parts of her body. So they shared a bed for an hour or two and he paid her well. He always paid them well.

'You,' the woman whispered.

'Me,' he answered.

Weak and dying, but at his appearance, she attempted some dignity. While holding her lips together didn't cease the coughs from racking her body, she daintily held a blood-crusted cloth to her mouth instead. When they eased, she shifted her eyes from Reynold back to Cilla. 'You brought him.'

'You're sick, mistress,' Cilla said with oily concern. 'The babe needs her father.'

A widening of blue eyes, a flash of fear that no tainted cloth could cover. 'That's not her father. I told you who her father was. I *told* you.'

Despite the mother clutching the child close to lay down with her, it sat up fully and crammed its mouth with its fist. A girl, but only because the mother had called it such. Black hair, but in this dim light and his distance he could not tell the colour of her eyes.

'We both know you didn't mean it,' Cilla said. 'This child has hair like her father's, not that dandy you pointed out with his balding pate.'

The woman kept her eyes and her conversation solely with Cilla, as if ignoring him or pretending he wasn't there would make him disappear.

He wouldn't leave now that he heard her terrified protestations. This dying woman was frightened by his presence.

His family connection, and their ruthlessness, was enough for her to worry, but wasn't enough for her horror, or the sense of helplessness in her gaze and the vulnerability straining her frail body.

He saw it all though she refused to look at him. Her body convulsed again, worse than before. Great racking contortions as her knees drew up and she curled around herself and the babe.

Reynold did not move, nor did the child. Whatever illness was taking its mother, it had been doing so for a long time. Long enough that it didn't concern the child. To the babe, the stench, the decay, the coughing was what a mother smelled and sounded like.

'I told you,' the woman said, her voice gasping, the coughing, the illness too much for her. 'I trusted you.'

'You're alive, you are, and so is your babe,' Cilla said.

The woman tried to draw breath. Too weak to protect her child from the servant who could easily pluck her away again. Too ill to protect the child from him. But he watched her push the child across her stomach until it rolled behind her so that it was wedged between her and the bench's back. As if her prone wasted body could be any sort of a shield against him.

It was *possible* this child was his. 'Is it mine?'

The woman never opened her eyes. Her pretending he didn't exist was her last and only defence against him.

'Is it mine?' he repeated.

'Of course it's yours,' Cilla retorted. 'Little demon's a year if it's a day. A year of me waiting in this filth and waiting on this corpse for you to return.'

'How could you…?' the noblewoman said.

'I did what you wanted,' Cilla said. 'What you begged so prettily for. What was it again? Not to let anyone know you were sick. Mustn't let anyone know such common illness affected your noble blood.'

The woman opened her eyes again, not to look at Reynold, but to the servant. 'I beg you… Save her.'

With hot certainty, Reynold knew it was no longer a possibility. The child was his… For this mother asked not to save the babe from poverty or sickness, but to save the child. From him.

'Why would I do that?' Cilla said. 'He's here to collect.'

The child… All his life women claimed pregnancy. None of them were true. The noblewoman ignored him, but he needed his answers.

'How did you know who I was?'

All eyes went to him.

'You don't…remember me?' she said.

No rejection in her reedy voice, only the slight sound of victory.

'Your man…a carriage.'

He always hired a man. A temporary hire, for a temporary solution. He found a woman who would suit his needs, found a man for hire to procure her and bring her to an awaiting carriage.

All his women were done this way. A protection for him, a protection for them. This significant memory of hers provided no more information for him.

'You couldn't have known who I was,' he said. 'Who told you? Who—?'

'It stinks and I don't need to stay,' Cilla interrupted. 'It's her, you know that now. You know that's your babe—I want what's my due.' She laughed a cruel greed. Gleeful that her plan for great wealth had paid off. 'I brought the happy family together. Don't I deserve something?'

He'd forgotten the wretch was in the room. With his spare hand, Reynold brought his purse to the front. Let the full weight of it sound as he jangled the coins. It was heavy. He'd purposefully filled it to the brim.

The woman's eyes bulged. For him, this wasn't but convenient coin. The enamel gold box at his home was worth more than his purse, but she wasn't a smart villain. Not smart at all, because she had threatened him.

'I said I'd reward you amply. I came prepared.'

''Cause I spoke the truth,' she said, her eyes remaining on the purse, not on the blade he hid in the folds of his cloak.

He walked slowly to her, raised the purse so it raised her eyes and exposed her neck. Her hands reached—and then…something that he had never done before. Something he was unprepared for: he hesitated.

The servant registered the blade and attacked with outstretched claws across his cheek. Feeling the sting, he turned the hilt and struck her across the head.

She collapsed to the floor like another bloodied rag. He stared at her incredulously as her chest rose and fell, as blood trickled from her temple. He hadn't killed her. He *always* killed them.

The woman on the bench gasped. Another flinch, another prostrating of her body, this time towards the child propped up between the bench and her. She truly was trying to protect the child.

'Please,' she pleaded. 'Don't.

He turned the hilt, aimed the dagger towards the deceitful servant. Willed his hand to complete the deed. For his own survival, he shouldn't leave witnesses. But he couldn't do it. Angry, he whirled on the other woman, but his eyes went to the babe.

Was it because of this child he held his hand?

'Don't take the child?' he bit out. 'You think I want her?' At some point, they all begged and pleaded with him for mercy. He never gave it. He shouldn't be giving it now.

Walking away was still an option. He could tie the servant up, drag her to some more disreputable area of town with coin in her lap. Let the vultures there complete what he should have done.

The noblewoman looked soon for the grave and the child, far too young to escape this tomb of a house, would die, too. He should leave. Instead he asked questions.

'What can I tie her with?'

Her brows drew in. 'There might be…tassels, by the curtains.'

Did she not see the condition of the house? No tassels were left. But the worn curtains he ripped clear across, the fraying silk tearing easily. Used correctly, it would suffice to immobilise the servant.

Pointing at the servant, he said, 'Does she know who I am?'

The woman gave a small shake.

'Does. She. Know?'

'I don't know how she found you. I never wanted her to find you. I never wanted my child to be yours. You don't deserve—' She gasped for breath. Slumped. Her eyes closed. He watched her chest still for a moment before beginning again. When she opened her eyes, they were mere slits.

She couldn't finish her words, but he understood all the same. That she didn't want him to discover the child, that he didn't deserve her.

How would she know he deserved no one? Who told her who his family was? Whoever it was had to die as well. 'Who are you?'

'Handmaiden,' she whispered.

To the Queen. She was as high born as possible without being a ruler herself. He knew she must have some noble blood, had figured her for an unwanted bastard. But she had been more. She had been one of the influential ones and she had fallen to this?

More importantly, if she was close to the Queen, she knew his family. Knew his wealth, his power, knew *everything*.

He grabbed the gown of the servant, who jerked

awake. Her eyes, registering his presence, widened before she fought him. 'Cease!' he ordered.

She clawed at his hands, kicked. Laughed. 'Hit me, did you? You'll pay for that.'

He dragged her to the iron railing. 'I'll pay for nothing.'

'Cilla,' the noblewoman whispered.

He grasped her hands to tie the ripped silk curtain around her wrists.

'You'll pay,' Cilla sneered. 'You'll pay or your daughter will never be safe from—'

The slice across the servant's neck was clean, precise. A mere splattering of her blood and it was over. His hand holding the dagger remained steady as he wiped the blood off with the servant's gown.

The woman on the bench was silent, but Reynold felt her shocked eyes on him. Knew the child was awake and watching him as well.

'You knew all along who I was,' he said, sheathing the dagger and standing to his full height. His eyes stayed only on the corpse at his feet as a familiar weariness overtook him. He was so tired of killing.

'I…' she said. He swung his gaze to hers. They widened in fear as they should. He didn't care what she saw in his eyes. She wouldn't live long enough to tell.

'I saw…you at court,' she said, licking her lips. 'Then in the carriage.'

No one had told her who he was…and she had told no one who he was. Even as she carried his child. While she couldn't earn coin, while she grew sick. A hint to his family and that child, squashed between her rotting body and the mouldy bench, would have been used against him.

Everyone was alive, so he knew she had told no one of this child because she didn't want anyone to know it was… It was—

Two steps over and he snatched the child. No cries, no sounds. Was it mute? Was it deaf? It was aware, as he was in that moment. Dim light, but enough to see what he thought he never would. Grey eyes. Black hair. A girl by all accounts. But his.

His.

An almost keening sound burst from deep in his chest. One he barely held in check. But the emotion was there and it flooded him, made his knees weak and he locked them tight. If he fell…. Below his feet was the blood of sickness and human waste.

His child wouldn't touch any of this. Shouldn't be touching him, but he couldn't let her go. Now that he held her, now that he knew the truth. That hope, that longing, coiled around his blackened heart. Everything within him changed.

His.

This child…this child was *vulnerable*. To him, to the elements, to his family. To the sickness saturated into the air they breathed.

'Foolish woman!'

He could kill her for risking his life, for risking his child's. Was his reputation so horrific she thought this was better?

The answer was obvious. Of course she did—and perhaps she was right. Death was here, but it was an honest one. He hadn't been honest since he was a babe. All softer emotions were wrenched from him. They had been replaced with survival, and tricks, and games and weapons a long time ago.

'What is her name?'

Brows drawn in. 'You…are different.'

Over several years, he'd threatened many, killed more than that. Relished his brother's murder by another's hand. Black deeds left scars visible to all.

'You…wanted to spare her.'

The servant. 'A ridiculous lie,' he lied.

'You want to keep…' a harsh breath '…the name I gave her. Different. You never asked for mine. It's Grace,' she whispered.

For the first time, he looked at the child he held. Grey eyes absorbing him. No greed, no cruelty. Nothing of his life or her mother's affecting her. Yet she watched him. Watched him. Grace. Yes, the name was hers.

'I'll send a healer,' he said, having no intention of returning.

The woman released a defeated sound. It was as grief stricken as the sounds he heard before she knew he was here. Before she knew he'd come to take the child.

'No,' she said, one hand raised to stop him. 'Take me.'

A rustling and she pushed the blankets covering her to the floor.

He was accosted by the sight, by the smell. This was the decay, not the house or the chamber pot or the bloody coughs. The decay was her flesh decomposing while she still lived.

She wanted him to kill her. Before he could check himself, he glanced at the servant.

Her eyes widened as she took in his hesitancy. 'You…can't?'

Of course he could. He needed to. It was…the child. He didn't want to kill in front of her.

'You'd let me suffer?'

Legs, shredded. Mere holes to her bones. She

was no more than a corpse still alive. And she was in so much pain. Why was he *caring*?

'No one,' she repeated, 'can save me.'

No. No, they couldn't.

'I need you to kill me. What will you tell her? That you let me die…in agony?'

For the first time in years, Reynold's heart sped in indecision. For once, he felt torn between what he should do and what he wanted to do.

He had hesitated killing the servant. He didn't want to kill this child's mother. Both were necessary if he wanted to truly protect himself and Grace from his family's revenge.

'You have Grace. Now do what—' a wheezing breath '—you came to do.'

Keeping a child wasn't what he came to do. Cleverly constructed life, carefully planned so his game could be played out.

'I came to kill you, the servant and the babe.' He said the words, but there was no heat in them.

'You won't kill her,' she wheezed again. 'You know…her name. Kill me.'

Grace. The name fit, just as the child fit in his arms. His child. Setting her on a broken chair, away from the rags, far from the spilled refuse. As far away from the stench of decay, from the heap of a crumpled corpse, from the death of her mother.

A child. So young. And though they'd just met, he hadn't protected her from the darkest parts of his life, from the stench of avarice, greed, fear.

Grace had watched it with her grey eyes. Absorbed it as she would his final act of the night. The act of taking her away from the mother who loved her.

That soft expression, that comforting hand on her bared head and the sobbing from before when she thought her child gone forever. This woman *loved* her child enough to protect her against him.

He straightened and took the few steps to the bench. Loomed over her as Death with a scythe. This woman, this stranger, laid still. No flinching to flee, no cries of mercy or coughing because her battered soul and body knew their suffering was about to end.

There were no more words to say. There were no answers and the longer the child was in this house, the more chance for her to fall ill. For him as well.

He held the blade up so the glint of the waning moonlight through the windows played with it; so she'd know his purpose. She kept her eyes on him, bent her neck to give him access. To make the blade cut cleaner, more swiftly. This way, if he chose, he could make it painless.

His hand trembled.

The woman's eyes flashed with alarm, hatred. 'Do it!'

He adjusted his grip.

'I intended to keep her from you,' she panted. 'Denied forever. Your child. Denied her. Grace.'

His body changed. He had the child, vulnerable, exposed to his family, to the elements. To this woman who couldn't care for her. But for a greedy servant, he'd never have known she existed. A child. His. A family he wanted and she had meant to keep from him. Hatred coursed and burned in his veins. Familiar. Needed. His hand steadied. Seething rage. Unfettered malevolence and he let this noblewoman see it all.

'You monster.' She spat blood. Her head lolled to the side. Her eyes full of anger, of relief, closed. She'd asked for mercy and he gave her death.

'Yes, yes, I am.' He raised the knife and held. The woman before him was already dead.

Chapter Four

One stroll through the marketplace and it was all too easy to discover the baker whose loaves were stolen. Gabriel picked his place well if he wanted to escape with four loaves. It was in the busiest part of the market and one of the more luxurious stalls with actual shelves carved like animals. The loaves of bread left were golden, baked from the finest of flours and artfully displayed. The baker's design was clear though the morning light was dim.

She'd walked past this particular stall many times to smell the honey used in each loaf. Never, ever would she had thought to be in possession of them or how the loaves must have smelled to a starving child.

Why hadn't Gabriel taken from one of the smaller venders where she stood a chance to negotiate? There would be no negotiating here.

Not with the crowd forming or with the owner waving the loaves. Not with his words describing Gabriel to the watch guards, who even now pointed in different directions.

Gabriel had stolen the fresh loaves while they were being unloaded from cart to stall when it was dark. But it had taken too long to travel from the bridge and now the day was dawning. Early patrons were there and they adored a spectacle as much as fresh bread. Gabriel could never scamper through the market again and they had months to go before the worst of the weather changed.

If caught, he wouldn't survive again. He'd already lost an ear and, though it was unusual, his hearing in that ear as well. To lose another and possibly never hear anything? She couldn't suffer it.

It was up to her to make amends. Once she was out of the shadows, the baker would notice his loaves and so would the guards. If they didn't accept her apology and offer of free work, she'd be sent to gaol, to the gallows, could lose her ear or hand. Any of those scenarios were unacceptable. She had three people depending on her now. She made a promise to return.

However, if she didn't return the loaves they'd search for Gabriel. He couldn't hide forever. With one ear missing, he was unmistakable. And since he was a known thief his punishment would be worse.

A child's future or hers?

There wasn't a question.

She stepped out of the building's shadows.

A few hours to return to the house and for Reynold to notify the most loyal of mercenaries of what must be done with the bodies.

By the time morning arrived Reynold was back to staring out of the window at the top of the building. Everything was as it had been before the servant approached him. Everything except the child who slept in his arms. Both of them needed washing. But not yet. Much time had gone by since he left in the late evening and nothing now could be left to chance.

He had to think. To plan, to add another factor to his games. Perhaps the most important one and he was already pressed for time. Time was his only true enemy. Not because of his death. That was a certainty since he'd been born to a father who had killed his brother. Since his own brothers intended to kill him.

Time was his enemy because his plan depended on it. Assignations. Manipulations. Hiding, concealing, enquiring after legends. All these matters required time, a schedule, which was why he hid in one home after another. Always hiding while he played his games. He was close to securing victory over his family this last year when an Englishman bungled the capture of the treasure, the Jewel of Kings, a legend much like Excalibur. Except the gem was real and his family wanted it very much.

He thought the Englishman a clever foe, but he was only a fool. A dead fool when he was found by his family. And so he remained ahead in the game, for only he knew the legend's true worth. Only he kept track of all the players in the game so he kept his advantage.

Until then the child, Grace, could not exist. This child was his, he did not want to let her go, yet he could not claim her. To claim her would spell her death. At least outside the walls of his home, he needed an alternative to him. Dark hair, grey eyes. Every feature of a Warstone and some that were his own.

Had he been this quiet at her age? He couldn't remember. She hadn't clung to her mother, to Cilla. She hadn't cried out. Just kept those eyes open, absorbing everything. Depending on no one, observing all.

'You like the shadows, too, my girl? You like to watch. So do I.' How many times had he stood in darkened hallways and around shadowed corners? As a boy for protection, to wait and see if the room was clear and safe, and later to listen to private conversations.

But she was only a child. His child. A liability. A gift. His greatest weakness. His mind never found problems, but for once he could think of no solutions.

A commotion in the marketplace caught his eye. The baker, Ido, was making a fuss again. The man thought his loaves of bread were sanctified by God. They were good, but not divine. He knew of one baker in a village south-east of Paris, where the loaves were superior.

A large crowd was forming. This was more than Ido being cross over an opinion of his bread, much more than being shortchanged coin. A brute of a watch guard clenched the arm of a thin black-haired woman. In front of them, Ido was brandishing two loaves at her as if they were weapons. The woman was pulling, trying to get away. A theft.

Commonplace, barely worth his notice. But he knew immediately, incredibly, what it was: a solution.

With rapid strides, he swung the door to his room open and gave the guards outside precise instructions and his bag of coin.

* * *

'Let me go!' Aliette yanked her arm to ease the manacled grip of the guard who held it. After her feeble attempts he tightened it. She'd been concerned with bruises, now she was terrified he'd tear her arm away.

It had been years since she'd been caught. It had hurt then, too. But when she left the shadows and approached the stall, her attention had been on the baker. The guard had caught her by surprise. A deadly mistake.

'I've returned the loaves,' she said.

'Ruined!' The baker hoisted the loaves over his head and made a slow turn. It was a gesture for the growing crowd. 'I can't feed these to pigs now!'

There were hungry, barely clothed children who were eagerly in position in case he dropped or tossed that ruined bountiful bread.

She should have kept them. But she thought it early enough that she could return them without him knowing. What she hadn't been aware of was the baker had already reported it to the guard, who dragged her across the market to confirm the loaves…and thus confirm the thief.

Very fine loaves, and an extremely arrogant baker. She was a woman grown and felt the scrutiny of shoppers. Gabriel would have been in tears with no chance to negotiate.

'They're not ruined. I returned them and I'll work for the other two.'

'Other two? I'm missing four loaves this morning. Four! And these...things! I'll never accept bread from your filthy fingers! If I sold it, I'd be ruined as much as these loaves!' He waved them again. A section fell to the ground and disappeared.

It wasn't true that Gabriel stole four, but with the bruising grip of the guard and the salivating baker, it wasn't the time to argue. 'I'll work for the others as well.'

'You'll go to gaol,' the watch guard said.

'Cut off her hands now!' Ido said. 'Gaol is too kind for one such as her.'

'No. Please! I meant no—'

The crowd parted and two men silently approached. One whispered low and heatedly in the guard's ear. The other flanked her right side. Neither touched her, nor gazed at the crowd. Neither acknowledged the abruptly silent baker. The men were identically dressed, hair identically cut. Their size the same, their build the same. Their manners the same. If not for the colour of their hair and eyes, she'd think them twins.

Hired mercenaries, but for whom?

A look at Ido told her much. His face unearthly pale, mangled bread fell from his hands to disappear before it hit the ground.

'See here.' Ido looked from one man to the other. He looked to the crowd who had backed several paces away. Some of them continued to jeer. Others had gone quiet or vanished.

'I didn't know she was part of his house,' Ido said. 'I have no grief with his house.' He scampered to shelved loaves and proffered several to her. 'Take these if you wish. They are the best I made today.'

The guard let her go. Startled, Aliette gaped as the mercenary gave him a small bag with the unmistakable jingle of coin. Without a backward glance he walked away.

But the mercenaries stepped closer to her. She couldn't run. The crowd that was left stood solid at her back, their attention on the baker who looked as if his hand was to be chopped.

'I was mistaken.' Sweating, Ido was almost stabbing her with the loaves he held. 'Take these. They're yours for free. Tomorrow's as well.'

'I don't want them. I told you, I'll work for the ones already eaten. Free me and I'll work twice what those loaves are worth.'

Ido stepped back. 'Free you. I can't—'

The men snatched the loaves in one hand and took her arms in the other.

'Wait! Who are—? Please!'

They dragged her away from the baker's stall. She yanked and fought, but these men weren't a fattened guard or an even fatter baker. These men were warriors. Deadly. Paid well, with weaponry tucked at their waists.

'Where are you taking me?'

They didn't answer. Panic set in. She'd been worried to go to gaol, for her arm, for her hand. For Gabriel. But this was far worse. In gaol, there were people to plead with, to beg for mercy. These mercenaries dragged her away from anything she knew to take her somewhere she didn't know. She'd made promises!

Stomping on a foot caused one mercenary to curse in surprise, the other swiftly wrenched her arm behind her back and brought her to her knees.

Sharp agony in her shoulder and she cried out. The other mercenary gripped her assailant's arm until the wrenching eased, but not enough for her to break his hold. Just enough to be aware of the two men over her, and others walking by, but not offering help.

She was in trouble. The kind with consequences she couldn't return from. The men didn't talk, but maybe she could talk to them. 'I need to return. Please, I don't want to do this.'

Nothing, although the second mercenary didn't ease his grip from his comrade.

'At least...tell me what you want to do with me.'

Silence while she was held down, while she heard the regular sounds of the marketplace. Shoppers going about their day while hers was turned upside down.

'Please—'

'Orders will be followed,' the kinder one said.

She waited for him to explain, but he offered nothing else. No words that all would be well, or what would happen when they arrived at whatever destination they took her to. All she knew was that these men weren't from this city. As large as it was, she would have noticed them before now, and she wasn't sure they were French because the accent was strange. Yet she was to go with them, away from Gabriel, Helewise and Vernon.

What were the alternatives? None. Slowly she stood again, but now her knees and arm throbbed. On and on they threaded her through the parting crowd.

Around the stalls and a building or two until they abruptly stopped at large double doors. It was one of the many tall residences in the area that overlooked the market.

'This isn't my home.' She wrenched her arm. If she entered, she feared she'd never return. 'Let me go.'

The doors in front of them remained closed. The men remained still, waiting for something.

For what? This wasn't a grand home that had servants. It wasn't in much better condition than the boarded house she occupied.

But the men flanking her were rich, or at least well provided for, and they had parted with that bag of coin as though it was simply a loaf of bread. The owner of such men should have had a great estate or, if in town, a residence in the more luxurious boroughs.

Two other men opened the great doors and her captors marched her through the entrance. The house was larger than it looked from outside. As if one house was constructed to appear like many. Gawking, she was walked through a courtyard. More men swiftly crossing the small space as if they had great distances to go, or important matters to attend.

The home was a crumbling palace and a battalion occupied it. All mercenaries, all men. There was only one commodity she had that would be of any use to them. One commodity that she fought to protect ever since it was the only thing she was left with: herself.

'No!' she called out.

Some men looked their way, but none paused in their duties.

When she dug her heels in, her capturers tossed their bread loaves to men around them and bodily carried her to another large door that was opened effortlessly by others. Nothing in this small room but stone and a staircase that looked new.

Up and up, her feet hitting each stair until they reached the landing. There they released her and she flexed her tingling fingers.

'Now what?'

Neither said anything, but both blocked the stairway down.

A short landing, nothing but three closed doors. Two at her front and another to her left.

'I'm to go through those?' She pointed to the ones at her front.

Again, silence.

A few stolen bread loaves had brought her to this dark door. Bread she hadn't eaten so she was hungry. Scared. But if going forward meant getting this day over with and back to Gabriel as she promised, it was what she would do.

Releasing the latch, she stepped into the room. The men behind her closed it.

Then there was only her. And a man cradling a child.

Chapter Five

Reynold did not wait to turn as he had with the wench before. He needed to know immediately if the thief he'd spotted at the market would suit his purposes.

If not, he'd have his men march her to gaol and start again. So he turned, expecting no more or less than what he always expected. Except... Something was different.

Maybe it was the night of no sleep, that underneath it all he felt his hand still tremble at a killing he couldn't complete and one he didn't want to make. Last night had shaken him and he'd altered his course from past deeds because he had Grace, who remained quiet and watchful.

It was different and he blamed the child in his arms for his reaction to the woman in front of him. Standing still, remaining quiet, letting her gauge him as a man with her large eyes.

What did she see? Dirt, blood, his weariness. Running, always running, and last night his mind unable to let him sleep since he held his greatest vulnerability. He didn't have the advantage he usually desired.

He never allowed strangers to simply stare at him. Customarily, he hid in corridors or corners and waited to emerge. He liked watching. The waiting made the person he watched reveal more than they wanted to.

Most never knew he was inspecting their mannerisms for weaknesses as they paced and twitched. As they lifted his enamel boxes off his tables or inspected his books. When he'd eventually emerge, to hide their moment of vulnerability they'd cover their shock with spilling words.

There'd been an exception to this once. Not so long ago, a maiden, scarred and far too loyal to another knight, taunted him out of the shadows, but she was a rarity. He knew immediately that this woman in front would also be an exception. *How* she would, he didn't know, because he'd been foolish.

For a while he ruminated on his situation and last night. He'd been standing in front of her, so that he was fully exposed to her, revealing his weaknesses and vulnerabilities. It was time to inspect her in turn.

She reminded him of a pixie. Despite the years of filth marring her skin and dishevelled clothes, everything about her was delicate and frail. The only abundance was the length of her thick wavy black hair, bound in an irregular plait, and the freckles across her nose.

If there wasn't such poignant awareness in her large eyes and the tell-tale sign of soft curves under her threadbare gown, he'd mistake her for a child instead of a woman grown.

Her eyes were not dark as he'd thought. Blue? Difficult to tell with the curtains closed in this room. But her hair was so dark it was almost as dark as his own. This would be useful when it came to his daughter, to his plan.

There were questions in her eyes. Fear, too, but not the sort he was used to. He couldn't put his finger on it, but she wasn't skittish as though she worried about her own life. Another's, perhaps. He'd seen that once before.

She was quiet, which surprised him, as she made a perusal of him, of Grace in his arms, and then her eyes took in the room.

His favourite room filled with tapestries, silks, comforts and stacks of books. Because it was hard on the bindings and parchment, he never placed the books upright if there were enough tables to support them. As his only true family, he liked to take great care with them.

Her eyes didn't gleam with greed as Cilla's or with awe. Instead, she looked curious. He should have met this thief in one of the bare rooms on the other side of the house. A room that wouldn't have revealed anything of himself. She now knew more of him then he of her. Since the fateful day he'd overheard his family's intentions to kill him, he'd never revealed anything of himself.

It was the child in his arms. Any act he did from this point on wouldn't be as he had done in the past. The game had changed.

Another turn of her gaze around the room. Another one of him. 'Why have you brought me here?' she said.

Her voice. Direct with an elegant lilt to her words. A common demeaned thief should have spoken with guttural accent like Cilla. Instead, she held almost a cultured accent that both intrigued and confounded him. It was a boon. A dark-haired woman with a pleasing accent and desperate to survive. He didn't deserve it, but Fortune favoured him greatly this morning.

Aliette had been afraid of only one thing her entire life. Darkness. As a child, she knew shadows hid bad people. As an adult, she avoided them for in a building's crevice was inevitably a man with a knife. Around a corner would be a guard or a hand to grab what food she'd scavenged.

At night, when Darkness came, she huddled in whatever sliver of moonlight she could under her bridge. Night was always worse, for she'd fall asleep and remember that, when she woke one morning, her family had left her in the night.

Darkness was cruel. And though logically Aliette knew the man before her stood in daylight, his surroundings were clear and every feature of him was there for her to see, every instinct in her clamoured the opposite.

This man before her was shadow and night. He was Darkness.

Dishevelled raven hair, dark tailored clothing and a black gaze lit with a feral light. He was clutching a child wrapped in a tattered white gown that drooped almost to the floor.

Blood. Unmistakably blood was streaked across his clothing and his cheeks. Mud splattered along his breeches, his arms and thickly encrusted on his boots as if he had tromped through freshly turned graves.

The child's crumpled swaddling was also streaked with dirt and blood, and it remained unnaturally quiet and still. As if it was dead…or pretending to be. She couldn't see its face for the man held it far too tightly to his chest.

Would it escape if he eased his grip? Perhaps it was a changeling he'd dug up for some ritual.

The room was no comfort from her thoughts. The sumptuous surrounding only confirmed her certainty that this man was Darkness. For Darkness was powerful and encompassed everything. Perhaps kings could surround themselves with such opulence, but she couldn't imagine they possessed such extravagance as this man.

Too long had it been since she had been to church, but she fervently wished she was there now so she could beg for sanctuary and stand under a hundred candles. To beg for Helewise, Vernon and Gabriel as well, though they weren't in this room with her.

For she had feared Darkness all her life and finally he bared himself to her. His ruthlessness apparent in the savage edges of his cheeks and square of his jaw. His arrogance drawn by the refinement of his nose and arch of his brow. But the eddying dark grey of his eyes, the lush frame of lashes and soft curve of his mouth bore him a cruel beauty. If this was how Darkness deemed to personify itself, it wasn't safe for any of them.

Because Darkness enticed.

'Why have I brought you here?' he said. 'It is an interesting question that you ask.'

Fanciful thoughts she couldn't stop that beat with the hammering of her heart. The low rumble of his voice did nothing to help her. Neither did the fact he found the question on whether she lived or died *interesting*.

'An important one, I think,' she said.

One brow raised. 'Extremely, but most do not dare ask it.'

The others he brought to his lair? Aliette shook herself to stop her errant thoughts. She wasn't a child anymore, and this was daylight. Despite the warning hairs on her neck, he could be no more or less than a mere man with a child. Mud, blood and gold aside, he was human and not the most important one in her life. Gabriel, Helewise and Vernon were above such fears. She needed to, she must, return to them. Whatever this man wanted, she wanted it over. She'd been gone long enough. Gabriel might leave the house and search for her. If so, Ido could snatch him for gaol.

'Whatever it is you want of me, tell me now and have done with it.'

'So much haste.'

'Yes,' she said, 'but not for my death.'

A quirk to his lips. 'Most of us aren't hasty for death.'

Us. He wasn't Darkness. Of course he wasn't. But he was dangerous. He had enough wealth and power to drag her here with no interference.

'Why am I here?' she repeated.

He adjusted the child in his arms. She saw tiny

fingers curl, but little else. For a child, it was un-naturally quiet.

'Do you have a family?'

She couldn't answer that and remain safe.

His brow rose at her silence. 'Do you have a father? And a mother?'

This was personal. 'Why do you ask?'

'You keep asking me questions…thief.'

She couldn't have heard him correctly. Surely this wasn't about something so trivial as the baker. 'Were those your loaves of bread?'

'Parents. Answer me.'

She shook her head. 'No parents. Is this over the bread? Did you watch me take it?'

'I watched you being caught.'

Relief that he hadn't seen Gabriel steal gave her courage to ask more questions. 'And that had you bring me here.'

'You know what would have happened to you if that watch guard took you away?'

'Do I look a fool?'

'You're the one caught for mere bread—perhaps you didn't know the consequences.'

Living the way she had all her life, she always knew the consequences. 'It's not mere bread when it means life and death.'

'Ah, yes, the important question. I don't want your death.'

'Rape, then.'

A curl to his lips as if she insulted him.

'I'm a woman. You're a man. Why else did you force me here?'

'Not. That.'

His answer was short, curt, the tone as if he found her question distasteful.

Aliette refused to be embarrassed. She was poor, street born and bred, her clothes barely serviceable. But some of it she purposefully created. She needed to smell, to grind dirt into her skin and clothes to deflect leers and lust. Life would have been easier if she was a boy. When she'd become old enough she'd thought to disguise herself, but by then she was all too easily recognised. So a girl, now a woman, she remained.

She should be pleased her filthy appearance worked as it had all her life. He didn't want her death, or her body, and he purposefully saved her from gaol and losing her hand.

'In truth, what—?' he began to ask.

'Why are you holding the child?' she interrupted.

Chapter Six

He looked perplexed. 'Because I have not put her down.'

A girl. Aliette had no reason to trust he wouldn't harm her, but he had held his hand so far and it was enough for her to truly pay attention to the man before her…and the child. 'What's wrong with her?'

Alarm crossed his strong features. 'Nothing.'

'She's too quiet. Is she asleep?'

He looked down at her. 'Her eyes are at half-mast.'

Awake, but listless. 'Is she with fever? Sick? Has she spit up?'

'I don't—'

She took a step forward and raised her arms. 'Give me that child.'

'No.'

He said the single word so evenly and decisively it was as a sword striking down.

It stopped her short, her arms outstretched, her stepping foot braced in the air.

'You may not take her,' he said.

Where were her finely honed survival instincts? This was not a man to be ordered about. She lowered her arms and foot and stepped back. 'I only meant—'

'Save me from well meaning intentions,' he said sardonically. 'That's not why you're here.'

She could not keep her eyes only on the man. She was a fool. Maybe he was Darkness. But for some reason, instead of heeding the warning in his expression, in his words and deeds, she stupidly took her eyes away from him.

It was the child. Jarringly innocent in this darkened luxurious room, a clamouring instinct had welled up and overtook her good sense.

If she survived this, she'd blame Helewise and Vernon. Gabriel as well, for he was frequently sick and needed her care. He'd been unused to street fare and exposure. It had taken him weeks to toughen to the degree he had.

'You haven't told me why I'm here.'

'I will, in my time.'

'In the meantime—' She couldn't let it go. It was unwell; she was certain of it. Maybe it was the fact she had been a neglected child, or maybe it was the care of Helewise and Vernon that compelled her. Either way, she asked, 'Is the child yours?'

He swiped a dagger from his waist. If she had

taken those steps towards him, it would be buried in her belly.

'Why do you keep asking me questions about the child?'

'You're…' she swallowed '…you're holding her in front of me.'

The blade looked well used and fit easily in his hand. It was a weapon this man had used many times before. He held still. So did she.

'The child isn't mine,' he answered, watching her watch the blade.

Her entire life she'd lived with Death and his scythe. If it wasn't the icy cold of winter trying to kill her, it was another person trying to survive. When threatened, she'd learned it was always the person behind the weapon she should be wary of. But this man wasn't like another thief on the streets trying to steal a blanket. This man didn't pull his blade to take something from her, for she had nothing. He pulled the blade because she asked about the child. He did it to protect the child—from her.

Fear from being kidnapped swirled with her usual mistrust. But his deeds ceased every emotion in her. She'd never seen a person defend a child before. Not like this. Certainly never her own parents and even a mother with a suckling infant put the infant aside if there was food to be had or a customer to pull up her skirts for.

Five winters past, it had been bitterly cold and she had come across what she thought were wadded-up old blankets. But instead of a treasure, it was a swaddled baby. Frozen, its skin pale, lips blue, with ice feathering along its tiny eyelashes. She'd cried for days afterwards. The babe haunted her dreams still. To this day she avoided that part of town in winter and found herself wary of piles in corners.

But Darkness drew a blade for a child who he awkwardly held and something ripped through her chest. She couldn't breathe right.

'You've gone pale,' he said, sheathing the dagger. 'Are you fainting?'

She felt far away. As if she was here, yet not in the same place she was before. As if she recognised everything, but nothing was the same. Because Darkness guarded a child from harm.

She swallowed. 'Have you…have you ever taken care of a child before?'

'No.'

'Can you put her down?'

His smile curved cruelly. 'Are you ordering me?'

He said it as though she was an insect who

could talk. 'I'm not ordering you. I…simply want to see her.'

He did a double take. Another. A cant to his head, waiting for something.

She wasn't about to do anything else. This was enough and he made it clear it was too much. Never trusting anyone, she shouldn't care about anything other than getting as far away as possible from this madman.

This killer. Who happened to cradle a child and was overly protective about her. But the child was too quiet. Aliette *needed* to see her.

'You can place her over there, unwrap her and I can see her from a distance.'

'You know something of children?'

'Is that why I'm here?'

'Hmm.' He took two strides forward. So swiftly she braced herself for a curled fist. It didn't come. Instead, he held the child towards her. 'She feels warm.'

'All children feel warm if you hold them too long.'

She took the child who, despite her length, was light, and carefully unwrapped the swaddling.

Thin, gaunt cheeks. Bone-like arms, a swollen stomach and sunken hip bones.

'How old is she?'

His brows drew in, his eyes searching the child as if asking her to answer. 'Around a year.'

She did know something of children and this condition, she knew it very well. Thin, emaciated. Greyish skin. Listless. An unwise anger swept through her. 'She's—'

'Yes.'

'She's...hungry,' she blurted. 'You're starving her! When was the last time she ate?'

At his mystified look, she demanded, 'Did you give her something to drink?'

Lips clamped shut and his eyes narrowed.

'You haven't fed her, or given her a drink? Has she been crying? Restless?'

Another bout of silence. Aliette had no patience with it. Maybe the wealthy had time for waiting, but if she stalled or waited for anything she'd have starved to death. 'She needs oats or bread all warmed with milk and honey.'

'You want me,' he said in that terrifyingly even voice of his, 'to provide that for you.'

'I don't know this place. These men don't follow my orders. How else am I to get it?'

'This isn't—'

'Whatever you want of me, I won't do it, not when this child needs me.'

He looked to the child and to her. He looked to argue, the superiority of his expression one she'd seen many times when a shopkeeper thought to abuse a street urchin. She stared him down. If he meant to kick or strike her, he could join the others. She'd survived many such blows over the years.

If he intended to kill her, there was nothing she could do to defend herself, though she'd try to protect the child first. But if this was her day to die, it was simply like every day she ever lived. In truth, she wasn't meant to have made it this long.

With another narrowed gaze, he pivoted towards the door, but not before she saw a flare of victory in his eyes.

What he thought he'd won Aliette didn't care about, as long as the child had what she needed. She'd seen enough suffering in her lifetime—the fact that this child was surrounded by gold and silk and was still hungry she couldn't tolerate.

Reynold left the room and closed the door. The two men who had escorted the thief were on the other side and he gave them the unusual tasks. If they wondered about the requests, they didn't ask. He paid them not to question. Although one of them looked behind him. To see if the thief was unharmed? He would have to be dealt with later.

When they marched down the stairs, he turned to go back into the room, but stopped. The door was partially closed and the thief wasn't looking his way, her attention fully on the child in her arms.

She was doing this walking, swinging motion and singing softly.

The morning sun filtered through the unwashed windowpanes delicately lighting its two occupants, the shimmering reds and greens of tufted cushions and the rich browns of well-polished carved furniture.

The woman was slight, not much more substantial than the babe she held. Her clothes were an odd, but practical mixture of layers. Two coarse surcoats, one much shorter than the other, over a thick, overly large chemise. She had no gown and her shoes had distinct holes. Grace's greying swaddling dragged on the floor as the thief swept them from side to side. Both were slight, filthy, their clothes unkempt.

The room was small and the subtle distinct tang of abject homelessness, blood and fresh dirt clashed with the resonating fragrance of lavender and lemon, the warmed silk from the tapestries and the musty familiar perfume of his books.

But she was perfect. Everything about this was perfect. Hair that almost matched Grace's and both appearing filthy from the streets. No parents to care for her. No one to suspect or question the child she held so carefully and sang to so beautifully was his.

Even more so now that her mothering instincts resurrected themselves. Against him, which both grated on and amused him.

The thief was the solution to keep Grace close to him. A woman of childbearing age in a desperate situation. She would be a servant to him and raise the child. He could then see Grace, keep her close through the years. And because the thief and Grace would be perceived as servants, his arrogant family wouldn't perceive Grace as his greatest vulnerability.

He turned to the mercenaries taking the stairs behind him and instructed them to place the food for the babe, the woman and himself on an empty table. He'd propose to the thief what needed to be done and she would thank him profusely for saving her from gaol and poverty. It was all too easy.

Although…there was that one moment of lapse in his control which was concerning. Her request to take Grace catching him off guard. The blade was out of its sheath before he thought to draw it. An indication of how much he cared though he hadn't had his daughter for a day.

Such action would be an anomaly from now on. People did not catch him unawares and now that he knew his feelings existed, he'd hold them in check so he didn't reveal anything more. Until he dismantled his family, not even his daughter or the thief could know him.

Chapter Seven

Aliette was startled when the door swung open and the two mercenaries who had carted her here carried in large trays with mouthwatering food and freshly poured ale.

They set them down, one of them glancing at her from head to toe before they walked out the opened doors. A moment later, her captor entered. Silently, steadily, he closed the doors behind him and stood with no direction of what he intended for her.

But the food was here for the child, and she wouldn't wait another moment. Whatever this man had told the kitchens, it was correct. A bowl, a mortar and pestle, cooked oats, and copious warmed milk all ready to be prepared.

Glancing at the man who hadn't moved from the doors, she set the child down on the bench and propped her with cushions. Another glance, as she prepared the bowl and dipped the tiny spoon in the mixture.

The near silence made her heart and her breath

unnaturally loud. For a clarion moment she wanted to fill that silence, but the way he held still made her think he was expecting her to question and accuse.

She wouldn't give him that satisfaction. Silence had done her well in the past when she needed to hide or surprise. So she sat with the child on her lap, covered her finger in milk and honey and dabbed it on the sweet lips until she took sustenance.

The man at the door shifted, she didn't raise her eyes. Her entire world now was this room and this child.

Another dollop and the child suckled, its incoming teeth gently scraping across her finger. Another, and another, until she sat her up and filled the small spoon.

Her dark, telling, grey-coloured eyes were distinct and explained much. Dark hair, dark grey eyes. Her captor said he wasn't the father, but the way he watched them, and the way he'd pulled the blade, told a different story...but maybe she was wrong. She trusted her instincts, but she didn't trust this man or anyone. Lies were too easily told.

Another shift and he strode to the chair nearest them, his dark presence and intent cloaking him.

He reminded her of a raven, perched, watching, waiting.

She watched right back. Out of the corner of her eye, she saw the way his thick lashes fanned his cheeks, the sardonic bowing of his top lip. The way his fine, almost beautiful hands folded in front of him as he rested his elbows on his knees. One hand perfect, the other marred by a large circular burn scar.

A growing tension threaded its way between them, but she ignored it. The child's eyes were wide and anxious, its body curving and contorting in her arms. A franticness to reach the food she was slowly and carefully feeding her.

She knew this feeling. When she was young, and days went by between any scraps, the hunger was a living, breathing animal that clawed and scraped. If she was fortunate enough to snatch something edible, she'd consumed it between blinks. But the feeling would make her nauseous. Her body rejected what it most needed.

She didn't want this child rejecting nourishment so she kept to the slow steady feeding, but not the entire bowl.

Standing, she adjusted the child over her shoulder. She was around a year old, but so thin and fragile. Walking, talking, comforting, she traversed the room until the child calmed in her arms and fell asleep.

The man in the chair didn't move, didn't speak.

She didn't care. She'd feed this child. Feed her again in another hour, then be on her way. She wouldn't risk more time here.

He hadn't taken the blade to her or made any threats. He had no reason to keep her here, so, logically, he must let her go. If that didn't work, the room was filled with enough precious items. Surely a threat to damage such beauty would warrant her release.

The child she wouldn't threaten. She could never go through with it and the man, who watched her care, wouldn't believe she could harm an innocent.

'She sleeps,' her captor said.

Aliette nodded.

'Yet you do not ask to go.'

It was a question that didn't need an answer. He'd let her go or he wouldn't, either way she intended to stay a bit longer for a second feeding. She shrugged.

'You also fed the child without feeding yourself. Two trays and you chose to feed her first.' With a huff, he pushed himself back in the chair. His relaxed position did not make him seem less threatening.

'This is all so…uncomplicated,' he said.

That warranted her looking at him. She heard the mercenaries outside the door shift their positions. Trained killers positioned to threaten her or protect him. Which begged the question—what did she have that he wanted?

For what was easy for this man would never be easy for her. Over the years she'd been caught, which always revealed three options for her: fight, pretend stupidity, or plead for mercy.

None of those would work in this situation; talking of the child was her only safe choice until he exposed his purpose for kidnapping her.

'She is a child and needs shelter, food, and gentle words. There is nothing difficult about it. It would do her well to be bathed, to have a change of clothing. She is soiled and, with the food, she will soil her clothing far worse.'

'I have ordered her clothing and a bath. They will be available in another room.'

Aliette was surprised at his forethought and yearned to go there now. But if her stay went beyond this room she feared it would change his expectations of her. She had no intention to stay here.

'In her condition and over the next sennight,' Aliette continued, 'she'll need to be fed and cared for as I have done. Anything less and her condition will worsen. It may seem simple, but there are concerns here.'

'Hmm,' he said. 'The child is a concern, but not what I meant.'

'Then what is uncomplicated?' she said without thought, without thinking, her mind on the supplies the child needed and Gabriel's worry.

'You.'

She stopped moving and looked directly at him. No, nothing of his relaxed stance changed her impression that he was shadows and dark. He was Darkness, swirling around the light in a dance that didn't make it any less threatening. She only had to misstep and a blade would be in her belly.

He quirked a brow at her, his mouth curving at the corners. 'Interesting.'

She didn't care what was interesting, she cared for his deeds, his words.

'You're not talking.'

He was playing with her. Making her wait. She couldn't remain idle the whole day. 'It's your turn,' she said. 'I asked questions that you have yet to answer. Further, you're the one who dragged me here. It would be appreciated if you would be courteous and convey the reasons why.'

'Haste again.'

'With good cause.'

Another brow, enquiring, looking for elaboration on her statement. She wouldn't give him more. It was none of his concern that she needed to return to her family. When it came to time, hers was important as anyone's. Rich or poor.

Another huff of air as if she amused or frustrated him. 'I want you to care for the babe.'

'I already am and I intend to wake her in a bit and feed her more. Then she should bathe and sleep.'

'It is good you let me know your intentions—what will you do when she sleeps?'

'Leave.'

He nodded. 'You are correct in thinking it is my time to talk, for I intend for you to stay.'

'Stay?'

'For the remainder of the day, tomorrow and the conceivable future.'

'You said—'

'I do not want your body or your death, nor by extension will my men. I intend for you to care for the babe, as you've been doing.'

No one snatched a stranger off the streets and ordered them to care for a child. Especially when that child was obviously theirs. He'd drawn a blade guarding the child, now he was giving her into her care?'

'You want me to care for your child,' she said.

'Not my child.'

'The mother, wouldn't she—?'

'You're her mother.'

She jerked, momentarily waking the child in her arms, and she walked around the room again until it was soothed. A year old. She should have been plump with dimples and too heavy to carry this long. She weighed no more than the swaddling wrapped around her.

'We both know I'm not her mother.'

'You look alike.'

It was true.

'You look alike,' she pointed out, certain he'd confess to the relationship.

He only smiled. 'Anything could be a deception.'

She'd play along if she must to understand this. 'If you are not the father and I am not the mother, won't the parents have some say in this matter?'

'She has no parents.'

'You're certain.'

'She has no one.'

Not true. She knew what it meant to have no one. 'She has you. She was in this room and you were holding her.'

'Now you are.'

An abandoned baby. This man took a trebuchet to her defence against her argument to leave.

'Everyone saw you with the child first.'

'You mean by the men who are in my pay?'

This man wasn't like anyone she'd met before. She'd always been able to bargain her way out of a situation. But every argument she could think of, he'd already anticipated.

Panicked, she blurted, 'I can't stay.'

'You're a thief, homeless, on the streets. Before I snatched you from that predicament you were to be sent to gaol to suffer for your crimes. Wouldn't staying here in this home, taking care of that child, be preferable?'

Darkness was a madman. 'No one snatches a complete stranger off the streets to care for a child. No one takes a thief and brings them into their home. You do not know me.'

'True, but you do not know me.'

Oh, but she did. Her instincts never lied. He was far more dangerous than his act of bringing in a thief. And she let him know she knew him. 'I saw your blade.'

'Yes…you did.'

Threats. If he set her free, she'd go to gaol. He'd insist; Ido, the arrogant baker, would as well. There her sentence would be an ear, a hand, her life.

That is, if he set her free. After all, there were other means to dispose of her. For all she knew, she was the second woman he'd offered to care for the child. Maybe another kidnapped woman declined his offer and it was her blood on his clothes.

'If I refuse?' she asked.

'You can't.'

He didn't say any more, but he didn't need to. It was the truth. She couldn't refuse though she had a compelling reason to beg. Pleading did no good with the mercenaries, but pleading was all she had left. She'd tried reasoning and that failed.

But what could she plead? He wouldn't believe the little bits of work she did or her scavenging were important.

She couldn't tell him she had others in her care. That would give him an advantage and put her family in jeopardy. All he would need to do was find them and threaten them and she'd comply with his demands.

Her only recourse was to agree, then escape. Gabriel wouldn't stay at home, might already be in the streets looking for her. Maybe he'd listen to Helewise and Vernon. They'd talked of a situation like this. That if she was caught to give her time to return.

She prayed he'd give her time.

Striding to the bench, she plopped herself and

the child down. It was enough to wake and feed her again, which is what Aliette did.

'That is your answer.' He indicated to the food, to the child.

'I can't refuse you and this child needs care. If you are so insistent that I'm the one to do it, who am I to argue?'

'The house and food for your belly doesn't hurt.'

That is what he thought compelled her. Shelter and food? Once it might have been enough, but her dingy room with her family was worth so much more than that. With them she laughed and told stories.

Darkness never smiled.

She smiled at him. 'If I'm to be treated as well, I'd be a fool not to accept.'

Narrowing his eyes, he stood. It forced her to raise her chin as Darkness loomed over her.

'I do not mean you or the child harm. I intend to give you a roof over your head and all the food you could want. A bath and clothes have been ordered for you as well and they are to be prepared for you in the room next to this one. You could have all this daily.'

'Until the child is well?'

He slowly shook his head. 'Food and shelter for years. Something you've never had.'

She hated that he guessed the truth.

'All this as long as you never cross me.'

'I assumed that,' she said, pointedly looking at his belt where the dagger was sheathed.

'And you must be the mother.'

'You want me to pretend to be her mother.'

'Not pretend. Simply make it truth. She will sleep with you and you will feed her. I will confer with the staff and find a place of employment for you in this household. But you must claim the child as yours.'

The threats were clear. Everything else was not. What was he not telling her? So much, but what could she infer from what he did reveal to her?

That he had a scratch on his cheek, blood on his clothes. That he meant every threat. That he couldn't be trusted with her life or the child's.

Still she had to ask. 'Surely there is someone else in this large house that would have taken this position.'

'There are only men. Although now that you are here, I will need to remedy that. You will be too noticeable otherwise.'

'What is her name?'

He took a few steps away from her. 'Grace.'

'And yours?'

Another few steps and he stopped at the door.

Looking over his shoulder, he answered, 'You will call me what everyone else calls me: Sir.'

It wasn't until the door was closed, Grace was fed and Aliette fed herself, did she realise not only did she not know his name, he didn't know hers.

Chapter Eight

The thief and child, despite their influence on his life, represented only a slight adjustment to his day since most of the activity acquiring Grace had been at night. Still, there were matters to attend to. Dispatching men to the neighbourhood where he'd killed the servant, ensuring there were no witnesses to his act, and if there were, to kill them immediately. He sent another group to walk the market and report if there was any gossip on his taking a thief.

Which left only a few men to guard. Not enough given his newfound vulnerability. So after he'd washed in the kitchens and changed, he stuck close to Grace. Did what he could around the bottom of the stairs leading up to his private rooms. From sound and a brief glimpse, he knew when the thief left his study and entered his bathing chamber. She was holding Grace and talking to her, then the door shut and all was quiet again.

A child. His child whom he didn't want to part with for a moment, yet it was necessary to in order to keep her safe.

Was she safe with a thief? With this one… perhaps. She'd demanded food for Grace and fed her before she fed herself. Maybe it was possible he'd found an honourable thief. But he would need to ascertain over the next day whether she was appropriate for his daughter. At that thought, the tightness in his chest eased. Another anomaly and a sign that his feelings for this child went too deep and too fast.

Was it simply because he longed for a family… because he remembered his younger brother's birth, remembered Balthus's first smile and the heavy precious weight when he held him? Was it because he'd wished so fervently that his brother's life, that his own, was with any family other than the great Warstones?

Mere hours in his arms and Grace already ruled his emotions and deeds. At first he could not kill the servant, then, when she threatened his daughter, he reacted before thought. He shouldn't be reacting at all.

Not enough time for this uneasiness inside him because he wasn't holding her. Illogical when Grace was in his care, and he'd done the best under the circumstances to protect her fate.

On finding and securing the thief, he'd surpassed all expectations. True, she was filthy and had no skills to aid his household, but both could be remedied with little effort.

There was, however, something about her that was different, that pricked his curiosity. Nothing about her appearance, though her eyes were riveting when she demanded he fetch her food. Maybe it was the way she argued. She was wary, but within a few breaths in his presence she'd fought him.

Or perhaps it was the way she cradled and sang to Grace. Affection wasn't something he was privy to. Perhaps her act of caring was what intrigued him. The thief had a lovely voice and sang like a— He stopped, craned his neck for a view up the stairs.

It was quiet. Reynold bounded up the stairs and stood outside the door. Still no sound. Asleep or gone?

Every instinct demanded he barge in. Every knowledge he'd gained against that impulse knew better. Prepared for anything, slowly, silently, he opened the door.

He wasn't prepared for what was before him. The steam from the hot water cast its mist, warming his hand and face with the scent of sage soap and softening the details before him. But the mist didn't hide a room blazing with light.

Not from the smallest of windows encrusted

in years of weather, but by the four sconces and two candelabras. Every flickering taper enveloped the woman emerging from the tub in a raiment of light.

Her back was to him and her dark unbound hair cascaded down. The wet tendrils clung to her shoulder, to her arm. One, unerringly curled along her spine as if beckoning him to look further.

He did.

Her skin was unlike anything he had seen. With her bathing, no longer were the years of living on the streets marring the absolute utter perfection.

In his life, he'd travelled far and to many countries. He'd witnessed and touched such statues to make ordinary men weep. But if there was marble more beautifully shaped or coloured than she was, he'd never been privy to it.

Her skin was pearlescent like that precious stone, shining and reflecting in the flickering flames that lit the room and emblazoned her. But the warm tone of her skin enticed and beckoned as no hard, cold stone could ever do.

And beckon it did. He was Icarus, standing on the ground, staring at the sun and longing to touch it. She was as slender as she appeared in her clothing. But it wasn't starvation's slenderness that made her so.

No, every fine angle of her was created as certain works of art are created. The firm straight line of her shoulders, the subtle arch of her spine, the exquisite curves of her waist pronounced everything about her feminine.

All of it highlighted by the flames, by the water that fell in rivulets along every natural curve of her before sliding headily down her legs and back to where it begun.

Not even a moment to glimpse before she bent for the linen on the side of the tub and wrapped it around her body, veiling everything from him.

That infinitesimal moment was all he had. It was enough to make him feel as if he had donned those fateful waxed wings. Enough to have flown too close to the sun and already fallen.

Only a moment to close the door. To absorb his rapid heartbeat and mutinous breath. To brace against the latch and pray it caught him in his free fall because his legs were too weak to hold him. Only a moment to know with certainty his body was no longer his own.

It was hers.

And he knew he'd don those ill-fated wax wings over and over again to reach where he shouldn't.

For if he was able to touch such purity, they were both doomed to fall to their deaths.

Aliette delayed leaving the bathing chamber. The steam and torches encased the room in warmth and light, and the little space held a certain peace she had never had before. Even Grace, wrapped in clean blankets, was sleeping securely in a basket, as if she felt it, too.

She knew it was a temporary peace because outside the door was an enigmatic man who couldn't possibly mean her well. Except for the three in her acquired family, no one ever did.

He demanded she play a role that she had no intention of playing. That she must be a mother to a child. Even if she trusted such a role, her inexperience would give away that Grace wasn't hers.

Whom did she belong to? He denied the child was his. If she took this as truth, then this child was another victim in a scheme she didn't understand. There was no reason a stranger would kidnap a child and her.

Who was he and why surround himself with mercenaries? A powerful man who expected to get his way and one she couldn't trust. She never trusted anyone, yet there were contradictions she was already aware of.

Because he guarded a child; because, though

dark, he was beautiful, he enticed. Aliette shook herself.

She must not forget how much he took away from her! How she longed to return to her family, who must be frantic. She prayed Gabriel stayed at the house. For while she donned fine clothes, watch guards could be hauling them to gaol.

Gabriel needed her far worse than this child who was secure in a house that held rooms full of books, gold, candles and a lit fire. So much bounty and wealth to assault her senses, and yet, Grace was hungry and thirsty. Wealth, but there appeared no one who knew what to do for her.

Oddly and yet more contradictions—there were no servants, only hardened, scarred men who had brought hot water to fill three tubs. One to bathe with scented soap, the other to immerse herself and rinse. A smaller one all for Grace. Another man, missing fingers, carried linens and clothing for her and Grace. None of them were the ones who had brought her here. None of them spoke, though she begged for answers.

At any other point in her life, she'd take advantage and amass the food and clothing before she was thrown on the streets again, but there were too many questions here to trust any of it.

Reluctantly, knowing she couldn't stay enclosed in this room forever, Aliette lifted the basket holding Grace, tucked it against her hip and opened the door.

She expected the landing to be empty, instead, her captor leaned against the opposite wall in the darkest corner. Leaning, but not resting. Still, but not passive. He was Darkness, readying himself. But he said nothing. He moved not a finger.

Alerted to the danger, Aliette froze. Something had changed in his countenance since he left her. Maybe he had changed his mind at her usefulness, or maybe he meant her harm. For he held himself like a sword about to strike. Taut, vibrating, cold steel.

Another part of him was hot, rolling, seething, sweeping away what little peace and safety she'd hoarded and replacing it with something else.

Fear and want. Wariness and longing.

If she spoke, if she moved, she wasn't certain which aspect of the man would react, so she did the only thing she could. Wait, as he was doing.

She knew immediately she had failed at such an endeavour. It had nothing to do with the fact that her usual reaction would be to charge forward and everything to do with how he was looking at her.

Elemental. All encompassing. As if she wasn't fully dressed and carrying a child-laden basket. He wasn't aloof with disdain, as Darkness should be. He gazed at her as a man. She'd seen lust before in others, accidentally encountered the act performed more times than she could count.

This wasn't the same. This time, she wasn't a child, she wasn't broken and on the streets. And this man…this man wasn't like any she'd met before.

A cruel beauty because he shouldn't be able to lure her. She'd avoided Darkness, avoided all men, but she couldn't escape him. It became undeniable and the longer they stood in the silence they created, the longer she felt the pull. The need to step closer to him, to break the quiet in another way, whatever way he wanted.

His chest expanded on an inhale, held as if holding his breath. And she could no longer resist. A step towards him…another until she was caught in the current of his mesmeric grey eyes. If possible, they darkened further, before his lashes lowered to shade any telling emotion. But she could feel it. Some…need, something gripping. Another step. Not so far now.

She tracked the distance with her eyes, with the feel of him almost near enough. What was he trying to tell her? She licked her lower lip to part them, to ask the question.

His breath hitched, he blinked hard, then Darkness swirled and drew away. She froze mid-stride.

A moment passed and then another while he held still. She was never good at waiting. Bracing herself, she headed towards the stair.

'She sleeps again?' he asked behind her.

Stopping on the top stair, Aliette didn't turn. Grace slept, her black hair no more than fluff against the whiteness of the bedding. It was easier to look at the child and not at a man whom she was to call Sir.

'A little food, a careful wash in water, she'd fallen asleep while I dressed her,' she said, addressing the staircase.

'Is she meant to be sleeping?'

Aliette had never cared for a child, but she'd seen others. 'They sleep when they sleep.'

When she glanced over her shoulder, he was no longer leaning against the wall. His gaze was avid on the child, his lips parted to ask questions. No, not questions. He was *concerned*. Yet he didn't make demands.

Watching him carefully, she said, 'Can you carry her?'

He had the basket in hand before she was prepared. His eyes soaked up the sleeping infant. Surely this concern was of a parent for his child? If she had a child, someone who needed and loved her, she'd announce it to the world. It made no sense why he would hide his relation.

Tensing as if he realised her scrutiny, he shot her a look. 'I'll show you to your room.'

Her entire being wanted to demand release, to plead that he find someone else. She didn't trust why he stole her from the streets. And she more than didn't understand her reaction to him on the landing. Why he affected her so, and why she felt the need to be near him...to touch him. In the past she'd avoided Darkness. Now she should be fleeing.

However, this man had no weaknesses, he'd tell her nothing and, if she ran, she wouldn't get far. And Grace needed her, so down the staircase she followed him into the large open courtyard and down another staircase that went underground.

One, two steps and a familiar fissure of fear trickled through her. The stone around her was different, thicker, colder and felt like ice under her feet. The fireplace in the hallway was unlit, as were most of the torches.

This hallway revealed doors to rooms showing beds. But her captor did not stop at these that contained natural sunlight from the lone staircase. Instead, he grabbed a torch and walked the narrow passage to the very end and opened a door there.

The air inside was unused with a smell of damp

and cold unforgiving stone. No windows. No light or avenue to escape.

'The other rooms are occupied,' he said, his voice devoid of any emotion, the heated tautness of his gaze completely gone. 'This house is not large. The other side that you have seen are my quarters, these are for those who serve me.'

'I am…to serve you?' Refusing to reveal her vulnerability to the dark, to the feeling of being trapped, she swallowed the tremble in her voice.

'You will care for the child, but you must have other tasks to do as well.'

'Why? You dragged me here and now you tell me what I must do?'

He turned away from viewing the room to address her. 'It's a wonder you do not curb your tongue. Do you want to return to the streets?'

Where was her sense of self-preservation? Frayed with the worry over Gabriel, the kidnapping, the dark hallway…this room. 'What do you want me to do?'

'What can you do?'

Nothing. She was good at nothing domestic because she had never had an opportunity before. She wasn't good at tasks outside the home either. She either stole what she needed, or ran errands for those too busy.

'I cannot cook.'

'There is a man who comes and cooks for me when I am in residence. But my men loathe kitchen duties. I'm assuming you can chop vegetables.'

She shrugged.

'Tomorrow we'll have a better idea of what you can do.'

'Why are you offering this?'

He looked at her for so long she was sure he saw all her imperfections and weaknesses. Darkness never looked for anything good.

'Are we to pretend you don't know your role? Are we to continue further discussions as if you have a choice?'

He sounded as every nobleman sounded when speaking to those beneath him. Except…there wasn't the bite of conviction in his voice she had come to expect. It was as if he said the cruel words, but didn't mean them. Which made no sense at all. He was wealthy and clearly of noble blood, of course he meant them to be cruel.

She didn't need to understand this man to know what she needed to do. She'd cooperate, stay alive for her family's sake and, when she could, she'd escape. Except, her room was a trap. 'Do I need to be put here?'

Reynold should turn away. The thief and child were fed and provided for; they required nothing else. He only meant to show her room, then escape from her and what he had accidentally revealed on the landing.

He must have exposed his turmoil, his sudden need for her, though he had stood in the shadows. He must have… Otherwise, why did she walk towards him?

Her footsteps behind him slowed as they approached the last staircase. And dragged as they walked the passageway to her room. He thought once he swung open the door and she saw the bed, stool and shelves she would gasp at her good fortune. Instead, she acted reluctant and now, by her comment, offended at her accommodations.

'There is nowhere else. The other occupiers are men and you are the only female. If Grace cries, you are far enough away not to disturb. It is better for you both here.'

Placing the basket by her bed, he abruptly swept past her again to the stairwell.

'Sir.'

He stopped. Everything in him rebelled at her using the formal address. After seeing her bathing, it felt wrong that she called him as everyone else did. He wanted her to…no. Turning, he said, 'I'll see you tomorrow.'

'It's still morning. What am I to do?'

He shouldn't care what she did. 'Care for the child.'

'She's sleeping. Do I have free rein of the grounds?'

Her wandering around his house, him catching glimpses of her around every corner? He wouldn't survive it. Not after all that he had seen in the bath. All that he imagined on the landing as she stared at him. He'd been one shuddering heartbeat away from taking her. 'No.'

'Where are you going?'

Escaping from the questions in her stunning eyes. Barring that, he hoped to do what he always did. Read, write messages, and make plans. This residence was only one of many hideaways he had built for himself. There were some houses he hid only coin and supplies, but had never visited. All so he was never caught by his family.

Relocating from one domicile or country to another was extensive, but necessary, and it occupied most of his life.

What he was doing today was nothing he wanted this thief to be privy to, yet he already knew his concentration for the day wasn't optimal. Even if he holed himself up in the study, he'd think about the thief and the child. In that sense, it mattered little where she was.

'Follow me.'

Without waiting to see whether she would, he ascended the stairs. A moment, maybe two, and he heard the quick patter of uneven steps as she grabbed the basket. He didn't offer to carry the child this time. He had little control as it was when it came to his daughter.

Especially with her soft warbling breaths emitting from the basket. Grace was awake and the thief was whispering to her. He wanted to tear the basket away, to peer into the basket at his daughter. To see if Grace would smile as his brother Balthus had once done to him.

To protect her, he made no such move. If he failed to keep his distance, his family would tear her apart. He did the only thing he could, hurrying his steps through the courtyard, widening his strides on his own staircase, to put distance between himself and the thief who was supposed to be his servant. Yet, how was anyone to believe that when he invited her to his private quarters?

Chapter Nine

Safely ensconced in his study, Reynold stopped to listen for the thief who did not hurry her pace. Perhaps she couldn't, perhaps she sensed he needed time.

There was no peace here. In his study, the sanctuary of books usually eased his reeling thoughts. But she had been here before and everything in him knew it.

The thief entered more quietly than she had previously. While he watched them awkwardly, she carried the basket over to the bench under the window. Setting it down, she withdrew Grace and walked towards the door.

'Where are you going?'

'She's wet. I'll need to change her in the next room. They left spare linens in the bathing chamber.'

Control, that is all he wished for, all he needed to stay alive. So how had his life irrevocably devolved to this?

After all, he couldn't ask her to his private rooms and not expect she'd need items to support her care of Grace. And, in truth, he didn't want her changing soiled linens near his books. But just the way she so expectantly went about her tasks was something he hadn't experienced before. Nor was the ease and familiarity in which she did them.

People didn't do tasks like these in front of him. Servants came and went, carrying trays and items he needed, but they were trained to be ignored and invisible. But this nurturing of a child wasn't covert. The thief didn't try to mask her demands or quiet her singing. She simply…sang in front of him. She merely walked around as if she'd lived here all her life.

Since she did these deeds with such ease, it was apparent they were ordinary motions for her. To him, they were…extraordinary. She, the thief who was now eyeing him with brows raised, waiting for permission he hadn't yet granted, hadn't a clue how her insignificant task weakened his personal defences.

'Very well,' he said.

Nodding, she whisked Grace out of the room. Reynold stood for a moment out of place in his own home and chided himself. It shouldn't matter if the thief and child were here or elsewhere in the household. He had games to play and no time to waste.

Sitting at his desk, he picked up the latest correspondence from his south-east messenger. Many more letters were in front of him, stacked, rolled, tied, sealed. These tiny encrypted and costly messages would contain vital information on how he could act.

Matters in his game were proceeding rapidly now his brother, Guy, had been killed by the Welshman, Rhain of Gwalchdu.

Up until that point, there had been four of them. Four Warstone brothers: Ian being the eldest, then Guy, himself and the youngest, Balthus. Four perfectly bred sons. Issue of the married royals, Henry and Joan of Warstone.

To the public, they had everything they could want. Many would argue they had the best of both worlds. That it was a blessing kings and the church were more powerful than the Warstone family. After all, kings and the church had responsibilities, Parliaments to cater to, wars to start, citizens to acknowledge. They had greater power, but much greater burdens. As to more coin, it was rumoured the Warstone family had more money than King Edward, not that they would acknowledge it.

So his family enjoyed their wealth and power, and they kept their arguments and divisiveness only among each other. That was his parents' sacred rule. The punishments were so severe for all the other petty faults—how to stand, how to eat, et cetera—that none of his siblings ever dared break it.

And because they never did, to everyone else they were unbreakable, feared. And it made for a hellish childhood. Since birth, Reynold knew only hatred and death. When Balthus was born, his mother trained him as she had her other sons.

Reynold despised the unkind words, the anger, the insidious whispers. He wanted to protect Balthus's innocence. The only outcome of his outbursts was his mother turning on him. Forging a pack of her and his brothers against him. His punishments became almost unbearable. Worse, she took Balthus away and it was a full year before he saw his little brother again. Just barely a boy, and the innocence gone, his first words to him were vitriol. His mother's hatred had been planted.

Unable to fight against such a force, Reynold learned if he was quiet, he was allowed food and a place to sleep again. When he hid in the shadows he was ignored and allowed to observe. This way, he learned much of his family dynamics of power.

Even when he hadn't been hated he was never the favourite. That would be Ian, the first born, who would inherit everything and damn well knew it. Superior and cunning like a fox. Ian was no fool and, since he'd had two twisted people to learn from, he was a formidable foe.

As a child, he wasn't cruel like Guy, who snapped the necks of cats and hung the carcases in the servants' quarters as a prank. And he could never be as eager to please as Balthus. His youngest brother would be beloved because he was the last.

Many years passed like this with him hiding and observing until, one day, he overheard his father and mother plotting. Whispering about a legend he thought was a childhood story, but they talked of it as if it was fact. How the Jewel of Kings, a gem, had been hidden inside a jewelled dagger. Much like Excalibur and King Arthur, legend had it that whoever possessed the Jewel of Kings would rule Scotland. A mere symbol, but powerful enough to capture King Edward's interest in obtaining it.

Reynold knew, then, that if he acquired the Jewel of Kings he would have power over his family. They couldn't amass anymore. His parents might have kept their machinations with whispers to kings to behead a few nobles, massacre a few towns or conquer a few highlanders. But his brothers held no such circumspection.

Ian's duplicity and cunning wouldn't be satisfied with piecemeal evil. If he gained all the Warstone wealth and power as verily he was aiming to do, no one was safe from harm. Especially not infants who smiled at their brothers.

So every duplicitous trick he'd learned at his mother's breast, every backstabbing ploy discovered at his father's knee, every disloyal stunt performed by his brothers he would do as well until he was victorious. Until he possessed the Jewel of Kings.

He already held an advantage through his many studies. All his books and travel revealed the Jewel of Kings might be more than a symbol, though with the uproar of Scottish politics that alone would sway many from one side to another.

No, the Jewel of Kings was more lasting than the borders of countries. It was a map to a treasure. A great treasure. One that could buy kingdoms and any man. Could influence the Pope himself. He suspected this was why it had become a legend, why so many wanted it to control their political turmoil.

The issue, however, was he didn't have the dagger or the gem, nor did his family. And the dagger and gem were now separated thanks to a bumbling fool of an Englishman.

Who hired him? Either Ian or his parents. For a

time while Reynold tracked the Englishman and his entourage of men and a cunning archer who never left his side, he thought he had some true competition. But with the exception of the archer, the Englishman had hired mediocre mercenaries. Like idiots, they had lost the Jewel of Kings to the Colquhoun family.

Another complication. A troublesome one, but he knew the direction he needed to take now.

The Colquhoun family might now be on his game board, but they were easy to follow—distinctive red hair would do that. At one point he was tempted to order the slaughter of them all. But the brothers had scattered. So for now they were safe. However, it was the people they came in contact with who were the unacceptable variables.

Because of those variables, he needed to take the players he knew off the board, the Englishman being one of them, his brothers the other. He was grateful to the Welshman, Rhain, for killing his brother, Guy. Not only was Guy's wealth split among his brothers, but he was taken out of the game with no familial backlash.

'She was more than wet.' Entering the room, the thief swept past his desk and sat on the bench. Adjusting Grace, she extracted a tiny bowl of porridge from the basket. Nibbling on the contents from the wooden spoon, Grace sat docile in her lap.

It was a picture in domesticity, and jarring to his thoughts, to his work, to his game. To go from spying, treasure maps and murder to—

He watched Grace reach for the spoon.

'She's awake, I can return to my room,' the thief said.

They needed to leave. Both of them, but it wasn't safe outside or in here with him. 'Stay. I didn't sleep much—I think I'll read for now.'

He tossed the unread opened message on the desk, swiped the nearest book and flung it when he realised which one it was. It was an accident, it must be because he hadn't touched the book in years. Yet he feared the reaching for the haunting story of Odysseus traversing years and adversities to return to a devoted wife wasn't by chance. That somehow he had done it because Grace and the thief were going about their tasks as only a mother and child could. As a *wife* could.

Glancing over, he caught the thief's gaze travelling from the flung book and back to him. Irritated that he inadvertently revealed anything to her, he swiped the next book. Only to realise too late she'd settled into his favourite spot in the room, the one with the most light and comfort. He was regulated to a modest chair.

He opened the book and shifted as he tried to get comfortable.

'I can move,' she said.

'I didn't ask you to.'

'There's more light here.' She shifted over and moved the basket.

He had killed a woman last night. He was clean, but the deeds had stained his soul…if he had one anymore. 'What are you doing?'

'Making room for you.'

Chapter Ten

He slammed the book shut, startling Grace. The thief clutched her close, placed her hand on the back of her head. As if to protect her *from him*.

'I'll leave,' she said.

'You'll stay.' Though he needed to stay away from his daughter, he rationalised he would need the thief nearby to ascertain more about her. That was reason enough to invite her to the study and not leave her down below.

A couple of steps and he arranged himself on the large bench. An immediate mistake. He was so near her on the sun-warmed pillows he could smell the sage soap that enveloped her skin.

Aliette continued to feed Grace little bites. His daughter's eyes wide on her face, on the food. A light to them that wasn't there at the first feeding. Though clean, her skin still didn't have the glow of health and it hurt to see her swollen belly, frail arms and legs.

A bit more porridge, and Grace slowed, wiggled. Aliette wrapped her in swaddling and held her close.

Standing, Aliette was all too aware of the gaze of Darkness upon her. He had washed and changed, but these clothes were just as black as the last. His hair was wet and now shone almost blue.

He seemed aggravated with her, yet he had invited her to this room and ordered her to stay. She didn't understand. He'd kidnapped her, didn't like her, yet displayed acts of kindness.

It was only fitting she made room for him on the seat. How often had she done that with Vernon and Helewise? But…her captor wasn't her family and she shouldn't have done it with such unthinking ease.

He was a man, a species she shied away from as much as she ran from Darkness. More than that, he was *this man.*

And he didn't react to her offer of sitting on the bench with ease. Instead, frustration and distrust flashed across those grey eyes of his. As if she suddenly presented some danger to him.

Yet he said nothing while she walked the room with the child over her shoulder. His book was open, his eyes downcast, the thickness of his eyelashes remarkable against his cheeks.

Inexplicably, she knew his attention stayed on her and turned her back, but could feel his gaze as if he could see her very thoughts. She walked further away from the bench, patting Grace's back until she heard the telltale signs of wind and saw the drooping of eyelids.

'She sleeps much,' he said.

Nodding, Aliette took a few more turns around the room and Grace's eyes fully closed. She wanted to close her own. The quiet of the room, the warmth of the child, the fact she was fed, cleaned, clothed in a chemise that was soft against her skin.

The man returned to his book, a certain tenseness about his concentrating expression. All these books and he had trouble reading?

She returned to the bench and adjusted the child. Her captor shifted his body so it angled towards hers, their legs and feet almost touching.

The bench was enormous, padded with giant firm pillows along the wall and numerous smaller ones that were generously stuffed. The light from the window was pale given an oiled parchment which covered some of it, but enough with the torches along the walls.

Except for Grace's gentle breathing and the turning of pages, the room became ensconced in stillness.

Nestled like this, Aliette could observe her kidnapper. His body was sleek, elegant, the broadness of his shoulders hinting a leashed strength that couldn't be hidden by his tailored clothing and refinement. As if this inscrutable man hid himself not only in shadows, but in manners and the finest wool.

But his powerful physique was noticeable to one such as she. Used to the streets, on who to steal from and who not. Her rich captor could be alone at night and drunk, and, no matter how desperate or starving, she'd walk the other way.

It wasn't only his appearance that gave him away, but in the well-rehearsed way he moved that made him a predator. Even now, with his legs stretched out, his ankles gracefully crossed, the deft cupping of his hand that held the book, the capable curving of his fingers as they turned a page.

He leaned back against the pillows, but that only accentuated his size, his status, his formidable position in her world. She didn't feel his eyes on her, so she risked glancing at his face.

Dark hair drying, eyes relaxed. His lips softly moving, reading to himself. Like this he was... Aliette willed the wild flicking awareness to die out, but failed.

Like this, reclined, at ease and reading in the light, the man was utterly breathtakingly beautiful. Disconcerted, she searched his features for the cruelty, arrogance and ruthlessness that must be there.

'Something concerning you?' he said, his eyelashes sweeping upwards until those dark grey eyes burned into hers.

Was she concerned? Yes. This man was only Darkness and Death. Like this, he became something more. Was this fascination with him why she reacted that way on the landing? Was she noticing him as a man?

'I don't recognise the symbols.' She indicated with her chin.

He pursed his lips as if to challenge her before he said, 'It's Greek. A philosopher named Parmenides.'

'You can read other languages?'

'A few. I can speak more. Does that surprise you?'

No. Darkness would know more than others.

'What is a philosopher?'

He frowned. 'A philosopher is a great thinker.'

'So they are opinions or advice?' At his nod, she added, 'Don't you have thoughts of your own?'

His lips curved. 'Too many. It's refreshing to read others especially when it comes to matters I cannot solve solely on my own. Do you know how to read?'

She shook her head.

He jostled the book. 'Yet you know these are symbols.'

'In the market, there is writing and numbers. I don't know what they are, but I listen. What you are reading isn't like any of them.'

He roughly exhaled, his calculating eyes trailing to the child. 'You should know how to read.'

'Your philosophers won't have advice on how to find food.'

'There is more to life than survival.'

'What would you know of that?'

His grey gaze stayed steady, before he rolled his shoulders and waved around the lavish room. 'It takes much to guard silks and enamelled boxes.'

Again, she thought of his voice and his words. How they contrasted with the tone and the look in his eyes. Why did she feel he was playing a role? That he wasn't what he appeared to be.

'Survival is not about gold. Is that what you learned from those books? It's good that I cannot read such foolish words.'

'If you fight me so much on this, I insist you learn to read. Let me.'

'No one teaches a servant to read,' she blurted out, almost laughing.

He remained silent; his indomitable will speaking volumes, and all the tentative peace of the day was gone.

'You kidnapped me today,' she stated when his expression did not change. She sat in comfort now and had fed a child who slept contentedly against her, when the truth was she didn't belong and her own family could be frantic. This man had blood and mud splattered on his clothes the day they met. He wasn't safe. Now, he wanted to teach her to read.

'Yes, and you have yet to thank me,' he said.

'Thank you?'

'From saving you from the guard, from the baker, from the streets.'

'I will not thank you for ripping me out of the life I had!'

A mistake. His eyes narrowed. 'Why wouldn't you want it? Are you telling me you intend to escape?'

'Any sane person would. I don't know you. You've fed me, given me clothes, invited to teach me to read. No one does that.'

He eased back against the numerous pillows. 'You don't trust your good fortune.'

'I have yet to know if it's good.'

'Tell me why you want to escape, what displeases you so, and I will try to remedy your discomfort.'

Never. As if she'd believe him, as if she'd jeopardise her family! 'Tell me why you kidnapped me. Why you want this child, but won't touch her. Tell me why you have her, but don't know how to care for her.'

He went still. Carefully, he closed the book on his lap. 'It appears we are at an impasse. I think I'll say good day now. I'll have food sent to your room for later. Ask one of the mercenaries where the garderobe is. Or the kitchens are near it if you want things to do while it's light.'

If he was allowing her to leave, she'd leave. Laying Grace in the basket, she lifted it with both hands and leaned the cumbersome weight into her stomach.

She was tired, trapped, with no visible way to escape…yet. But she would find one, and he could find someone more suitable than her to care for the child.

'Tomorrow, I want you and Grace here after midday but far before light fades. You will be learning to read and to do sums.'

Arguing with him would achieve nothing. He had told her to find the garderobe and kitchens. That gave her plenty of free rein to find exits and weaknesses in this house. Almost to the door, he called her out.

'Thief.'

Not her name and she liked he didn't know it. Even so, she couldn't ignore him. He'd raised his voice and could wake Grace.

'My men, when they brought you here, did they speak to you?'

The men who brought food, water for the bath and clothing, had ignored her. But there was one who said a few words. The kind one who stopped the other one from breaking her arm.

Ah, now she understood why they had ignored her questions. This man had ordered them to be silent. What would happen to the kind one if she said he did speak? Nothing good.

'They've ignored me,' she said.

'None of them spoke?' he said, overly loud again.

Trying to keep quiet, she shook her head.

He canted his head, peered at her overly long as if she was someone or something of infinite puzzlement to him.

Impatient, she shifted the child's weight. 'Are we done...sir?'

He blinked and shook his head. 'You weren't meant to have secrets,' he said softly. So soft she almost didn't hear him.

But she did and it was true, she did have secrets. Perhaps for the first time in her life, she did and it surprised her. Made her feel...stronger than she had before. It was a power that she never had. Because she had secrets and he wanted to know them.

Of course, Darkness always wanted everything. But in the dead of night he had taken away her first family—she wouldn't let him take her current one. 'And you have too many.'

She turned away, but not before she saw a gleam of light to those all-knowing eyes and a quirk to his lips. Darkness enticed when he almost smiled.

At that realisation, she hurried out of the door to crash the cumbersome basket into one of the two men who stood guard outside.

The exact two men who had dragged her here. Then she understood her captor's loud voice. And by their fierce frowns, and eyes that gazed pointedly at her, they understood it as well.

Chapter Eleven

Aliette woke the next morning to Grace's restless turning. She pushed herself off the floor and took the few steps to the basket. Gathering her close, she rocked the child, who startled before she stilled.

'Who are you, Grace?' she asked. 'Where is your mother and why are you so unwell?'

Wide grey eyes soaking in her every word. The child looked as if it had known only suffering in her short existence. Had she been suffering here in this house, this fortress?

Because after her walk around yesterday to find the kitchens and the garderobe, Aliette came to the only conclusion she could. This place was a fortress. One exit and entrance, and far too many patrolling men.

If she was locked behind bars, she'd have less security than she did here. But there were comforts, too, fine clothing and fare for all and none of the men suffered.

Which meant Grace was a newly captured being, just like herself. And her father...for

Aliette knew her captor must be Grace's sire... had had blood on his clothes the day they met. Whose? The mother's? Because she couldn't conceive of anyone willingly giving up any child. If Grace were hers, it would take someone killing her to separate them.

Could her captor kill? Without a doubt. Was he capable of killing the mother of his child? That she couldn't reconcile, just as she couldn't reconcile her attraction to him.

That feeling of needing to be closer to him on the landing. And if he did kill Grace's mother, what did that say of her?

He wasn't...heartless, but what did she know? A day in his presence didn't tell her who he was. He was different than other nobles whose conceit wouldn't even deem her worthy to talk to. But his kindness was hardly enough to compensate for murder. Maybe if he was sorry for it, or if it had been accidental... Or maybe he was playing a role and he wasn't cruel Darkness at all. The way he protected Grace... Maybe he was... What was she thinking? Her thoughts were dark. Was this what one day in his presence brought?

She didn't even know his name. And she didn't know why she or Grace were here. Too many secrets. Still, she couldn't abandon Grace. She knew all too well what it was like to be left behind.

And how were Vernon and Helewise faring—was Gabriel keeping warm?

Squeezing the child once more, she changed her linens, adjusted clothes, cleaned their faces and hands with the cold basin water that had been brought last night along with a light fare. Little things, but luxuries to her, and the room wasn't as freezing as she suspected it would be being so deep under the stones.

Perhaps it was the fireplace at the opposite end of the hallway. The one by the stairwell that hadn't been lit yesterday or when she finally went to sleep, but someone had stacked it with logs in the middle of the night and it was blazing away.

It made the hallway comfortable. She carried Grace in the basket up to the kitchens. Three men whom she hadn't met were there. One was making bread, another preparing vegetables and, off in the corner, near an open door, the third mercenary was hand-dipping chickens in a vat of steaming water.

She set the child down far enough from the industry in the kitchen, but near the fire. For now Grace remained quiet. She suspected the child stayed quiet because of neglect. That she was weakened. She hoped it was that simple, that more harm hadn't—

Aliette refused to think those thoughts. Nothing could be resolved just now.

After meeting the cook yesterday, she knew to come here. She'd hoped for some companionship, yet no one talked in greeting or to tell her what tasks to be done. So she grabbed a water-dipped chicken, laid it within a large linen in her lap to gather stray feathers and plucked.

This was a task she knew well. The market sellers demanded their fowl to appear faultless. So she learned the subtle quick tug that released the feathers, but didn't harm the skin.

That's when the man who was tearing his fowl to bits stopped his task. Glancing at him, she was relieved to see his gaze was on her plucking fingers.

Ah. Opening her linen so that he could see, she pinched a few of the feathers in the wing's crevice and tugged. She did it a few more times, more slowly than the first, until he adjusted his chicken to mimic her.

She did this for a few more turns of the bird before gathering it tight in the towel again to keep the feathers in place. The quiet made it easy to hear Grace's restlessness. Two full meals yesterday and the child needed more food, but Aliette had never been in a position to simply ask for food before.

Just when she was certain she'd have to stop her work and return to her room where she had hidden a roll under her pillow, the mercenary who'd been slapping at the dough nudged her shoulder with a bowl of porridge that he set on a table. It was large enough for her, but it had been cooked long and the oats were mush.

'Thank you,' she said, her voice sounding unnaturally loud among the quiet mercenaries, and she made a startling realisation. They'd been ordered to ignore her, but she hadn't been ordered to ignore them. They couldn't talk to her, but there was nothing to say she couldn't talk to them.

Laying her plucked chicken on the pile, she walked to the sink to wash her hands with the hot water available.

She had never washed so much in her life, but she had Grace, who looked like a stray speck of dust could fell her, and the blood and feathers weren't pleasant to breathe, so they couldn't be good for her.

But what did she know? Maybe…maybe these men did. After all, one of them anticipated Grace would need the mush and handed it to her. Who were they? All large, one of them in clothing she'd never seen before.

'Where is the cook?' she said, not expecting a reply. 'I'm supposed to assist him, but I'll have trouble assisting if he's not here.'

Nothing.

She picked up Grace, who was thankfully dry, and set her on her lap. Pretending to address Grace, she talked to the men. 'Well, what do we have here, Grace? Hot porridge which the nice man made for us. You should tell him thank you, when you can. Because he didn't have to feed either of us, but he did. Just like that man who allowed us to sit and help pluck chickens. That man made us feel useful and needed. If we're to be here, we need to be needed, don't we—otherwise, why would they allow us to stay?'

Carefully spooning and blowing on the mush, Aliette continued to feed Grace. 'And didn't you sleep wonderfully? Was that because you were warm because someone lit a fire? I wonder who that could have been. That was a courteous person as well. I think I'll thank that person, too. It helped us sleep so much better.'

And on and on she talked to Grace until she was fed, alert…almost content. Far too quiet, but maybe no one talked to her as she talked to her now. Aliette had had a brother once, whom she thought of fondly when she could bear the memory. He had been kind, hadn't he? Maybe she learned her ease of talking with Grace from her brother.

Or maybe it was with Gabriel she began to realise children needed more than food and shelter. Both she and Helewise had talked to him long into that first night. It soothed him and had done something for her as well. A wish that someone had talked to her on those first long nights alone. Gabriel...she missed him, feared for him. Helewise and Vernon would comfort, but couldn't provide for him. Were they starving?

She shoved away the bowl of porridge and returned an awake Grace to her basket, which wouldn't hold her for long. If Grace gained her strength, she'd be pulling herself up, crawling, walking, and there was no place in this kitchen that would be safe for her.

Perhaps she could request a corner to be cleared and a fence of sorts to be erected. She'd seen those before and they penned the children to a safe area. She snatched another chicken to pluck. Was she truly thinking she'd be here that long?

The feathers flew. This one, too, had been dunked in hot water to release the feathers. The pile had grown since she fed Grace. How much food did they need? One, two fowls per man? Too much food!

And yet, here she was fed, clothed, sheltered

as if she'd lived in this luxury all her life. None of it felt strange to her.

Maybe it was the quietness of the kitchen or the ease she was able to talk to Grace. Certainly, nothing about this situation should feel natural. Surrounded by hired swords who patrolled and killed. Kidnapped, stuck in this fortress with no means to contact Gabriel. Yet, here she was methodically plucking feathers alongside mercenaries.

They didn't feel threatening, even though their silence confirmed their loyalty to her captor. Thus, they, like their captor, couldn't be trusted.

But maybe in time, with familiarity, she could persuade the man who saved her arm yesterday, or this man who gave her porridge. Maybe she could plead with them to send a message to Gabriel. She knew she'd receive no such leniency from her kidnapper, no matter how fiercely he guarded Grace against her, no matter how longingly as he looked at the child. She wouldn't risk telling Darkness of her own family. He could take—

A hand on her shoulder and she started. Everyone, but the man who'd plucked chickens, was gone. His hands were now clean, his expression tentative. Voices were coming down the hallway. It was the sound of the cook she'd met yesterday.

How long had she been lost in her thoughts? The man took the plucked chicken from her lap, laid it with the others and helped her up. Did she look as unsteady as she felt? She'd barely be able to pick up—

Grace! No basket, no child. 'Where is she?'

He pointed to the door. She washed her hands and followed him out to the courtyard. It was a sunny day despite the cold. Several men were training, most were watching. One was holding Grace. The kind one who had saved her arm, who was too handsome for his own good. He was bouncing her about while another man talked to him heatedly, as if advising him on his foolish deeds. But whatever was said in such seriousness, the kind man turned his back and laughed again, his face going into the crook of Grace's neck to make the most ridiculous sounds.

The child didn't say a word. The mercenary next to the one holding Grace, however, did. And though she hadn't stepped fully into the court-yard, she heard it.

He was cursing at the other mercenary and when he saw her, he announced something in a foreign language and marched away. The whole courtyard of men turned to her.

Head held high, she strode towards the laugh-ing man and lifted her arms to take Grace who was supposed to be hers. He didn't dispute her claim and the knot of uncertainty in her stomach eased. Did she worry over this child already? What was to be done when she escaped?

Stay occupied, keep moving forward, that was the only solution for these thoughts. Aliette knew she'd have to remind herself often in the coming days. Prepared to change Grace, Aliette patted her bottom, it was...dry. Which was an impossibility. 'You changed her.'

The man simply raised his brow.

'This is ridiculous.' She had had enough. 'Whatever that man said to you is just ridiculous. He can't expect me to be here and not talk to anyone. What if there's a fire? Will no one call out to warn me?'

'If such an event should occur, a general cry of alarm would be raised so that all would be expected to escape,' said a voice directly behind her.

An all-too-even voice that was so richly textured that she shivered.

Holding Grace firmly to her chest, Aliette turned.

'And I can and do expect much of you, thief,' Darkness finished.

Chapter Twelve

Even with the sun beaming this man wasn't tangible to her. Among men who were giants among men, who no doubt killed and if possible, something worse, this elegant man was something other to her. Intimidating. Absorbing in a way that fascinated her.

Everything that was natural in the kitchen wasn't here at all, because her reaction to this man before her wasn't ordinary.

Once she was older and more sensible to avoid men, she ignored them. It was safer that way, but also, she never needed to be close to them in any capacity. Especially not the way she'd seen the local whores or the more desperate street urchins be with them.

When that occurred, Aliette saw too much. Some received food, others coin, but Aliette could never sell her body. Not out of a sense of purity, but because she was broken. Because her parents had shattered her trust the morning she woke and they weren't there.

No. Always, always, she thought she was broken, damaged, ruined. That whatever passion, fake or genuine, she witnessed, whatever soft affection Vernon and Helewise displayed to each other, would never be hers no matter how she longed for it. How could she trust another soul like that?

For her there was only survival.

But Darkness could not be ignored or avoided. Though he stood in a calm manner, though there was no frown upon his face, though he was merely looking at her, everything in her reacted.

Nothing felt broken in her as she took in his startling appearance. For the first time, there was a flash of something alive and whole within her. It sped up her heart and shortened her breath. Her hands prickled and grew damp and a heated weight sunk within her very core. Lower yet the longer they stared at each other.

Pure daylight above and something of his flaws should have been apparent. Something to mar the fierce beauty of him. Instead, the sun above highlighted his perfection to her. Sunlight highlighted the darkness of Darkness. She wasn't a fool. She knew what this was. She simply hadn't expected it. Never with anyone and certainly never with him, but she was…attracted. Enticed. *Tempted.*

She didn't know if she was more irritated at

herself or him. 'This is absurd. I don't care what you expect or don't expect. If you—'

'Follow me,' he said, swiftly turning towards the staircase she knew went to his rooms above.

She stood, aware of all the eyes around her. Instead of being intimidated, she looked at the men. Truly looked at them. Yes, they were large and no doubt dangerous, but none of them looked at her with hatred or evil intent. Some looked…well, most had no expression at all. An expression she was sure was convenient when it came to battle. Some, however, were shocked and the one who had been holding Grace was overtly amused.

'You all think this ridiculous, don't you?' she said. 'How am I expected to work or perform any task if no one speaks?'

No answer, but the amused one's expression changed to warning.

All right, she'd find no friends here, so she'd pursue the man who made such absurd demands if only to have a proper argument. She pivoted in the direction of the basket, only to slam into an extremely unmovable body.

Not even the cushioning of Grace between them softened the fact that his hands grasped her arms. That his rigid stance forced one of his legs between hers.

He stood as if bracing himself, bracing her for the fall she was supposed to have, but her body had no intention of doing it. In fact, oddly, she leaned into his weight, which pressed the whole of Grace into his chest, but also gave her other touching points. Her elbow, a stray lock of her hair caught on his shoulder.

Nothing, he said nothing. She was incapable of drawing back. The scent of him, the heat of his hands. She'd never been held this securely before in her life. A child braced between them and they shared the barest of connections. But it was enough to withstand the harshest of winters, the bitterest of life's heartache.

Just his hands holding her steady and she felt—

'Bring the basket,' he said low, not breaking his gaze with her.

A blur of movement out of the corner of her eye, a mercenary picking up a basket, while her captor deliberately extracted Grace from her arms to wrap her in his.

And her heart. Her heart that hadn't been working properly around this man since he guarded Grace against her the first time stopped.

Because his gently cradling Grace did something to it, to her. This wasn't like before when he had held her swaddled, both covered in mud and blood. Both threatening against her because she was forced here, because they were unknown.

But a day had passed since then. She knew Grace better and now she knew something of her captor, the mercenaries who surrounded him, this fortress.

It wasn't much, but it was enough. A sliver of difference that somehow was enough space for other emotions to tumble through. Like the traitorous heat that acknowledged him as a man and then acknowledged that she desired him. Like this image of Darkness enfolding a child into his arms. She hadn't been wrong yesterday when he guarded the child. Grace *was* precious to him; he truly cared for her.

Such an infinitesimal difference between one day and another, but enough. Assaulted by her observations, her abandoned heart wouldn't work like it had before and she didn't know if she wanted it to. For why would she want to go back to a time when she thought all infants were abandoned to freeze to death or learn to survive? Why would she want to forget how he looked at her on the landing as if she wasn't broken?

Yet life had taught her not to trust any of this. It was a lesson she must remember until she could escape or was left behind.

* * *

Reynold didn't bother to see if the thief would follow this time, he simply took the child and expected it. Where else would she go?

He had told her she must remain with Grace. Told her what would happen if she didn't. He told her and the very next morning his daughter was being passed around from one mercenary to another with no thief in sight.

The fear, the anger. The possessive rage that struck through him. He wanted to rip their throats. He didn't want his own hands to touch her, but these men were paid to kill and did it well. He didn't want their murderous calloused hands on a child who had already suffered so much.

When he saw the thief wasn't near his daughter, his anger grew cold. He had warned her that she must be the mother. A true mother wouldn't abandon a child, not ever, and, unless she was dead, not to these men.

These men… The closer he came to the courtyard, the more he heard. Their gentle singsong words, Louve blurting sounds right in her neck. Instead of being terrified, Grace's eyes widened in delight. No sounds, no laughter, or giggles or happy cooing. But she *liked* it.

So he'd stayed in the shadows of the courtyard

to observe. Because, unlike him, these men knew how to hold a child. Baldr, who he knew had siblings, but no gentleness, even changed her soiled linen. And all the while, Reynold watched them be careful, gentle…at ease with her in a way he hadn't been, but wanted to be.

His men knew he was there, but no one engaged him. They never did and he preferred that, but this time around, he expected the child to be placed back in the basket and for them to continue with their training. Instead, they continued to hold her.

And that's when the thief arrived. Took Grace in her arms and made her incendiary mutinous comments.

That wouldn't do. It was one concern to watch his men shirk their duties and hold a child, it was another for a homeless street wench to question his rule in his own domain. Because in that moment, he wasn't sure if his men who sang, talked and held a child remembered who was in charge.

The thief certainly didn't when she stormed through the courtyard and held out her arms for Grace. One day she'd been here and she expected Louve to hand Grace over. Yesterday, she had sat on his bench as if this was her house. All with a certainty that astounded and frustrated him.

Grace was one change, having the thief as a

mother was another. He wouldn't, couldn't, tolerate any other differences in his life. He would remain in control here as in all aspects of the game until he won.

It was that feeling of loss of control that prompted him to demand she follow him. Instead, she stumbled against him. His first instinct was to steady her, to steady himself. But the longer he held her the more unbalanced he became.

And he didn't want to move at all or, if he did, it was to pull them both closer. Until he clasped close to his chest, to his heart, his daughter and this unknown woman. This woman whose eyes were as wide and absorbing as Grace's.

But nothing about her gaze was innocent. Eyes warming, pupils dilating, a flush that bridged across her cheeks and nose. The rose red of her lips parted, slightly damp with the tip of her tongue and softening.

Just as her body was softening against him. Incredibly, her delicate body pressed more against his. A leg brushing, a hand, her hair laying along Grace's back and across his chest. This woman, who hadn't expected to stumble into him.

Until he was at war with himself. One part wanting to shake her and make her come to heel. The other part all too aware he touched her in an almost embrace with his daughter between them and he couldn't let her go.

And his body, his soul, the very marrow of his bones knew exactly why. Because he saw it. Something he shouldn't for both their sanity. He saw it.

She wanted him, too.

Reynold couldn't climb the stairs to his rooms quick enough. If he stood much longer in the courtyard, his men would see his reaction to them both. One he struggled to contain.

He strode into the study and whirled for one moment. Why did he come here again when it brought him no peace before? What was he to do with the child in his arms?

Light chatting by the thief, absolute silence from the two men coming up behind her. One carrying a basket. The other wine, bread, some fruit to break his fast.

When they had arranged the tray and basket, and turned to leave the room, he said, 'Close the door.' Something he rarely ordered. Always he wanted the door parted to hear intruders, to ease access for escape.

More and more with the thief and the child, he needed it closed. With one simple pull of the latch, the doors were shut, cocooning them inside. Reynold couldn't contain his restlessness.

Holding the child, he picked up a trinket, set it down, adjusted a pillow and ambled completely around his desk until he stood in front of it again. His child simply watched his every action.

His child.

'Didn't I make it clear what would happen if you disobeyed me?'

The woman eyed Grace in his arms, her lips pursed, a question in her eyes as if she wanted to demand her back. He wouldn't oblige.

'I haven't disobeyed you,' she said finally.

'I told you to remain with the child. I came down from my rooms to see her being passed from one mercenary to another. You weren't in sight.'

'That's disobeying you?' she said.

'Do you know who they are? Hired swords. Men who—'

'Murder or worse,' she interrupted. 'You're angry because I was gone for a moment, when it was you who invited murderers in a home with a child?'

Just like that, she turned the game on him. Reynold wasn't fooled. He wasn't at fault. 'Do you think that in this house I would be on the defensive? I told you yesterday that you were this child's mother. Maybe given your background you don't know what mothering means. Maybe—' Reynold stopped.

The woman before him had paled, her eyes shocked wide with his words that struck deep and quick. He'd sliced his sword into men who bore such a look.

Clasping Grace more firmly, he stepped until his legs hit his desk. My God, he had hurt her. Truly hurt her. With words. He meant to, but not like this.

Before he could recover, before he could soften his statement, her eyes narrowed and her chin jutted. The pale expression gone, in its place was an expression of intent, of determination, anger.

'How long were you watching your murderers handle Grace?'

'How long was I aware?' His thoughts running rampant on what he'd unintentionally done and why it mattered, Reynold couldn't comprehend what she was talking about. For years he'd hurt people with his words and his swords. Why would it matter if he hurt her? She was at fault. They were always at fault.

'How long were you in the courtyard watching Grace being passed from one mercenary to the other?' she said. 'Because it couldn't have been long.'

'How do you know it wasn't long?' he said. 'Are you saying you allowed them to take her?'

'I have *allowed* nothing since you forced me here.'

'Don't pretend you had somewhere better to go.'

Her lips clamped shut.

Secrets. Could it be possible that one such as her would have them? 'What are you not telling me.'

A sound of frustration ripped from her throat. 'What is this? I agreed to take care of Grace, but you have no right to my thoughts!'

'Thoughts?'

'I was thinking. That's all. Plucking a bird and thinking. That's what people do when they're not reading other's opinions and advice. When I was done, I went to the courtyard. It's good the men took her from the kitchens. There's blood, innards. The air is full of feathers, dust from the flour and the fire doesn't draw properly.'

This was her confession, that she was lost in thought. A pathetic excuse. Weak.

Except when she said it to him, gone was Artemis brandishing her arrow, now she looked vulnerable. As if she had revealed a true weakness. What were her thoughts; what didn't she want to reveal to him?

He didn't know this thief, no matter what he had witnessed yesterday morning at the market. He'd only seen her in the clutches of the guard, he didn't know if she had taken the bread.

After that, she cared for Grace, fed, bathed and held her gently. Yet he was the one who accused her of not knowing how to mother. As if...as if he understood that kind of care. *His* mother was trying to kill him.

As for his men, his soul and hands were more bloodstained than theirs. They knew how to hold and talk to a child. Every time he held Grace, she felt breakable and he felt ill at ease with the flood of longing to hold her tighter. For him—

Self-reflection. Thought. When had he doubted himself? Never. Not once since he realised he must defeat his family. Foolish to do so and he would stop now.

This thief was dangerous to him. It wasn't only the fact his body recognised her, it was her thoughts, her deeds. He couldn't predict what she would do or say and, in one day, he couldn't predict men who were paid to protect him.

Chapter Thirteen

'Very well, then,' said Darkness.

'Very... What? I can have thoughts?' Aliette didn't hold back the bite to her words. For good measure, she looked at the door, which was closed. There was only one way to remedy that. 'Can I have Grace before I leave?'

The man patted Grace's back. She wasn't certain he knew he did it. She was aware, however. Everything from the courtyard still flooded through her, the clumsy way she stood, the uneven way she breathed. She knew exactly how close he was, the parting of his legs, the crook of his arms as he cradled Grace to him. She almost felt those long fingers drum along her own back.

'No, you cannot,' he answered.

She huffed, pivoted on her heel. Did he think she had all the time to waste with whatever it was he wanted of her? 'If you don't want me taking care of the child since I left her to your men, release me.'

'Why are you so eager to go.'

'I'm not eager, I merely don't want to be here.'

'I require you here today. For her sake, you need to learn to read.'

'There are tutors for that.'

He kept his silence. Constantly, this silence. Him, his men, even the child. 'You don't want other people here, do you? Didn't you say you'd hire others? I was in the kitchens all morning. I saw no evidence of others.'

She walked near to him; enough to become painfully aware of herself around him. Her very skin felt too tight with a weakening underlying trembling that she internally willed to calm. 'What is this place? It looks like one house from the outside, but it's not. You took many houses and combined them, but no one can know that. Do your neighbours know of the armed men? Like a secret. Which begs the question, are you intending for me ever to leave?'

He brushed Grace's head with his hand and sat her in the basket. Her hand immediately went to her mouth.

'How can she be hungry?' he said.

How can he not know this child? 'It's her teeth. A way to soothe them coming in.'

'She's not crying or distressed.'

She wasn't and that worried her. Grace had been fed and slept well. She was sitting more and, though painfully thin, the weakness was lifting within one day. Still, she didn't speak. Who was this child?

Aliette crouched before the basket and ran her hand over the child. 'No, she's not distressed. But—'

'But?'

She wouldn't put words to her worries. Simply kept her eyes on the child versus the man who now walked from table to table until he released a book from one of the stacks.

'Do you know stories?' he said.

Vernon and Helewise told many and he wasn't entitled to know any of them. 'When would I have time for stories?'

'I only have one copy of this in English.' He flipped through some pages. 'You can hold it while I read.'

She stood. 'How can you read it if I'm holding it.'

'I know this version of the story well. Simply look at the book and I'll speak each word slowly.'

He held the book out. She shook her head.

'Why not?' he said. 'It's a story, that is all, not some other person's advice.'

'I've seen books before. There was a priest at church, cradling a Bible in his hands. It was colourful. I drew up close to it and could almost see it before he hurried it away.'

At her words, the soft confusion in his expression was destroyed by something which blackened his countenance. 'Do you think you're not worthy to read it?'

'That's not it.' She looked at her hands and shook her head. 'Yesterday I didn't have a dress or shoes. The food I ate was from a pig's trough. In one day, someone is handing me a book.'

She was spouting words that had no meaning to a man who had lived in a palace. Her life had only ever been survival. Here, kidnapped and held prisoner, it should have also only been about survival. Teaching her to read was a kindness. A gift. Darkness didn't give gifts without taking something away. Would she never see her family again?

She glanced at the man beside her. His face implacable, his eyes steady. 'I don't suppose you'd understand.' She shrugged. 'Learned people read. Wealthy people own books. Books represent a life of abundance.'

'Abundance,' he said. 'Interesting thought when I always thought they were all I had.'

His words were said so softly, evenly, she didn't at first react. When she registered what they were, she wasn't all certain they were meant for her.

Then he blinked, cleared his throat and she knew with certainty the achingly distant words weren't meant for her, but she heard them all the same. *She heard them.*

'You are...crying,' he said, his voice a roughened timbre.

Embarrassed, she wiped her cheeks. 'It's the books. They're beautiful, aren't they?'

Reynold didn't understand this thief he'd kidnapped because he needed her, a woman, a pretend mother. Now he found he was needing her in other ways. Ways that were difficult the more time he spent with her. It'd only been a day.

Her dark waving hair unbound, flowing against her shoulders, the serviceable brown of her gown. He didn't like that. It wasn't right against the paleness of her skin and the blue of her eyes. Her unbound hair would look magnificent against a different coloured gown, but not as fine as her own bare— He couldn't think of the bath, not now, and remain rational.

The discussion of books was dangerous as well. The way she gazed with wary hunger at the book in his hand. Her telling him of her life of survival. His own confession. She'd looked at the book as if it was all that she could dream of. For him, they were precious, but meagre to the stories inside. When she heard them, what would she think of the books then?

'You should read.'

'Such a skill isn't useful in my world,' she said.

'Grace needs to learn and you must be the one to teach her.'

'That'll be years away.' The alarm on her face faded to mutiny. 'Are you saying I'll never see the outside again?'

Logically, he'd want his daughter outside these walls and, of course, he'd soon have to change home again. Not that she needed to be aware of that. He never told his own men until the last moment.

If she thought herself trapped, he could alleviate her fears. 'You help in the kitchens and it is only right you go to market for supplies...with a chaperon, of course.'

One eyebrow raised in challenge, she said, 'With one of your mercenaries?'

'Who else?'

Snatching the book, she plunked down in the bench's well-padded corner, once his spot and now hers, and tucked her feet under her. Setting the book on her lap, she opened it to the page he had shown her. The correct page. So...though she protested, she had noticed. What else did she see in his home, in him?

He burned to know her thoughts. With the parchment's illustrations twinkling brightly on her lap and the weak winter sun framing her dark hair, he could not want her more.

To cover his need, he sat on the bench and adjusted his body not to touch her. For in this delicate moment, he knew if even her drab clothing brushed against him, he could not control his impulses.

He was all too aware he had almost held her in an embrace in the courtyard. He knew the radiance of her bared skin was more beautiful than the illuminations of gold in his books.

He began to read, and slowly revealed the tale of Orpheus and Eurydice. Of a man who risked all to save his wife from Hades, only to stumble at the end. To turn around too soon and watch her fall back to the Underworld.

Each page he read again, knew every word, every picture. Knew when to tell the thief to turn the page.

Watched her roughened fingers lovingly lift each sliver of paper, watched her eyes widen and absorb the tiny inscriptions, the few pictures drawn. Saw her close the book when the story was completed and pressed her hand against it as if to keep it permanently there.

'He played the lyre,' she said on a shaking breath.

'It was said Hades wept iron tears when Orpheus played. I did not think this is what you would talk of.'

'I can't talk of the rest. Why did you pick that one? Out of all the books here, why was this the first story you wanted to tell me?'

Insightful. It hadn't been random when he chose it. It was a reminder for himself not to lose his own way. Guy, his brother, was dead and he was close to procuring the Jewel of Kings. Having Grace, seeing the thief bathing…he could not lose his way.

'It's a lesson.'

'A lesson?'

'Orpheus was warned what would happen if he looked back too soon. All the toil, the hardships, the trials he went through to save Eurydice from Hades. He risked his life and, because he wanted to give his wife comfort…or wanted to give himself comfort when he doubted she was behind him, he forgot his purpose. Just when he was to gain everything, he looked back and lost it all.'

'Oh.'

Such an insignificant comment, but there was a wealth of meaning. 'You don't agree with me.'

'It's not for me to agree or not.' She pointed to the book. 'It's only a story, is it not? Not some opinions or advice from a great thinker.'

He rested his arm on the back of plump pillows.

'I gave you an opinion and thus you can give me yours about the story. I can tell you don't agree with what I said. Don't you have an opinion?'

'I have opinions on many matters.'

'Tell me them.' The words were out before he thought about them or why it mattered. 'You were lost in your thoughts today, surely you can share a few.'

She frowned. 'You kidnapped me and hold me prisoner here. Why would you care about my thoughts?'

Good question and one he couldn't answer without revealing more of himself. 'I never said I cared, just that I want them.'

'Are you always this arrogant, or is it just to me, a mere street thief?'

He revelled in her rebuke of him. 'Ah, it appears you do hold opinions that you're willing to share, but perhaps I was merely born this way.'

She shook her head. 'You talk to a mere thief. You give respect to your men. You surround yourself with stories that contain adventures and thoughts of great thinkers and you read to me about the foibles of people. You don't act like a man who was born a certain way, but a man who knows it's the journey that makes him.'

His heart stopped and he didn't dare answer her with the truth or how much he wanted to believe her words. That he wasn't simply his father's son, that he could be something different. 'Such great thought and you still won't tell me about your feelings on some characters in a story.'

She huffed as if disappointed in his flippant answer. It had been years since he'd answered anyone with the truth. For all their sakes he couldn't start now. Still, her disappointment didn't sit well with him.

She straightened on the bench as if to get up. He didn't want her to leave. 'Maybe you're right,' he said, pleased that she stilled. 'I've had wealth all my life, the books are only more of that wealth, but the stories—the stories inside the books are abundant to me.'

Her eyes so blue and clear they were like looking at an untarnished sky. He held his breath, wanting to know what she would say next. He couldn't help but feel that she knew him somehow and that he could share these tiny bits of his soul with her. That—

'Read me another of these stories.'

A lightness hit his chest at her demand. He had…almost laughed. To cover his reaction, he reached for the next book in the stack.

The afternoon wore on as he picked more Greek tales. Food came and she fed and played with Grace on the floor. When it came time, she settled her in the basket to sleep, adjusted her own body on the bench again. Her head leaning against the back pillows, her arms half-tucked under her.

The last book, like all the rest, she did not want to hold. This time, he relented. Her eyes were slumberous, her breath evening out. The book he chose often put him to sleep. Within moments, her eyes closed and stayed that way.

Reynold quietly shut the book. He didn't dare move. Not because it would disturb the two females sleeping peacefully in his sanctuary. But because he didn't know if his legs could hold him.

What possessed him to bring her here, to teach her to read? Grace did need to learn, but there were tutors or he could teach his daughter.

These books were his family and he merely opened and *shared* them with a thief. Had she in that moment of bathing possessed more than his body? He risked asking her opinion. She told the truth without ever knowing how many times he asked himself: was he merely a product of his sire and dame or could he make himself something else?

It seemed she knew his very soul. Then, through it all, he almost laughed? It was too much, too soon. Just as it was when he first held Grace.

Grace. Knowing the thief slept, and it was only him, he bent down to the basket, extracted his daughter and settled her belly on his chest as he rested again on the bench. He revelled in her soft snorting breath, the little rustle movements as she found a comfortable position against him.

She smelled sweet. As if innocence had a bloom all its own. He noted the differences between his callused hands against the folds in her white skin. He turned his left hand to contrast the scar he endured to the perfection in her dimpled fist, and made his own vow: that no matter what he was, or who he had to be for her, a stranger or her father, she would never suffer as he had.

The thief had suffered. Just a few sentences to indicate what her life was like before him and he wanted to know more. Time. Maybe with his daughter, with this woman who drew him to her, time would be in his favour.

How much time did they have? The thief slept quietly now, but if he closed his eyes, if he left the room, the house, this very city, he would know she was here. Just her presence, the light fragrance of his sage soap not masking her scent. Something beckoning him. Then there was that something else almost tangible between them.

Similar to an instinct or a sense. A bond, internal and vital, which lured and intoxicated. A corporeal ability he didn't know he possessed or was capable of until she arrived. It uniquely tied him to her, with a fierce presence he didn't have the ability to fight.

It wasn't something he could negotiate with, battle, draw his sword and gut. He could send no battalions of mercenaries or release one lethal arrow. At present, he could find no freeing himself from her, though he knew he must.

For now, she slept and, a few heartbeats later, so did he.

Chapter Fourteen

Days went by, and Grace kept Aliette to a schedule. She gained strength. Slept less. Took the spoon and anything else in her vicinity she could grab. She didn't talk or make a sound, but if Aliette watched her closely enough there was communication.

The mercenaries kept their silence, though they gave up on stopping their own conversations and she gradually learned their names and personalities. Some of them fenced a large corner in the dining hall for Grace to play in since she had taken to crawling out of her basket.

Her captor had stopped in his tracks, stared at it, but continued to do whatever it was he was doing. Except in the afternoon, when the sun was just setting and he called her to read, he didn't seem to keep to any such schedule as she and the men had fallen into.

Sometimes he'd be in his rooms all day, sometimes only a few moments before storming down the stairs and handing tiny leather pouches to another man, who would saddle a horse and not return.

She continued to search for ways to escape. When all else failed, she watched the main doors when they opened. She realised after a few days there were a core of mercenaries who always stayed and others who came and went. On the sixth day, there were two who pounded at the great door outside. Their horses were in a lather, their own clothes were stained, torn and, when they dismounted, they collapsed.

That day, Darkness hadn't asked her to read and he'd stayed in his rooms far into the night. She knew he was awake when everyone else slept for she saw the lights burning upstairs.

Since she arrived she hadn't been able to sleep. Not unless she counted that day when she fell asleep in the study as if she hadn't a care in the world and was safe from any harm.

But the room had gone quiet, the fear of the day had wrecked whatever strength she had to avoid dangerous situations and her captor's unexpected kindness with the book shattered her sense that life was only about survival.

When she had woken, she found him in the same spot, his expression contemplative as he watched her. Realising her captor watched her sleep wasn't what brought heat to her cheeks, but the fact he didn't look away…and neither could she. Not when he cradled Grace against him. Both of their hair so dark; their lashes unnaturally long. Grace looked so slight within his large hands, against his powerful body.

She had wanted to ask him a thousand questions—why deny Grace was his, why act as if he didn't want her when he tenderly held her against him? His heated gaze turning challenging until, as if sensing the tension between them, the child woke and she bid him goodnight.

Another sleepless night, for Darkness kept her wary. She knew why she couldn't sleep, she just couldn't raise an argument why she should be moved. But it wasn't only the dark keeping her awake, but her circumstances. Surrounded by men who should have terrified her, but didn't. She watched the mercenaries train with their knives and bodies. With her and Grace, they were nothing but gentle consideration.

And her captor… Darkness was still all arrogance and ruthlessness. He most of all should have terrorised her, but over the course of the days she saw more of the man. The fact he whispered words to himself as he read Greek, but not the other languages.

The careful way he had watched her when she woke from sleep. How he held Grace and conversed with his men. His need to control, the respect he gave them. He was curt, rude, formidable and reluctantly kind. His kindness, which always seemed to disquiet and surprise him, tugged at something inside her.

She could no longer deny that the time with him was changing her perception of him. It was more than his kindness. No longer was she wary with him. In its place was something inexplicable. An awareness that felt...shared. It was there in ways she couldn't explain. A feeling when he sat with her reading, in the way he enquired about Grace, in the lives within the stories. In caught glances that lingered.

Those should have alarmed her, but her heart—her heart, which she thought broken—recognised him. The longer they spent together the more she wanted to...speak of it. That maybe he felt the recognition, too. Which made no sense, given his obvious wealth and status, but still the feeling was there.

But more than that, it was remarkable because of who she was, what she had become when her parents abandoned her. With her new family, her heart no longer felt alone, but there was still something jagged inside her and she couldn't trust.

Somehow, she felt she fit here, in this fortress,

surrounded by mercenaries, on a sumptuous bench being read to from beautiful books. Fit because of Grace, who had brought them together and whom she cared for deeply.

She shouldn't trust any of it, not while she was kept separated from her family. And not when her captor was thoughtful to her one moment, cold to her the next.

No, despite her feelings, she couldn't trust her surroundings, or Darkness, who had worn blood-spattered clothing. Whose blood? She feared the answer, the truth. Because the more time she spent with him, the more she doubted it could be Grace's mother's. There was loyalty and reluctant kindness here. *Why* would he murder Grace's mother? And yet…how else had Grace ended up in his care? And where was her mother now? Why was she becoming more certain he played some role with her, with himself? No man denied being a father, then cradled the babe against him while she slept. No one shared stories with a servant.

So many questions.

The only certainty she had were her old fears. Her dark room downstairs frightened her despite the fire which now always burned in the passage-way. Only the courtyard provided enough light in the dead of night, but that open space had nothing to block the icy winter wind.

The weather was changing for the worse and, while she was locked up, safe and warm, the house where Vernon, Helewise and Gabriel were staying was cold and draughty. The fires they did light were barely enough to heat their extremities; they could never risk more than that. She had intended to procure more blankets. The ones they had were past worn. She hoped they were alive, fed, warm. She hoped they were still there and she'd see them again.

Damned. That's what he was. Reynold swept out of his bedroom and into the study, bounded out the door and down the staircase. The men on guard took note of his departure, but they did not follow him.

Wise decision.

The days were disappearing despite the few hours slept. Another night, and the house was quiet while everything inside him clamoured and roared. Such a din of thoughts he could not cease.

The thief was torturing him with the secrets and mysteries of her. Since that first night there had been changes. Noticeable ones, but nothing overt, nothing he couldn't…and didn't…control.

Except one. When they were alone in the study.

When he could smell her soft scent and almost feel her fingers as she turned a page. The way the stories lit her eyes. The soft parting of her lips, her soft gasps of delight or dismay, tightened his body to unimaginable degrees. Still she would not give her opinions on the stories, still he wanted them.

Mysteries. Secrets. He'd see her watch the doors, a longing on her face as if everything she wanted was on the other side. Why?

And more questions when every room she entered she saw mercenaries light additional torches and candles. As if she was afraid of the dark. How could someone who lived on the streets be afraid of the dark? Such vulnerability should have been wrenched from her long ago.

That fact that it wasn't… Everything in him yearned to be near her at the same time he needed to stay away. He found himself turning right instead of left in his home because he knew where she'd be and he wanted to hear her soft babbling to Grace. The next moment he found himself turning again to avoid the play of candle flames against her features.

Worst of all, he found himself wanting to talk. To share. Not those bits he couldn't—the game, or his family—but other aspects of his life. When he read a book or the places he went. Share his life as if it was a story just to see her eyes brighten. He held himself back, but the weakness was there simmering ever closer to the surface.

He rushed across the empty snow-covered courtyard to the dining hall and burst through the door. The room was surprisingly empty as well. Though he had the house specially built for defence, a few men were required to keep watch. The men by his doors were awake, there should be others walking about as well.

The fire was dim in the dining hall so he threw a few more logs on it. The passageway's fireplace near the thief's bedroom was well-lit lately. The quarters he put them in were the most secure as well. Only one entrance and a long hallway with many men in between. It was a safe haven for the thief and his daughter, but more than that it was a means to escape.

What no one knew was the exit under the bed. A spot in his home to escape should his family find him. It was the safest place for them to be. However, the room put them too far away. He couldn't hear them, smell his child's scent as he held her, or admire the curls of freshly washed black hair.

He wanted them both for different reasons, but he wanted the same result. He wanted them near him.

All the worst for the messages. The Englishman had gone rogue, separating from his usual troop and kidnapping a Colquhoun child. Part of the game? A threat to seize the dagger? He had no way of knowing, though he'd been trying.

There was also the recent activity at his parents' home. For every man he sent out they had been sending twenty more. Foolish if they wanted to stay anonymous to their deeds like him, but fortuitous because it was all the easier to track them.

But was the activity his parents' or his brothers'? They all kept their base in his childhood home further south. He last knew Ian's whereabouts weeks ago, which was unreliable information. He could be anywhere. It'd been months since he knew of Balthus's location and that was unacceptable.

'I thought if you were to brood outside your rooms, you'd need some wine to do so.'

Reynold didn't turn from his task of stoking the fire. He knew that voice.

He'd taken Louve in his employ on a whim from an enemy. No, from a forced ally. Reynold thought he'd fall in line with the other mercenaries, be paid and keep his mouth shut. But there was a certain insouciance about him, as if life was humorous, and Louve never could stay silent. To make it worse, it was as if he sought out Reynold's company and, over the past year, Reynold had caved and allowed certain liberties of his time. Unfortunately, it gave the mercenary ideas that he could freely talk to him. Like now.

Straightening, he turned to see Louve carrying two flagons and two goblets. 'What are you doing here? You're not on duty.'

Louve set down the wine to pour it. 'You're not the only one she keeps up at night.'

Was the thief haunting all his men as well as him? Were they, too, flapping their waxed wings and trailing closer and closer to her? He didn't know what occurred while he plotted and planned. Hours, days he had been toiling and all the while these men, these hired swords, had been circling—

'Careful, you're showing your human side.' Louve dragged a chair to the fire.

Reynold scowled, which made most men cower. Louve merely raised his brow. 'Leave me be.'

'I'm thirsty—*sir*. Did you insist on her calling you that as well? Since you're keeping her like you are me, it isn't reasonable.'

'I'm not keeping her. I'm—'

Louve smirked. 'Didn't think that one through? There's a child involved, of course you're keeping her. She'll want to know your name eventually…as will your daughter.'

'Not my daughter and don't talk about her,' Reynold said. He needed a mindless distraction this evening—instead he got Louve. A distraction, but also an irritation. The wine, however, was welcome and the fire was warming. Reynold dragged the other chair and sat down.

Louve stretched his feet to the fire. 'The woman doesn't sleep in the room downstairs.'

If the thief didn't sleep in the room, where was she now and why had no one notified him before? Reynold lifted the goblet to his lips and took a slow drink to hide his reaction.

Louve huffed in amused irritation. 'When she *does* sleep, it's in the hallway outside the door. She makes sounds in her sleep. The men and I have taken turns to check on her.'

Reynold swallowed, held himself steady. 'And the child?'

'Inside the room. Sleeps peaceful enough.'

But the thief wasn't at peace. Were these sounds she made ones of distress or something else? Did she sleep that way to protect Grace, or because she didn't like the room?

'Are you attempting to understand why she does it?' Louve chuckled. 'The men and I have a good guess.'

Reynold refused to bite. But he remembered the thief's slowing steps towards the room, her eagerness to go somewhere else. His inviting her to his sanctuary. Was she still afraid of darkness?

'Still not used to conversation, are you?'

Reynold didn't converse with anyone, especially hired help who came and went. In fact, he constantly hired new mercenaries to keep his anonymity. Instead of loyalty, he paid them well and they were useful for one purpose. 'I dislike time wasted.'

Louve shot him a glance. 'I've been with you too long to cower before your façade of the great nobleman talking to mere servants. I know what we do with the extra food around here. I know you give away great treasures to the poorest of monks.'

His mother had beaten into him the many ways to present himself at court and how to behave before those lesser than him. When needed, he found himself using such façades to protect his most private of thoughts. Presenting enough disdain and contempt kept most people away from him. Most...except Louve.

'Are you pretending to our new guests you have no soft underbelly?' Louve continued. 'Are you presenting her with your family's disdain for the poor and the weak? Since she's staying, she'll see your underhanded compassion just as I have.'

Reynold felt like growling. 'Tomorrow, you and I will train.'

Louve stretched his neck. 'Then I'll enjoy tonight all the more, since tomorrow night I doubt I'll be able to move. What do we try first? Wrestling or just swords and daggers?'

Humour again. Reynold took another sip. He'd kept Louve too long, they'd become too familiar with each other. He feared Louve knew all his secrets, but kept his silence on them all the same. If that was the case, where did his loyalties lie?

'Silence again?' Louve said. 'I would think you'd have become accustomed to talking. There's a woman and a child in your home now. That's inviting a mountain of conversation, *Reynold*.'

And an avalanche of vexing moments like these. 'They are servants—nothing more than you are to me.'

At Louve's burst of laughter, Reynold almost broke his gaze from the fire. Almost gave a reaction.

'So you have a child,' Louve said. 'And have brought a stranger in to care for her.'

He wanted to deny it. But Louve had seen him

bring her home. 'You must not mention them outside this house.'

Louve whistled low. 'You already gave the men the lecture and the false story on who they are. You haven't fooled any of us.'

Reynold knew it and still he risked it. With their knowledge of Grace, he would either pay to keep them silent...or have them killed. He kept his eye on Louve, the mercenary, and the truth of the words. What he saw there made him...wary. 'You don't intend to betray me.'

'You have to know the men talked and we made a pact. No one desires to harm women and children. Especially not them.'

Loyalty among hired swords. Unheard of. Yet Reynold believed him. Had he grown soft? He held Grace and now he was someone who cared and surrounded himself with loyal servants. It was too fantastical to be true, but something felt...unlocked inside him when he held Grace.

He suddenly wanted to ask Louve a thousand questions; stand up and do a thousand more deeds. A chaotic mess he'd hadn't felt in years, if ever. None of his immediate thoughts or deeds were suitable. Especially when Louve watched him so carefully. 'You know what would happen to them if my family discovers the truth.'

'That is a secret only I am aware of and, since you and I are friends—'

'We are not friends.'

'You can't kill or bribe me. I'm here for other reasons.'

'Name something other than friendship.'

Louve shrugged. 'Curiosity. She's not the mother. I know you too well for that. And, usually, pretending your daughter is a servant's would be a clever scheme, except…you are different with them. It's apparent they mean more to you. And now you're trusting and sharing your secrets with me.'

He hadn't meant to share anything. If his family detected any weakness, his daughter would be killed. Reynold looked away from Louve's knowing eyes.

'My trust is earned because I pay you.'

'Not all who are here are similarly motivated.' Louve adjusted in his chair. 'You should know some of the men are delighted. Some have families they left—a woman and child remind them why they work for you and what they save for. Some, however, think them a liability.'

Though he wanted to brandish the goblet, Reynold set the wine down carefully. 'Who are the ones who think ill of keeping them here?'

Louve swirled his drink. 'I'll take care of them.

It's why you've kept me, though others have left, isn't it? To do these odd tasks you can trust no one else with. They will be no threat.'

There was no negotiating with this man. A whim to take him in and he hadn't seen at the time there would be an issue. Now there was. Louve called him by his name and drank his wine, was too independent to control. But he believed him.

That didn't mean he'd leave his child and the woman kidnapped to care for her without protection. 'Very well.'

Louve raised a brow. 'Are you trusting me now?'

He never trusted anyone. Lately, he was beginning to not trust himself. Standing, he said, 'I know where you sleep and where you go when you leave this house.'

Louve huffed, but the sound of laughter was there in the frustrated sound. 'You trust me.'

Reynold strode from the dining hall and out to the courtyard. The blistering wind did nothing to cool his temper. Damn Louve and his conversations. He worried about his family discovering Grace and now he worried about men who were supposed to protect him.

Louve was correct. He *was* different. Because above it all, he worried about Aliette. Did Aliette sleep now outside her door? Did she use a quilt? It wasn't warm down there. Was the door opened or closed to Grace?

Swiftly he took the stairs and strode past the men's quarters. Why would she do this? Down the darkened hallway, he slowed his step to approach silently, until he saw her.

A quilt, nothing more, partly covered her. The door behind her back was opened. He could glimpse the basket with Grace sleeping peacefully.

The woman, asleep, gripped in a nightmare, was not. Louve said they checked on her because she made sounds. These weren't sounds. The thief was *whimpering*, her hands were clenched, her body curled as if deflecting blows.

She was fighting something he didn't want to see and knew she wouldn't want him to know.

Crouching down, he almost touched her, but didn't dare. If he did, his own self-preservation would crumble. His tearing need to clutch her close, *protect her*, frightened him.

'Get up,' he whispered. 'You're dreaming, wake up.'

A jerk of her hand, a stop to the heart-wrenching sounds. Her eyes opened wide and she gasped a choked scream.

He did touch her then. On her shoulder, which

was cold against his bare hand. Damn Louve. Damn her. He wouldn't leave her like this.

'You're moving to my rooms.'

She sat up. 'What…happened?'

He didn't know what compelled him. What need was clawing at him to hold and protect her. 'There's no time for explanations. It's late and I'm tired. I'll carry Grace and the basket, but you'll need to bring spare bedding.'

'But—'

'Do you want me to carry you as well?'

Scrambling to stand, she pushed her hair out of her face. 'I'll follow you.'

She capitulated too easily. No further questions, even her soft exhale was one of relief. She had been suffering from nightmares, cold floors and God knew what else. All this time they'd been reading in the study and she had told him nothing.

Entering the study, he lowered Grace's basket to the floor, took the bedding from the thief's arms and tossed it on to the padded bench. Then he opened the door to the right. This was his private chamber, stark of any comforts. He didn't deserve them when he slept.

He had a purpose to achieve, to rid the world of his manipulative family, and sleeping was a vulnerability he could ill afford. He only slept and dressed here and, even then, he never lingered. Thus, the room contained only a few chests, a perch to hang his clothes, and a bed.

Even so... The bed linens were crumpled, the pillows pushed to the floor. His turbulent emotions depicted in the sharpest, most intimate way. Was his need for her here this transparent?

Never. He moved her because if she didn't sleep, she wouldn't care for Grace as he needed her to. He'd never questioned himself before. He'd be dead if he did. If he questioned her role in his game—any of their roles—they'd all be dead.

'This is your room,' she said numbly, taking in the room's meagre contents.

'I will sleep in the study on the bench. This will be yours and Grace's room from now on.'

'But—'

'Don't question what I order, thief.'

She looked to the room, then back to him. 'This is too much.'

'It is necessary.'

She frowned as if she saw through him. Her next sentence proved him right.

'I can't keep calling you "sir."'

'Everyone does.'

'But—' she looked at Grace in his arms '—it doesn't feel right. You've asked me to care for the child. She'll want to know your name.'

He frowned at that. 'Despite the unusual circumstances of your arrival, you are a servant. All those who serve, call me sir.'

'I don't serve you.' She opened her mouth as if to argue more. Shook her head once, twice. 'Why do the stories represent abundance to you, but not the books themselves? The other day, you said the stories were all you had.'

It had been a mistake to tell her. 'It matters not. It is late.'

'Is it because your wealth is meaningless? Why would it be meaningless?'

He needed her not to look at him so closely. 'Why are you asking me these questions? Is it because you have nothing that you can't comprehend that such wealth would have no meaning?'

He regretted his cruel words the moment they were said. But instead of temper or tears, her lips curved in a knowing smile. 'You do that. Change subjects, become cruel or conceited when you don't want to answer something.'

'I told you that is who I am.'

'I watch you. It is as if you're trying to be something you're not.'

'We should sleep,' he said instead.

She pointed to him, to the room behind her. 'You read to me—you're giving me your room. There's more between us, isn't there?'

'Such haste since we hardly know each other.'

She flushed, but her gaze grew determined. 'There you did it again. You don't mean that. And I said it because it's true. Because...'

There was a connection and one they shouldn't explore. 'Giving you my room means nothing. You have nightmares and my men aren't sleeping.'

With a small huff of breath that could have been exasperation or disappointment, she said, 'Won't I keep you awake?'

'I don't sleep the way they need to.' With her so near, he wouldn't be sleeping at all. 'What is it about the dark that upsets you?'

Her eyes became contemplative. As if she was trying to solve a problematic puzzle. 'There is something about Darkness, but I have so many questions.'

He already knew, before she asked, that he wouldn't answer them.

'Tell me about Grace,' she said.

'No.'

'You say you're not the father, but then who is?' she continued. 'Who are you to her and why did you bring me here? There's enough help here to take care of her. You didn't have to rescue me from the guard. And you rescued her, too, didn't you?'

All logical, reasonable questions and ones he would never answer. All pointed and accurate observations and ones he never meant to reveal.

'Silence,' she said.

'You haven't answered my own questions about the dark.'

Almost smiling, she took a step closer. 'I don't know what it is about the dark, but the longer I'm in it the less I feel broken. But there's too many contradictions. I don't understand it.'

He didn't understand her words, but he noted her step, the startling nearness of her. Pivoting, he tucked Grace into her basket and snapped the linens to spread on the bench. But he didn't get that far.

The thief was by his side, searching his gaze that he purposefully turned away. It was a mistake bringing her here into his home, an error to think a thief could care for his daughter and no one would know.

He was a fool to show her where he read, worked, where he slept. No one was allowed in this room. A lapse in judgement, an error, but she was looking at him with wonder on her face.

There's more between us, isn't there?

He couldn't answer her questions. He was disintegrating. One feather at a time plummeting at her feet the longer he stayed in her presence.

'You need to go to bed.'

'You kidnapped me, took me from my—' She shook her head. 'But you've fed and clothed me. The mercenaries, despite their not talking, are almost kind. I've seen your care with them. You hold Grace like you never want to let her go.' Another step closer so that her body was pressed against the bedding he held like a shield.

'And I shouldn't want, should I? But I'm not used to waiting, and wondering. I need to ask— why did you move me to your rooms? No one else is invited here. Just me, day after day. Why?'

Her soft questions he could withstand, but her eyes… Her imploring eyes battered him like gusts of harsh wind demanding more. As if she asked one question, but there were others, so many others she didn't dare ask.

But he felt them all the same. His body knew… He could hear the flapping of useless wings. His entire body urging him to drop the bedding, to *take*.

Their doom if he did.

'On the landing…you looked at me.'

He couldn't stay in his game and think of her bathing. He couldn't answer her and keep his control. He had to give her something else, not him. 'Tomorrow, you can go outside these walls— a mercenary will accompany you. Is that what these questions are about? If you gained freedom, would that ease your fears?'

A look of surprise and then a gleam of tears. 'Yes, yes, it would very much.'

It was the utter joy in her gaze that was his undoing. Joy that gave strong currents to his futile toiling. He dropped the bedding and cradled her face before he realised he had flown so close.

'Stop watching me. Stop asking your questions,' Darkness whispered against her lips. 'You're not safe here.'

Aliette suspected none of them were. Not in this fortress, not in a bedroom void of forgiveness. Not in the dead of night. 'Neither are you.'

A shiver of his lips against her own, but she didn't move while something was held in balance.

Something she didn't want to end. Not while he swept his thumbs across her cheeks and tugged at her hair behind her ears. Not while his elegant fingers held her as if she was more precious than illustrated parchment.

Waiting, when it felt as if he'd finally answer her with the truth. She wouldn't stand for it. Gripping his wrists, she pulled herself up, closing that breath of space between them until her lips touched his.

The pinch of fingers tightening in her hair, the hitch to his breath before he tore his lips away, took a step back, and another. His gaze rushing from her, to the bedroom behind, to the richly laden tables. He grabbed one solitary book, clenched it between his hands before he set it down. It was the same book he had picked up and set down countless times before. And his expression... It was as if the book simultaneously comforted and wounded him.

His eyes darting to the book he set down and back to her, he pivoted and almost tripped over Grace's basket. A harsh exhale of his breath, one that she couldn't match. She'd lost her ability to breathe. He hadn't kissed her. He didn't want to.

Without looking at him, she bolted to the basket and hefted it. His eyes flickered to the child again as if he was helpless to do so.

She didn't know what was more unexpected. Darkness longing to cradle a child, or her wanting to leave Grace with a man who had torn her from her life.

He acted as if they were strangers and a part of her knew that. Her captor didn't starve babies and would know how to hold them if Grace had been born here. No, this dark man kidnapped Grace away from her mother, away from her family.

At that thought, she waited to feel what she should have. Something of her own past. Of being abandoned and knowing she'd always be so. If not for Vernon, Helewise and Gabriel, what kind of woman would she be?

Perhaps more cautious, timid. Less naive. Not grasping him and trying to pull him closer. This man took her away from her family, despite everything else, she must not forget that.

'Do you want her tonight?' she said.

He jerked as if from a trance. 'No, she's yours.'

She didn't believe him. His words said one thing, his deeds another. He stared at the child, a line between his brows, his lips slightly parted, softening them. A fierce caring.

Had her parents ever looked at her so? She wasn't prepared for that thought or for this man to display it. Her heart couldn't take it.

'Many winters ago,' she said, 'I came across a bundle of blankets heaped among a pile of refuse. I thought my luck had finally turned. A bit of cleaning and I'd have protection, warmth, shelter.'

His brows drew in. 'It wasn't blankets.'

She shook her head. 'It was an abandoned infant. Frozen. His little fingers curled as if holding on to something precious.'

'You didn't take the blankets,' he said, giving a hard swallow when she nodded. 'Why, when you needed them and could do nothing for a baby who was dead?'

'Because that child was left those at least. It showed they cared, didn't it?'

'What happened to you—why do you have no parents?'

He didn't deserve the answer to that question. 'If I had such a child, I wouldn't have left them behind. If I had a child, I'd claim her.'

His scarred hand clenched, once. Twice. 'Do you think I don't want to?'

She felt the truth of those words though they were hardly a confession, but more an admittance to what she knew. More than that, he told her that though he might not want her, he did want Grace. And so, when she stepped back into the bedroom, her hand on the door to close it between them, she had to give him something.

'My name—'

He looked at her then. He looked and his dark gaze didn't let her go.

'My name is Aliette.'

Chapter Fifteen

Aliette attempted to hide her giddy step as she gave Grace over to the scarred mercenary for a few hours. She was off to market, free to leave the fortress and walk the Paris streets again. But she couldn't hide the grin she gave the two guards at the doors who held them wide open as if she was royalty.

Sweeping outside, she ignored the mercenary at her side. He was one of the men who had taken her from her family. The one who stopped her arm from breaking, but even so, he was her enemy for today. Because with him, she knew she couldn't escape. Still, she hoped to catch a sight of Gabriel and see that he was safe. Or there was the issue that if he saw her first, then—

'You could have said I spoke.'

Aliette jumped. She couldn't help it. Though the voice was soft and melodious, she'd grown used to the mercenaries not speaking.

'I'm sorry,' he said.

'I suspect you're not,' she answered. 'Were you just waiting to frighten me to death?'

'I was waiting until we were out of range of the others.'

Around the corner and she knew where she was. So close to everything familiar and she still couldn't reach her family. Her longing for them was acute.

'You're truly not supposed to say a word,' she said.

'I suspect the order was not only to protect you, but us as well. We're not *usually* trusting of others.'

'Usually?'

'Why did you tell him I didn't speak that day when he asked?' he continued. 'You could have.'

So many days ago! 'This is the question you want to ask of me? Not who I am and who is Grace and what I'm doing there?'

'That is easily answerable.'

She stumbled. He gestured with his arm to help her, but she waved him off.

This man appeared to be kind, but couldn't be trusted. He was handsome and, the way he held himself, he knew it. But he was not soft. He might not be scarred or battered like some of the others, but if he was with these men, he could hold his own. A deadly predator among other deadly predators.

'How do you know who I am?'

'You're the woman he brought to care for the child...' He paused. 'We don't ask questions about our past.'

Nothing of the past, but that didn't mean she couldn't ask questions of the present. 'What would he have done if I had told him your friend wrenched my arm and you gave comforting words?'

He stopped and regarded her for a moment before he resumed walking. 'I am heartened you took my words as they were meant. They were all I could conceivably give you when Baldr was there.'

Aliette waited only a step or two for more information, but none came. 'Will you not tell me more? I know nothing. I don't know who he is, or how you know the baby is not mine. But she's his, isn't she? Where is her mother?'

Brows drawn, he said, 'I can't save you. But if I could, if I knew, I would have. How is your arm?'

No answers. But they were talking of mercenaries and captors and broken arms. 'This is ridiculous. What is your name.'

He gave a chuff of surprise. 'Louve.'

Easily done, she wanted to press her luck. 'And him? Will you tell me his name?'

A quick smile. 'He wants all to call him "sir." I call him by his name to vex him.'

'And yet he does not harm you for it. So why shouldn't I know it?'

He stepped to the side. 'You haven't been with him long, but I know you are clever. You must have seen some contradictions with him by now. Saying one thing and doing another.'

Complications and contradictions with Darkness? A man who kidnapped her and fed her, who wanted to hold a child, but wouldn't, who looked as if he wanted to touch her, kiss her—

Louve smiled. 'I can see you have. The man who has taken you in is…complicated. He has to be many things and in the past he was forced to be many things. Sometimes I think he forgets and falls into habit with his deeds and words. Sometimes, I believe he purposefully uses his past to protect his future.'

'I don't understand your words at all.'

'And I can't tell you more and keep his friendship.'

'Friendship?'

Louve shook his head. 'A slip of the tongue.'

The mercenary looked too pleased for that to be the truth. 'He doesn't want to be your friend.'

Louve lifted a shoulder, which was all the truth she needed for proof that Darkness was complicated, contradictory and held far too many secrets. 'Tell me something else. Anything.'

He glanced down to her. 'All you need to understand is he hasn't told you his name and so neither will I. Come, we need to move on.'

Aliette fell in step with the strange mercenary. His explanation of Darkness rang true, but she didn't know why. He was full of contradictions, but why he felt he had to have them to protect himself, when he obviously held wealth and power, was dumbfounding. As was this mercenary.

'You're not like the other men,' she said. 'Why do you work for him?'

His gait lengthened. 'He pays well.'

'But you don't do it for the coin.'

He looked away before he laughed. 'Everyone works for coin.'

Louve was trying to appear at ease, but he wasn't. For one, his eyes didn't reach hers. For another, his laugh wasn't all that easy.

A few more steps before he slowed, and glanced her way. She saw not the mercenary, but the man he was. 'You want the truth? Maybe I wanted a different life.'

It couldn't be true. 'How terrible was your life before that you would choose him?'

He looked away, but not quick enough to hide his discomfiture. Then she remembered. He didn't say he wanted a better life—he said *a different life.* Louve hadn't fled a worse life, he'd fled a better life.

Aliette struggled all her days. Never did she think, not once, she'd be living as she had been with a warm bed and meals waiting for her when she wanted them.

In her opinion, someone would have to be witless to flee a good life for a bad one. But in the little time they spent together, she knew with certainty that Louve wasn't dimwitted.

Which was the reason to stop conversing with him. He was the enemy and kept her away from her family. It'd be easier to search for her family without him, or if she was taller, and there weren't so many horses blocking her views.

It'd been too long since she had seen Gabriel—he might see her first and rush to her aid. She prayed that wouldn't happen. If only…

'I know you're intending to escape,' Louve said. 'The food you've stashed in your gown is noticeable despite your cloak,' he said. 'No doubt the others noticed that, too. You're too slight to hide much. You're about as large as Cook now.'

Aliette clutched her cloak tighter. This was her only chance to help her family. She had to take the risk. 'It's not for me.'

'Then *not* planning to escape.'

She'd seen Louve train, she couldn't outrun him, nor did she have the element of surprise. 'Not now.'

'What will you do with that food?' he said.

How much to tell him? 'I need to give it to some people...then I'll return.'

Near an abandoned building, Louve stopped his easy gait, and adjusted his stance. 'I'll wait here for you for no more than an hour.'

She couldn't trust such a boon. She couldn't trust this man.

His gaze softened as if he guessed her thoughts. 'If you don't return, he'll kill me.'

'You didn't have to tell me that,' she said. 'I'd return only because you are giving me this time.'

A flash of a smile. 'You truly are what you appeared to be.'

'What is that?'

'Honest. Kind.'

She'd never been described as such her entire life. 'Why is that surprising?'

'Because he never touches the innocent ones.' He pointed ahead. 'You best be going. The time we talk counts.'

Aliette wanted to thank him for allowing this. She knew the risk she took and she didn't mean for him to take one as well. If he found out, Darkness would no doubt—

'Go!' he said, laughing. 'I can hold my own.'
Aliette ran on ahead.

'Child!' Helewise called the moment she stepped through the window.

The smell assaulted her. Days away and she instantly knew the chamber pots hadn't been emptied as frequently as she had done it. It clashed with the smell of rotting food and unwashed bodies.

These were smells she'd grown up with all her life. One fortnight away and it was as if she never grown up here at all.

'It's me,' she called. 'I've returned!'

She entered the other room. Vernon and Helewise were huddled in a corner. A few burning embers in a metal pan glowed at their feet. The sunlight was dim, but it was the most secure area of the house. They could talk, have a fire and not be seen.

They were safe. 'You're here.'

'Where else could I kind go?' Vernon said.

The joy of seeing them dimmed with her guilt. Her fault they were here. Regardless...

'It's so good to see you.' Eagerly stepping forward, she clasped the food around her waist as she crouched before them. 'I've been so worried. I'm so sorry I was—

'Aliette?' Vernon said, his gaze going from her head to her hands to her knees and back again. 'My eyes...they've worsened!'

'Not your eyes,' Helewise said, a note of disbelief and archness to her voice, 'that's our Aliette with fine clothes and hair. And I smell food, too.'

Vernon scuttled back and hit the wall. 'What have you done?'

Neither of them had ever behaved this way to her. Had her appearance changed so much already? She'd bathed, true, and her hair, usually bound in a cap, hung free. Her serviceable gown was a sturdy brown wool, which fit her perfectly with no discernible holes. She suspected the chemise, which was fine and the softest item she'd ever touched, was not meant for the poor, but if they were foolish enough to spend the coin, she would only take advantage. As she took advantage of the warmth of the thick green cloak that was lined with fur around the inside edges that weighted the cloak against wind.

'I was able to bathe,' she said.

'And a bit more,' Helewise murmured.

'Here.' Aliette swept her green cloak away from her body and dislodged the three loaves of bread and leg of pork. 'This is all for you.'

Helewise avoided her eyes. Aliette swung around. No one was there. What was the matter—? Why would Helewise not look at her? She never— Oh. They thought…they thought she had sold herself.

Of course they did, they'd been on the streets long enough. This type of bounty could never be gained by mere thieving. Still, it was the hurt of their opinion that surprised her.

Over the years, Aliette had built defences against people's judgements and it was easier to push people away, to not trust, to survive. Except she'd somehow developed these slivers in her defence since she'd last seen her family. Enough for her to wonder about life in a house with food, clothing and warmth. Enough to wonder about reading and a future of days filled with something else besides survival. About a child whom she could truly keep.

Slivers to the walls she held herself in that allowed her to see Darkness cradling his child, to be fascinated by his beauty, to want to kiss him. And enough to be hurt when he rejected her.

Maybe they should look at her warily, she didn't even know herself anymore. And all the worse because she would inevitably be tossed to the streets again.

For now she needed to explain this bounty she'd received. But how?

'Where's Gabriel?'

'Out to find food,' Vernon said.

Guilt. She'd been living in luxury and he was risking himself. 'Not to steal?'

'I think he learned his lesson the day you were taken.'

'You know.'

'Gabriel followed you,' Helewise said, 'and saw the men take you away.'

'He was meant to stay with you.'

Helewise gestured in a placating manner. 'He felt responsible. We couldn't hold him here.'

Gabriel was terrified of roaming the streets alone. He'd always let her take the risk—for him to be so brave was a miracle. 'And since?'

'Do you need to ask?' Vernon said, no kindness to his voice. 'It's been almost a fortnight, child.'

Guilt was the least of her feelings now. These weren't mere slivers in her defences, she'd developed cracks. What had happened to her? Hadn't she learned her lessons already. She'd wanted her family, but she needed to stay strong for them. Not...thinking about days of sitting on a sun-warmed bench, reading.

'Where were you taken?' Vernon asked. 'Why do you have such clothes and food?'

They'd glanced at the food, but neither had taken it. This wasn't the joyous reunion she expected. Her family was starving. They should be eating with abandon.

'The food is for you. Please eat as much as you like.'

'You're not staying.'

She didn't belong here. No, that couldn't be true. If she didn't belong here, then where else? This was the home she had found for her family. It was a good home and she would return when she could. 'I can't stay. I wanted to talk to Gabriel. To ensure—'

'He's taking care of us, Aliette,' Helewise said.

The mothering tone in her voice made it all the worse. 'He's a child!'

'No, he's not,' Vernon said. 'You never told us what you've done. Who took you?'

Were they concerned for her or for themselves? Her loyalty was, should be, to them. Not to a man who kidnapped and confused her. Maybe if she remembered that, this feeling of vulnerability would disappear. 'A man has a child and he took me to care for her.'

'To dress you like that?'

Simple clothes. She knew they were after she saw what the mercenaries, what *he*, wore. Yet they were a luxury.

'I know none of it makes any sense. Anyone who can pay for such clothes should be able to hire a servant instead of steal them, but that's what he did and I'm there for now.'

'I don't understand,' Vernon said.

She smiled at him. 'I don't trust it either. But the child, Grace, needs care, and I can't just abandon her. If this visit goes well, I'll will try to return every day this week with more food.'

Helewise pointed to the pork. 'More than that?'

'Much more.' Aliette's thoughts flooded with the platters of delicacies she'd been privy to over the last few days. 'Tell Gabriel to stay safe and stop looking for me. I'll return.'

Encasing her found family in an embrace eased her heart. In the dead of night, her parents had left her never to return. She also had left her family, though she didn't mean to. For days she worried they wouldn't be here when she returned.

'You'll be here when I return?' she asked.

'If we can,' Helewise said, her eyes softening. 'If we're not, we'll try to make it to the bridge. Will that do?'

Aliette brushed the tears from her cheeks. They were, and continued to be, her family.

'That didn't take long.' Louve pushed off the wall.

Aliette jumped and glared at the smirking mercenary. 'You're not surprised.'

'You look lighter than when you left. Where's your cloak?'

She lifted a shoulder. 'I must have dropped it somewhere.'

'We can replace the cloak, but Cook will notice the missing pork.'

Aliette knew she'd taken a risk stealing so much, but, if she couldn't return, she wanted to ensure they had as much as possible.

'I don't know what you're talking about,' she said.

'I'll tell him I ate it,' Louve said.

He wasn't lying. 'Why would you do that?'

Louve exhaled. 'You are too trusting! You just confessed you took the pork.'

'You already knew.'

'Yes, but you confirmed it. I could report everything to him.'

She shrugged.

Louve's brows rose. 'You expect me to report it. Now I'm offended. Don't you care for your life?'

'Everyone cares for their life.'

'But you—' Louve stopped himself. 'You care about others more.'

She ignored him. It was the truth.

'I thought I'd admired you before, but I only do more so now. My God, he found a prize with you.'

'I'm no man's prize.'

Louve stopped. 'What do you know of men?'

The feel of her captor's calloused thumbs rubbing away her tears. Her wrapping her hands around his wrists, pulling on his strength, knowing it would be there. Heat rose to her cheeks. With her complexion, she couldn't hide it.

'Nothing! You know nothing. You're not only—How did he *find* you?' Louve muttered other words which made her only blush further until he glowered. 'I've been around the field or two, and I've been with that man for some time. Trust me when I say you're his prize.'

'He's done nothing—'

'Oh, I know and so do the other men. So it's bold of you to steal from him. He's already a sword drawn, but since you've arrived, he's been stabbing at anything and everything in his way. He hasn't been training with us, either afraid he'd cause true harm or because he doesn't want to unleash something that can't be stopped. And today, I'll feel the brunt of that. Word of advice when it comes to him? Watch his deeds, then you'll know the man.'

'Are you—? There'll be consequences. Don't help me.'

Louve pointed behind to where her home was. 'I already did. Understand I'm allowed liberties and we'll both take advantage of them now. Is food the only commodity you need?'

'What are you saying?'

'Whatever you're doing or whomever you're feeding, I'm certain they need more than food. You doubt I would procure them, or that it's safe?'

When you were as poor as they were, there was too much need. Could she risk trusting this man? For her family, she'd do anything.

'I need blankets, kindling and some boots. For a boy about this size.'

Louve froze. All sense of humour gone. 'Is there a man?' At her confusion, he continued, 'Is there a man that you're feeding?'

Vernon wouldn't want Louve to bring him clothes. After today, Aliette wasn't certain he'd appreciate it. But he was there and he did need food.

She nodded.

'Does *he* know?' Louve said, his voice heated with urgency. 'Does he know there are others, that there's a...boy, too?'

She shook her head.

Louve whistled low. 'Oh, this will be interesting.'

Chapter Sixteen

'Where does she go?' Reynold said, welcoming Louve's swift turning.

'Finally you arrive,' Louve said. 'I expected you days ago.'

Reynold had kept to himself over the last few days. Didn't dare look out the window when Aliette left in the mornings. He knew his obsession with her was mounting, knew he had to be more careful or his men would know he had taken on two vulnerabilities.

Aliette. She'd been different these past days since he allowed her freedom, which was more for him than her.

She'd kissed him. Her hands circling his wrists was such exquisite pleasure he hadn't reacted swiftly enough to avoid the tenderness of her lips. She might not understand it, but there was no returning to any life she had before. When the game was done, she would be truly his.

Even so, he wondered if he could wait to the end of this game. He had never shown weakness before, but teaching her to read and relocating the thief and Grace in his room were weaknesses. Wanting them closer was stupidity.

Surprisingly, the move from her room to his eased some tension between himself and his men...as if they approved. He didn't care if they approved, he cared about her comfort.

Certainly not his own. Knowing she was sleeping in his bed tormented his body in ways he never knew it could be. Not even the pain his mother subjected him to, to cleanse weaknesses, burned worse.

In the meantime, he read with Aliette in the afternoons, watched how the burden on her shoulders lifted and her longing looks to the doors eased. He thought it was merely her being outside, that she could see that though he'd kidnapped her, he wouldn't limit her life. But everything about her was different. Playing with Grace, singing to herself, not skittering past dark corners.

Too many changes. Too obvious. She was *happy* and it made him suspicious.

'You did not expect my arrival,' he said. They were in the middle of a square, people conducting business, greeting each other. Louve looked for all the world like a traveller resting and Aliette was nowhere in sight.

'You ordered protection, trusted me enough to look after those you care about,' Louve said.

'I don't trust you. I pay you.'

'Do you?' Louve replied. 'I think we both know why I'm with you.'

'You're not spying for him. If you were sending messages on my deeds, you'd be dead.'

'I'm an observer, nothing else. Thus far I see nothing of your deeds that jeopardise his interests.'

'You are too loyal to your childhood friend.'

'You can never have too much loyalty, Reynold. Something you should learn about.'

He hated the use of his name in public. Reynold glanced around. More people filled the square, two women were walking entirely too close, but there was no sign of Aliette. 'Loyalty to him, yet you work for me.'

'The work is not why I stay. I find our late-night chats over wine enlightening. I have no intention of jeopardising such camaraderie.'

'Why do you continue talking as if we have a friendship? We are not friends.'

Louve's lips curved. 'I think that has something to do with *your* learning loyalty.'

'I learned there is no such thing as loyalty before you were born.' Reynold rolled his shoulders. 'Talking about enemies is wasting my time, tell me where she goes.'

'Nicholas isn't your enemy.'

'Don't say his name out loud.'

Louve flashed a smile. Louve found every moment humorous. Reynold didn't, especially if Warstones' spies heard Nicholas's name. That would be enough to jeopardise his game. Nicholas was a knight who owed him a life favour and he was repaying that debt by hiding considerable amounts of Reynold's coin deep in the bowels of his estate.

If Reynold needed to disappear, or have access to his wealth, an enemy's land was the very best of hiding spots. Though there was a risk if his family discovered this, Nicholas took the chance. After all, Nicholas helped kill his brother, Guy, and Reynold had let him live. Hiding coin was a fair exchange.

The only hardship was that Louve had been with him since.

'You'll tell me what you're so worried about someday,' Louve said. 'Or am I not to have already guessed your family is involved?'

Cracks in his game. No one was to know about his family. And worried was not an emotion he felt when it came to them. Rage was more accurate. 'I'm done with this conversation.'

'Well, you should improve your conversations with Aliette. You're not leaving a very good impression of yourself.'

Reynold took the bait this time. Any information he gathered could only protect his daughter. 'What was spoken of?'

'You can't threaten me for answers,' Louve said. 'You also can't keep hiding your true self from her in some vague idea to protect her.'

'Tell me what she's doing.' At Louve's closed expression, he continued, 'I will punish her when she returns.'

Louve canted his head. 'You wouldn't.'

'Don't profess to know what I am capable of. I surprise even myself.'

Louve pinched the bridge of his nose. 'Reynold, there's more. I don't think she means you harm. You took her off the streets and she had a life before you. She doesn't understand what—'

Enough. 'Tell me where she's gone.'

Exhaling, Louve indicated with his chin. 'She's gone that way. I promised not to follow her, but I do wait here for her return to bring her back to you.'

'Promises? Waiting? You're loyal to her as well. It's a wonder all of your promises do not conflict.'

'She'll return soon,' Louve said. 'Let her explain first. Talk to her properly. Tell her.'

Reynold didn't like that this man knew more of his thief than he. Not. At. All. Leaning in, just enough for his intent to be clear, he said,

'Remember, mercenary, I made no promises to her and know no loyalty.'

It was the prickling on the back of Aliette's neck, the frisson of awareness that always accompanied the presence of her captor, that warned her. Not the sudden dimming of sunlight, as she imagined.

Though Darkness was here. She saw it in the face of Gabriel as he looked over her shoulder before giving a squeak of alarm. She witnessed it when Vernon and Helewise stilled like mice caught in a predator's gaze.

For her, she merely needed to stand from her crouch and turn. To see her kidnapper, in all his dark glory, before her.

'Well, my little thief, who have we here?'

Her captor's sweeping gaze took in her derelict surroundings, her threadbare family. No doubt assessing how easily it would be to kill them. They shouldn't be worth his notice. She knew the destruction Darkness wrought, yet she risked it anyway. It was she who had brought this danger to them and she who must draw him away.

Praying he would follow, she marched away from her family, through the few rooms on the ground floor and carefully up a rickety staircase to a landing. She chose the only room with a door.

His steps were unnaturally sure. He had no fear the broken stairs would fail him as he strode in front of her again. A mistake to enter as she did. The door was behind him and she had no access to close it. To give them privacy, to give her family time to flee.

She hoped they'd disappear by the time he came down again, but she couldn't hear anything over the roaring in her ears.

'Grace is well cared for,' she said. 'I returned every day.'

Watch him, Louve had said, but what did she see? He simply kept his grey unwavering gaze on her. His slow blinks, the rise and fall of his chest the only movement. It didn't matter, she knew his intent.

'I took fewer meals for myself to atone for the difference in what I stole.'

His brows lowered; brackets framed his lips as he clenched his teeth.

The longer he stood there, the more nervous she became. She swallowed.

His eyes deliberately tracked that movement.

The roaring in her ears died out. She knew better than to show such weakness. Either her family stayed quiet to hear what would happen to her, or the floors were thick enough and this exchange wouldn't be heard.

But they would hear her body fall should he slit her throat. There was no one to help her now. And he *waited*.

'Just get it over with, whatever it is you want to do.'

A quirk to the corner of his lips. 'Such haste and this time with your life.'

'It's mine to do with as I please.' As long as he didn't harm them she could take anything. 'But theirs isn't.'

'Who are they?'

Everything. 'No one. Fellow people I housed with.'

'You don't know who I am, do you?' he said in that voice that constantly tested her awareness of him.

He stood in the squalor of her home, but he might as well be surrounded by his gold, books and fine furnishings. Darkness's domain held no bounds, but did she know who he was?

'No,' she said.

'Despite my wealth, my men, the way the villagers fear me?'

'None of that tells me *who* you are.'

A frown. 'You are aware I can send you to gaol. Have my men take you out of the city and break your legs…kill you.'

These were his threats? Her need to survive

gave her fear, her need to protect Gabriel made her strong. She would take whatever punishment he met. 'Do you think you can do more to me than anyone else? I've lived on the streets all my life. Everyone can send me to gaol, break my legs or kill me. You are no different.'

Stillness. A canting of his head. Assessing her as if she was someone he hadn't sat next to for hours every day.

'There you are wrong, thief.' He paused and she heard the weight of it as if he was to reveal a burden he carried. 'My name is Reynold. And I am one of the four sons of Warstone.'

She couldn't hide her reaction.

'You know my family,' he said.

'I know the name of the English king and the name of his English sword, Warstone. There are stories everyone tells. It does explain your accent.'

'My mother's French and my father... So now you know who I am.'

She didn't. It explained the books, the gold and silk. But a man who had castles shouldn't be living in a derelict house in France. Grace shouldn't have been starving and her snatched off the streets to pretend she was her mother. Especially, when everyone he surrounded himself with knew the truth.

She knew nothing. Nothing, and felt like laughing. She was in great danger. But it had nothing to do with his name and everything to do with him.

And the longer she stood there in utter inability to explain this, the more Reynold lost the superior menace he mantled himself with. For once, he seemed unsure. As if her reaction to his name shocked him. Did he expect grovelling? Gratitude she'd shared his company? Fear because his family was powerful?

Where he came from didn't make a difference to her. And it surprised her that he didn't understand this. But his amazement slipped through the slivers she'd made in her own defences. Though it made her vulnerable to him to reveal why she didn't care, she told him anyway.

'Kings mean nothing to me. Warstone means nothing to me,' she said.

His eyes narrowed, his lashes shading any further emotion, but the suspicion was there in his voice. 'You live on the land they own. Eat food people pay taxes to consume. They might mean less to a homeless poor thief, but even you are touched by their power. No one can escape them.'

She'd brought him up the stairs to protect her family. She stood before him offering reasons not to kill her. Now…now she didn't care. Because he stood there and she could see that disappointing look on his face, as if she was beneath him. Which changed her emotions from apprehension on what he would do to rage. Because he simply didn't get it.

Kings. Warstone. Kidnappers didn't have power over her. Only Darkness had power over her. Just Darkness—which wasn't this man. No matter her imagination or how he appeared, her captor was merely a son of some family. He'd never starved or begged for his life. He'd never cried in the middle of a square and had no one come to his aid.

He was a man who was born to privilege and thought he was entitled to snatching people off the streets to play some game she knew nothing about. He had no right over her. None! And if it took cutting her heart out and throwing it at his feet so he could gape at all her pain and agony, she would do it. She would and then he could get out of her life.

'I don't fear *you*, your family—kings.' She pointed at him, pointed at her own chest. At her own useless nothing self. 'Because you could do no more harm to me than my family did when they abandoned me!'

Utter silence. Utter stillness. A storm suddenly died; Darkness's turbulent rage was subdued. 'How old?'

'What does it matter?' She waved her hand impatiently. 'They left. In the middle of the night, while I slept, they left. I've been alone ever since.'

'How old?' he bit out.

He sounded as though he wanted to know. She knew better. 'Five. It's been fifteen winters since.'

He waited. She wouldn't. In many ways, she was better off without her family who thought they knew better. Now she could live her life the way she wanted. Pick her own family, her own house. As long as she didn't trust or depend on anyone, as long as she ignored the jagged pieces inside her, she could survive very well on her own. 'So now you know who *I* am and we can forget whatever this is that you—'

'They come with us,' he said.

'What?'

He took a step towards her, the floor creaked ominously, and he shifted his stance wide. 'Those people downstairs aren't *no one* to you. You risked my wrath. You brought them food, you starved yourself to make it happen. You, the frail couple and that twig of a boy will return to my fortress now. They come to my house because they mean something to you.'

Darkness cared for no one. This was about something else. 'Whether that child is yours or not doesn't matter to me. And I have no intention of telling anyone your house is a fortress and you have a hundred men there. I don't care what you're doing here.'

'Your concern is taking care of Grace, that is all. She needs a mother and that is what I expect. If her mother has…relations so be it.'

This couldn't be true. He must not understand. 'You know my own family found me worthless and I am no carer for a child. Downstairs are people I vowed I'd take care of and I won't abandon them. Ever.'

'You're simply telling me what I already surmise, Aliette. You're not uncomplicated after all.'

She wasn't— Ah. That word he used on their first day. He said her agreement to taking care of Grace was easy. Intending to escape, she held to her secrets. Now she'd revealed all to him.

'No,' she answered.

His eyes swept the empty broken room. 'There's nothing else here worth saving. I also expect them to be bathed, clothed and fed within hours. I won't have them staying in my home in their present condition.'

He meant to take all of them. Darkness was truly a madman. 'You can't mean this.'

'They left you with no blankets, didn't they? Unlike that frozen babe you found, your parents left you with nothing.' At her nod, he continued.

'And at night, when it was dark? You woke up and they were gone?'

She didn't need to repeat it.

His frown deepened. 'You will all go. Don't question me again. I can and will do this.'

And he had every means of disposal to do it. 'You'd force us.'

'You care for the child, and I won't force or harm them if you come willingly. Furthermore, they will have the same privileges you have had these last weeks.'

Aliette's umbrage over his arrogance vanished. It was she who was stunned by his reaction. She who probably gaped at him now. No one took in people such as them and didn't expect something, especially Warstones, and yet, he didn't ask for a thing. 'I don't understand.'

He stared at her for so long, she felt Darkness enclosing her, wiping out all sight and muffling sound. 'It's better that way.'

If it was her alone, she'd refuse. Staying with this man was complicated and made her think of things she shouldn't. But if he gave her a day of unlimited food, shelter, clothing, for Gabriel's sake she'd take it.

'How long?' she said through the closure of her throat. Dots were swarming before her eyes. She was about to faint.

'For as long as you are with me.' Pivoting away, he added, 'We leave Paris in three days. This location has been compromised.'

He left, his steps as sure and determined as when he followed her in here. She waited to hear something from downstairs—nothing—and she crumpled to the ground. It eased the spots, but not her breath.

Gabriel's light bounding steps before he was immediately at her side.

'Does he mean it?' he asked, a gleefulness to his voice that underscored the fact she hadn't been dreaming. Reynold had just offered shelter, food, clothing to her family. 'Does he mean it like you meant it when you said you'd return to me? Is it that kind of promise?'

'He meant it.' Reynold never said anything he didn't mean. Why he offered his help, she didn't know. Except Darkness guarded and cared for his child. Was it possible, for the first time in her life, to trust?

She descended the staircase, her eyes met Vernon and Helewise, who looked a mix of her shock and Gabriel's joy.

The rest of his words sunk in. Reynold meant to give them shelter, but they were to leave Paris. She could barely get them to this house.

And what did he mean by *compromised*?

Chapter Seventeen

Hours later she settled Vernon and Helewise in the room at the end of the dining hall. They were clean, fed and exhausted. Gabriel took it all in as if his every wish came true. Sniffling, but far too exuberant for sleep, he skipped around as mercenaries gave him a tour.

Such a turn of events and one man was responsible, but Reynold disappeared the moment they arrived, hours ago, and it was time to confront him.

Never in her life had she thought she would seek out Darkness and demand answers for his deeds. But she'd exposed all her secrets to him and he'd revealed nothing to her. Simply ordered her about as if he had all the right to do so. With her family involved, she couldn't risk it.

Sweeping past the two guards, she swung open the door to his study and heard the distinct metallic clank as a mercenary closed it behind her.

Sitting behind his desk, Reynold was scribbling a message. He did not raise his head when she took the steps necessary to face him.

The scratching of quill over parchment was louder than the roaring in her ears and the thumping of her heart. But it did not hide her uneven breath and she refused for it to take the place of words.

'We need to talk,' she said.

'We do.' He dipped the quill in the ink and continued his message.

His raven hair fell over his forehead and shook along with his slashes. His expression grim, dark, his brows slanted down, a fierceness to his countenance as if he battled a foe. Though she was seeing him more clearly every moment they spent together, he still seemed cloaked in shadows and night. He still held his secrets. She needed to *know* more.

'What is it you're writing?'

He stopped, but kept his face down. 'It doesn't concern you.'

'You took my family into your care.'

'And yet again you do not thank me.'

'Not *thank* you!'

He looked up. 'Will you argue I kidnapped them as well? Let us be clear. By hiding them from me, by my discovery of them, it is you who have kidnapped me!'

He brought it on himself. 'You could have left us all alone.'

Tossing the quill in the pot, he answered, 'We've set the foundation that you are the mother to Grace. I could not let you go because I will not let her go. The fact you come with others is a complication, and one I never wanted.'

She didn't lie to him. 'They aren't my true family. They were struggling, starving, and I...we... help each other. You only asked whether I had parents.'

'Aren't you clever.'

Not enough. 'Where is Grace's mother?' She needed answers to questions she should have demanded on the first day. 'Why do you think you have to hide she's yours—? Why do I have to pretend I'm her mother!'

'For *her* sake,' he interrupted. 'For all our sakes, we must. I have enemies more powerful than me. If I cannot hide inside my own domain, my God, we will hide the fact she's mine outside this fortress. You don't know the acts I have wrought. I will do anything to keep her safe. I will not falter.'

She did know about surviving, but what did he have to survive? It was rumoured his family were wealthier than the kings of England and France. 'Why can't you falter?'

The fingers of his left hand, the burned one, flexed. 'I won't tell you. Don't ask.'

'Why do we have to wait three days?' With his

silence, she added, 'I will not follow blindly in this. I can't. You have my family.'

He exhaled. 'For a messenger. When he arrives, we leave.'

'What will be in that message he carries?'

'What did I tell you about your questions.'

It wasn't safe. But what did he care for safety? He had everything. Wealth. Protection from his men. Protection…she didn't have. Was it possible he was trying to keep her safe?

No one had ever done that before. She wanted to ask him more, though she knew he'd give her only silence. But what had she learned of him after their hours together?

He was curious and wanted her secrets and opinions. Ones that she had been withholding up until now. When he got frustrated with her, he tended to reveal more of himself. In those moments, he stopped playing a role she was now certain he was playing. He stopped watching and hiding.

'The message is important,' she said.

'Life or death.'

'This is like Orpheus, isn't it?' she said. 'You don't want to falter at the end like Orpheus freeing his wife from the Underworld. When all was at stake and he looked back only to lose her.'

A gleam to his eyes. 'Exactly.'

'But that's not the only meaning of the story.'

His eyes narrowed; his jaw clenched. Victory. He hated when she withheld opinions. But he held his secrets. With so much was at stake, she deserved to know.

Ignoring his glare, she strode to one of the tables, found exactly the book she wanted and sat down on the bench to read.

She didn't need to look at the man behind the desk to know her deeds struck him. He didn't like secrets of any sort and this one she'd delighted to withhold from him over the last sennight.

'You're reading a book,' he said.

'You taught me.' Days at his side, she'd learned his ability to wait was a tactic. She didn't lift her eyes. This time, *she* would wait. She turned a page, then another. All the while she felt his gaze on her.

'For how long?' he said.

'A while now.'

Even sitting as she was and him half-hidden, she could feel the tension, see him vibrating with some unknown force. He more than flexed his fingers now, he clenched his burned fist. 'You had me reading to you.'

She lifted a shoulder and turned another page.

'Why did you pick that book?'

Because since the first day he had brought her

in here he'd kept picking up this particular book and setting it down. Because he looked tortured, knowing this story existed. Out of all the stories in this room he avoided this one and she didn't know why. It was a secret and she wanted him to break. She'd do anything for her family. Needed to know the danger they were in.

'I like the title: *The Odyssey*,' she said.

'There are other more interesting stories.'

'I don't think so.' She closed the book, ran a hand down its spine. 'It's lovely. Far lovelier than anything else in here. Why is that?'

He now rubbed his thumb along the burn in his hand. 'I had it commissioned.'

Wealth. She knew he had it in abundance, but this was something else. He loved his books… and so he had them made. 'You ordered this book made.'

'From some monks at a monastery in Spain.'

'Have you ordered others?'

At his curt nod, she looked around his room, then down at her lap. 'Where are those?'

He made some sound from his chest. As though he was surprised, and pleased. 'Those I gave to the monks at the monastery.'

'Were they expecting that?'

'What do you think?'

She thought it made him angry and uneasy

he was sharing details of his life. Especially details that displayed a more generous man than she would have guessed. But he did it in some vague desperation to stop her reading this story.

So she returned to reading the story. 'It seems to be about a husband trying to return to his wife.'

'A trivial endeavour. If you can read, there are tales here worthy of your new skill.'

But he had the book made, unlike the others. She flipped through the pages. 'Odysseus suffered to return to Penelope, didn't he? It reads his mother died of grief while he was gone. He must have been gone for a long time.' A few more pages. 'Oh! He lost some ships. Did he make it to his wife? Perhaps I should read the ending first.'

He slapped his hand on his desk. 'Put it away—it's not yours.'

Ah. 'You took me and my family away from our life, from our things. You told me I had no choice. None of this is mine, you made sure of that. This book.' She set the book down and stood. Her fingers went to the laces on her gown. 'The clothes I'm wearing aren't—'

'Stop!' His chair banged against the wall as Reynold stood. Swift strides and he was grasping her arms in his calloused hands. 'You have changed everything. Everything! And you're not even aware of it.'

A quick yank that lifted her to her toes, a growl, and his lips slammed to hers. To take as she had. His game, his life. To punish. Because he could do it no other way.

But punishment turned to desire, to lust as her lips and her body yielded. Her slight body pressed to his, shivered, his hands drawing her closer, wanting those trembles to be his as well. *His.*

She wrenched her lips away. 'What are you doing?'

'Stopping you from asking your questions. You need to stop for both our sakes.'

She didn't pull away, her hands on his chest feeling the pounding of his heart, the battering of his breath. The kiss was too brief, a mere taste. Not nearly enough for the pain he would feel when he lost her. He could wish his family would kill him first to save him the pain, but there was no chance of that.

'I need my questions,' she pleaded.

'Never to gain my answers.' He never answered to anyone, even God himself. Especially God. Morals and commandments, all of it had to be forsaken. Unable to hold back anymore, the scent of her, the slightest of heat from her frame, her breasts, pressed delicately against him. He had to have more until she stopped him.

He kissed along her jaw, behind her ear, along

the cord of her neck until her gown denied him further access, then he rested his head on her shoulder just to breath her in.

'I do it for your own good,' he whispered. Revelling in her hands curved into his tunic as if to keep him to her while was trying to hold her in this moment for as long as possible, until he had to let her go. Just this little bit more. 'I'm trying to—'

'My own good!' She shook her head and he lifted his own to meet her gaze.

'Your men, your fortress, are excessive,' she said. 'Only a man in the greatest of dangers would have such force. And you mean to move us from here. Who is threatening us?'

He could never tell her that.

She wrenched an arm away and hit him in the chest. 'Stop leaving me in the dark!'

He growled, yanked her against him again with his one arm and cradled her face with his free hand. He couldn't look at anything but the bluest of eyes, the purest of souls. She didn't know what she asked. If he told her, she'd never be the same.

One brief taste of her; was that all she'd grant him? 'You feel in the dark, do you, Aliette? You want answers to my secrets I hold.' His thumb brushed her cheekbone. So soft against the cruel and permanent disfigurement of his hand.

Against the memory of her kiss that he would feel forevermore. 'I should never tell you.'

'Why are you doing this? Stop touching me.'

He couldn't. 'Don't like it, do you?' He brushed his knuckles along her jaw. 'Should I tell you how I received this scar on my hand? Maybe then you'd cease your questions. Follow me blindly like you so desperately should.'

'Your scar? No, that's not—' She jerked her head away. 'You're kissing me. You're touching me as if you want to—'

He lifted his hand. 'Want to…what, Aliette? What do you think I want?'

'Let me go.'

Never. It was everything he could not to tighten his hold. 'Tell me.'

She clenched and lifted her jaw, her eyes promised retribution. He looked forward to it. But for once, he didn't want to wait.

'I'll tell you want I want,' he said. 'You.'

She slackened and he truly did hold her closer. 'Why are you surprised? I'm holding you. I kissed you.'

She shook her head. Denying him. 'You refused me when I kissed you.'

'Refuse you? I'm trying to—' He drew in a breath. 'I watch you *sleep*, Aliette. I find myself walking hallways I have no need to just because I know you're nearby and I might catch a glimpse of you.'

Her lips parted. Her eyes widened, not with desire or anger or anything but disquiet and confusion. 'You watch me sleep?'

'Now I've scared you.' Like the monster he was. This time, he let her go, stepped away as he should have before.

'You weren't frightened when I told you who I was, or that there are enemies out to kill me... and thus you,' he said. 'You understand, though are being obstinate, that the more people involved the harder it will be to achieve what I need— Mistakes will be made. Of course they will. I've already done them!'

What had he'd become? Weak. Caving to his need for her. Revealing everything.

Confessing like the pampered nobles he derided all his life.

'I had Grace mere hours before you were brought here,' he continued, there was no point hiding this. 'I can't let her go or claim her. But what else to do? Her mother's dead and I believe she's mine. I couldn't leave her, though it may be kinder in the end. Her presence jeopardises everything and still I brought her into this home. I found you fighting that watch guard. With your hair, you could be her mother. I could then pretend she was yours, my servant. It was an acceptable easy solution.

'But I miscalculated how difficult it would be to keep away from her. You weren't fooled. My enemies certainly won't be and all the worse because I can't stay away from you either.'

This was his home where he reigned. Where was his worth? Gone. Aliette obliterated his control by her very existence. He was telling her everything because he was compelled to.

Her family had abandoned her and she had found her own. Fought for them. My God, she had no idea what that did to him. Standing in that derelict house before her, two people crippled, half-blind, a boy with a damaged ear, who hadn't heard him enter when he should have.

He thought he had pulled Aliette off the horror of the streets. The truth was she was their angel. It tossed him dangerously close to her. Every bit of wax he slapped against himself dripping off, his pathetic feathers falling. He plunged with the full realisation his body and soul were irrevocably hers.

And she simply stood there, her blue eyes wide. Observing his downfall.

'Do you come inside the room when I'm sleeping?' she whispered. 'Reynold, do you open the door and…?'

'I've said too much.' He blinked. Her words, making no sense, brought him back to his own. 'I'll leave you now.'

'No, don't. Tell me. Are you close when you watch me sleep?'

He gave her everything, and she wanted more? 'Your hair over the pillow, the whiteness of your skin. You look… You look like an angel.'

'I don't wake,' she said.

She didn't. 'Goodnight.'

He was halfway to the door before she stopped him. Just her hand on his arm, but it was enough to turn him. 'Don't go. You don't understand.'

'I understand I've said too much, that I shouldn't be here this late at night.' He waited. 'That I frighten you.'

This shouldn't be happening. She shouldn't feel like this. She shouldn't want him. A man with blood on his clothes, a kidnapper, but he read to her and he took in her family.

Watch his deeds, then you'll know the man.

'You should frighten me because of where I come from. And there are matters—' She shook her head. 'I've lived on the streets all my life. You don't live on the streets and sleep. Always rest in short bursts and even then you are aware of your surroundings at all times. And worse, I'm a woman. It's far, far worse for me. But…' She looked around the room, at him, and his bedroom behind her.

'I have questions,' she said. 'Just one. This one you must answer. Did you kill someone the day we met? You had a scratch on your cheek, your clothes had blood.'

Stricken grey eyes. 'Don't.'

'Don't ask? Or I don't want the answer who you killed?' she said. 'I think I already know, but I need to hear it from you.'

'It will solve nothing. I have already stated being in my household is a danger to you. If I let both of you go now, as I should from the beginning…' He shook his head. 'There are spies, it probably is too late. I can't…won't send you back out.'

'Is that what you've been doing? Keeping me away from you. Protecting me. Watching me sleep?' She'd never been safe at any time of her life, even when cradled in her mother's thieving arms. What danger Reynold told her couldn't be worse.

'Because of you, I slept for the first time in my life as if I trusted you to keep me safe…protected. You've taught me to read, you've taken care of me. Tell me whose blood you wore that day,' she whispered. 'Tell me or kiss me.'

Chapter Eighteen

He shook with tension. Aliette could see, feel Darkness, and it was advancing towards her.

'You'd kiss a coward,' his said in that even voice that sent shivers through her.

'I want…to trust you. But I don't know what is truth and what isn't with you.'

He briefly closed his eyes, the fanning of his lashes not softening the harshness of his drawn features. 'I've shown you, and all this time, I've been trying to tell you, I *shouldn't* tell you the truth.'

Because it was terrible. Because he had killed Grace's mother. Who else? Despite her speculation, his words blasted against her like a torrent of squalls. The consequences of it were too vast to comprehend and she failed to reconcile this man before her with the blood that had splashed across his chest.

Watch his deeds then she'd know the man, but what did this say about him? To end a life was one matter, to end Grace's mother's life quite another, and a thousand questions surfaced.

None of which he would answer. He didn't answer *this* one.

She should be frightened, appalled, repulsed. He expected it. And yet, Reynold was *tortured* by the thought of it. The grey of his eyes darkened; the waves of his hair slashed against his forehead. His chin lowered as he kept his gaze with hers, accentuating the sharpness of his cheekbones, the angles of his jaw.

She thought he possessed a cruel beauty. It was the truth. Beautiful, lethal…and yet… He had cared about that life he took; he cared about confessing to it. This determined man hadn't wanted to do it. Why, she didn't know, but it was important to her to tell him the truth because…he hadn't rejected her. Because even before Louve told her, she was watching him, seeing the contradictions of him. How he said he wasn't Grace's father, yet guarded her as if he was. Because despite everything, deep within her very soul, Aliette trusted him. It was there in the deeds she'd done when she was with him.

'I'd kiss you,' she said.

He swayed in surprise. 'Even knowing what you know.'

She knew so little of this man, but what she did know was he wouldn't have done it lightly.

With Grace as his daughter, he must have fought against it….and lost.

'What do I know?' she asked him. A man as dark as he, surrounded by mercenaries and a fortress… She was not so naive as to think he'd only killed once in his life. Reynold was a man who had killed many and something about taking this life agonised him.

'I know you have blood on your hands. Yet I don't know if it matters. I still slept when you were near.'

'It matters.' His brow lowered. 'I've killed many, Aliette. I've raised my blade to Grace's mother. I have done deeds I would give no confession to.'

'Raised your blade? You…didn't kill her.' The icy relief was short lived.

'Is there a difference? I killed her servant that night. There was blood on my hands, on my clothes. Grace's mother died anyway.'

Aliette did not know what she should think. Something haunted him. Was he sorry for the deeds?

If so, could she reconcile it? She'd never killed, but how many times had she taken food from others to feed her family instead? The first lesson her parents taught her was that life was harsh and unforgiving. That difficult decisions needed to be made to survive. Underneath it all, if she took food from others, didn't that mean they'd starve?

She shook her head. 'The real questions are why you did what you did. How did Grace's mother die?'

'Too many questions I will not answer.'

She didn't expect for him to answer the ones he did. But she was beginning to understand why he wouldn't. 'Because there's something terrible out there waiting for me...for you. You took in my family and you're not leaving us behind. You're protecting us. Why?'

His entire frame vibrated with the gust of storms inside himself. As if he'd barely held himself in check. 'I'm the one who brought danger. I'm not safe,' he said, the beckoning of his voice jagged with warning...with longing. 'You don't know what you've done to me. What I've become with you. What *we* will become.'

His words were meant to push her away, but they called to all the abandoned pieces inside her. He'd killed, but if he truly didn't care, he'd tell her. Instead, he'd called himself a coward. And he stood away from her. Waiting again. Waiting for her to reject him. Expecting it because of deeds he wrought. But his deeds...were both good and bad, and she didn't know why he did either of them. Yet, she knew how he felt about them; and she knew how she felt around him.

'I've only ever had one fear in my life. That was Darkness and I know him now.' Stepping forward, she placed her hand on his jaw and kissed him. His lips gave just a little. Just a hint of softness, but the rest of him was like stone.

She pulled away. Rubbed her thumb along his lower lip and revelled in his frustrated exhale.

'What are you doing to me?' He leaned his head into her touch.

'I was kissing you,' she said, rubbing her hand along his jaw.

'You shouldn't,' he said, his eddying grey gaze mesmerising her.

'You made that clear, but you're not kissing me back,' she said. 'Why?'

'I…wait,' he said.

'You watch,' she added.

He nodded.

She thought so. How many times had she seen this look of his when she woke from her rest, when she lifted her eyes from a book? Now she felt she could ask. 'What is it that you see when you look at me?'

His eyes roamed her features as if he hadn't seen them before, hadn't watched her sleep. He must have memorised her every flaw by now.

When his eyes returned to hers, they seemed that much softer and warmer.

'Won't tell me?'

He shook his head.

Never. Never had she met a man more stubborn, more in control, used to command and rule. But control wasn't all that was there. She felt... he was staying away.

This man who had taken in her family, offered them everything she had ever dreamed of providing and he took nothing. She wouldn't stand for it.

Stepping back, she undid the laces of her surcoat and let it drop. Watched the expansion of his chest as he drew in air, the flutter of his lashes as took in what she revealed.

Not much. The lines of her neck, her wrists, the tops of her boots. The chemise was the finest of linens, but thick, it being the coldest of winters and necessary. Even with the fire behind her, there was not much for him to see.

But she felt vulnerable to him. As if the outer layer of clothing was an emotional one she was unaware of until now. Fisting her chemise, she lifted it slowly, stopping at her waist. Watching the colouring in his cheeks flush, his nostrils flare and now the telltale sign that what she did was affecting him: him fisting his burned hand.

That emotional response was enough for her

to forgo her vulnerability and toss the chemise over her head and behind her. To stand before him naked.

Even in the comfort of his sanctuary, a fire blazing in the hearth, and the coloured linens hanging on the walls to block any draughts, there was a winter chill that showed no signs that spring was mere weeks away.

She felt that chill, the crackling fire and his eddying gaze. 'Are you watching now?'

Another rove of that lushly framed grey gaze brushing against her legs, hips, the slight indent of her waist. A caress to her belly only to encircle her breasts before they stroked up the tender columns of her neck and his eyes met hers again.

The grey was brighter now, his lips curved. As if he was pleased, or...amused.

'What is it that you see?' she demanded.

'Your boots,' he answered.

Never had she undressed in front of anyone. It wasn't safe. Not only for her virtue, but the Seine's water was unclean and anyone could steal her clothes. Even so, she was aware of how her body compared to other women.

As a child she had wondered what she'd look like as a woman. Hunger kept everyone thin, but she was...miniscule.

For hours she had heard Reynold convey the

stories of Psyche, Sirens and Aphrodite. In comparison, she was nothing like the lush women he revered with his voice. Scrawny wiry body and the brown sturdy boots encasing her feet like clods of mud stuck to her feet. The stockings that flopped over the top because they never fit her properly looked exactly how she felt: useless and ugly.

She knew it was the truth, too, because she was naked...and Reynold commented on her boots.

Maybe she had kept her virtue all this time not because of her filth and stealth, but because no man would bother with her. Of course. Just like her parents.

'I'm sorry,' she said. Who tried to seduce in boots? The thought of removing them was embarrassing. How was she to entice by clumsily bending over to untie leather laces with shaking fingers? Instead, she pivoted around to grab her clothing.

A sharp inhale from him. 'What are you doing.'

'Dressing.' She wanted him to kiss her, not laugh.

'Stop,' he commanded.

Like hell—she picked up the chemise.

He was on her in an instant. Shocked, she straightened and his fingers wrapped around her wrist. 'Drop it.'

With him at her back, she ignored him.

'Haven't I explained how much I desire you?' he said.

That was before she'd exposed herself to him. Before she'd showed him her nothing body. How she was like a girl instead of a woman. No hips, no breasts. She barely had legs. The top of her head didn't reach his shoulders.

'I was asleep under the covers,' she said. 'You couldn't know I looked like nothing.'

'I know exactly what you look like. I watched you bathe, Aliette.'

Shocked, she dropped the chemise. 'You saw me in the bath…'

'That first day, I didn't hear you and didn't trust you. I opened the door—your back was to me as you reached for a linen to dry yourself.'

She remembered that time in the bath, where she had felt safe, secure, cocooned. And all the while he was there. Of course he was, his presence was probably why she felt safe.

'That was the moment for me, Aliette. When I wanted you. I haven't been able to stop watching you since.'

He pressed against her back. The whisper of his clothes, the warmth of his body. His breath fluttering her hair as he bowed his head to her. He released his fingers around her wrist and trailed them up her arm across her collarbone until his hand clasped her opposite shoulder.

Then, anchoring her, he pulled her closer.

She felt the abrasion of his tunic's soft wool, the hardness of his chest and stomach, the strength of his legs. The power in his arms that encased her.

Then...she felt him. Against her lower back, his hips cradling hers, the hard, relentless length of him that was undeniably male.

He exhaled low, almost a growl, as he pressed tighter. '*Everything* about you calls to me. Everything. The cascade of your dark hair caught beneath my arm. The glimpse of your left shoulder, the softness of your skin under my palm.'

The enticing scent of him, sage and steel and man. And a heat that felt far, far hotter than the fire that blazed in front of her.

'How can you think I don't want you?' he said, releasing his grip and trailing his fingers across her collarbone. 'You are perfect. Right now your height allows me to see the full length of your body. The exquisiteness of your breasts, your hardened rose-tipped nipples that have peaked at my slight touch. Your mons, covered by the softest of dark curls. Are you as affected by my touch as me? Are you soft, wet, swelling even now? All of this was hidden from me when you bathed. To see more of you now is my undoing and you think I don't want you. I crave you, Aliette, and loathe those boots for covering any part of you.'

Trailing fingertips down her arm until he linked his fingers with hers. Lust's heat flared from her very blood outward until her skin felt as though it would burst with want of his touch to soothe it. The brush of his clothes wasn't enough, the length of his body pressed against hers wasn't enough. She wanted him laid bare and surrounding her as night does the day. The boots had to go.

She shifted. 'I can take them off.'

'No.' He turned his hand within hers and gently drew her around until she faced him. 'No, let me.'

Then he said nothing, and removed his hand from hers. Keeping his gaze upon her, he, in that elegant way he had, knelt before her. In all her days, she had never imagined Darkness kneeling at her feet, but that was what Reynold did.

She couldn't breathe.

Everything in this room, in her life, narrowed to this moment. Reynold's dark hair at her fingertips. In the firelight, it was blue like a fathomless inkwell. His warm breath fanned against her skin, and she knew just where his gaze fell at the juncture of her thighs.

Everything about her was shivering and heavy. She felt swollen, wet, and wondered if he could see what he was doing to her. But he said nothing. Only, the next breath he took was deeper, stronger, and the next exhale brushed across her skin like a caress. He did it again.

It was as if he was taking her in scent and sharing his own with her. The moist heat of it tightened everything about her. Her nipples chafed against the cold air; her skin prickled.

Her limbs felt weak and heavy, her breasts swelled, the tips almost painful points. Her fingers flexed, wanting to sink into the dark strands of his hair as he lowered his head. She watched his fingers encircle her left ankle exposed at the top of her practical boot.

She flinched at the startling touch. An upward brush of his calloused fingertips along her calf to stop at her knee sent an arc of heat until her entire body pulsed with it. Then he took his touch away.

Was this what he would do with her? Torture her with touches until one breath hitched to the other. He held only one ankle. If he moved to the other or captured them both, her knees would buckle.

Damn the boots. If Darkness wouldn't surround Day, then Day would throw herself at him.

'My boots,' she commanded.

'So much haste,' he murmured.

'It's my life.'

He lifted his lashes. 'Am I Death?'

She felt as though she was dying. Especially when the teasing light drew away and his eyes and mouth twisted as if he was in pain and his gaze sunk helplessly to her breasts. Upon a low moan, he gripped her hips and slid his hands up her belly to cup them underneath, trapping the points in the juncture of his thumb and finger.

The tips peaked painfully and her gasp was swallowed by his own sound of need.

'I want those boots off you, Aliette. *Need* them off you,' he said, flexing his fingers as if trying to gather the entire globe into the heat of his palm. They were so small they'd fit, but need had made them unmalleable. All he could do was repeat the scrape of his fingertips over the top of them. 'Bend over and take them off for me now.'

Bend over… Oh. If he put his mouth against her breasts now, she truly would faint. 'You're closer.'

His head fell against her belly. 'Now you wait?'

Her hands captured the blue strands of his hair which were coarse yet silky through her trembling fingers. 'You could do it faster.'

He gave a jagged laugh and released his grip, but not his touch which was a weighty caress along her sides to the back of her thighs. With rough haste, he tore the boots and stockings from her feet.

She expected him to stand, to carry her away to his bedroom. To undress himself and take her as man does a woman.

She'd seen men slamming women against buildings, or drunk and slipping in hay bales in the back of wagons. Nothing could prepare her for this: Reynold kneeling, staring at her feet.

She wiggled her toes at him.

He huffed. 'You'll wait.'

Encircling her ankle, he caressed the top of her feet, pressed his thumb on her inner sole until she shifted to widen her legs. A low hum of approval, he cupped her foot and lifted her leg.

'Reynold!'

'Hold my shoulders.' He held the delicate bone of her ankle, brushed his cheek against her calf. The coarse bristles scraping pleasure along the limb that was no longer her own.

'What is it that you're doing?' she said.

'What I want.'

Another brush, a kiss. He lovingly caressed her leg until she visibly trembled. 'My boots are off.'

Silence while she was achingly aware of his touch, his lips, the widening of her stance so her swollen folds felt the chill of the room.

Gripping his shoulders, she stated, 'Your clothes are still on.'

He lowered her limb, but didn't release it, and looked up.

'I wanted you to kiss me,' she said, releasing his shoulders.

'I am.'

He gazed at her and waited. She waited with him.

'Are we…done?' she said so softly and he could hear the soft questions in her voice. The ones that undid him.

How to tell her he was savouring her now that he could? Her deeds felled him. Her words…a redemption on his stained soul. He had confessed to his worst crime and she accepted him. He was unworthy to touch her, yet she demanded it.

Tell me or kiss me.

The slenderness of her legs, the narrow arch of her hips. A waist he could span with his hands. Her breasts… Delicate buds with nipples the colour of the deepest centre of a rose. His hands ached; his mouth watered to taste.

Were they stopping? He *couldn't.*

'Never,' he said. Continuing to kneel, he unbuckled his belt and with one hand ripped his tunic off his back.

Her widening blue eyes were all the confirmation he needed. She was untouched. How was that possible? And yet, she trembled and looked at him as if he was a bounty before her. Her eyes darting from his bared straight shoulders, the smattering of dark hair on his chest that arrowed to breeches he didn't dare unlace now. Not until…

'Hold on to me.'

Her hands hovered above his shoulders. 'I don't think I can.'

He knew what she meant. It undid him to touch her bared body. His breeches and braies pained him. Keeping his gaze on her, he kissed her foot and caressed with all the tenderness he could manage before he rested her ankle on his shoulder, shifted and felt it slip down his back.

Bringing everything his body ached for before him.

'Reynold.'

It was his name. He didn't recognise it now.

The colour of her. As red as her nipples, swollen, wet. Her scent flaring his lust. She was exposed to his every prayer and depravity, and he breathed her in.

Fingers now gripping his head, he dipped. Nuzzling his mouth, his chin, along the outside, coaxing her folds to unfurl before he laid wet open kisses. A sudden tightening of her nails in his scalp. The sharp pain that she might want a say in this. He stopped.

'You're…kissing me,' she said.

He nodded. Words were beyond him. When her fingers eased, he did it again, ending with suckling the nub.

One hand slipped to his shoulder, the other tangled in the hairs at his neck, and brought her against him. Then, then he tasted her. One long swipe of his tongue and another until she was shivering, until she pulled his hair. Until the tightness of his breeches felt like a blade against his need for her.

Again and again, while her body swayed over his, while her hands slipped against the sweat gleaming his shoulders, his torso, while he gripped her hips to press her tighter.

Hunger. He knew only hunger and wouldn't be sated until she came for him.

'Aliette, give yourself to me.' He thrust with his lips, his mouth, his tongue.

Her gasps of pleasure turning to whimpers. 'I can't. I can't.'

Denial from his every desire. Maddened, he yanked her against him. Supported her in his arms, laid her on the ground as an offering to him. Fell upon her like a starving man to feast.

When her legs curled into herself, he took advantage. Using his shoulders, his body to support her legs and ever so gently circled her entrance with the tip of his finger.

She held her breath at that telling touch and he eased his kisses. When she gave a sound of capitulation, he knew this was what she needed. This tenderness, this loving. This *savouring*.

It would kill him.

'Come for me. Come. I've got you,' he said the litany over and over, his warm breath adding to his gentle touch. And then—and then she did. A fluttering around his finger, her back suddenly arching, a keening whispered scream.

Tenderly inserting his finger until he reached her maidenhead, his mouth descending upon her to prolong, to fulfil, to—

A pounding of sound. She jerked beneath him.

Her clit against the tip of his tongue, his mouth covered with her essences. All he wanted was more. *More.* Splaying his fingers, he pushed her legs tighter against her body, opening her further—

Thunder reverberating under his bent knees; Aliette yanking her left leg from his grip. He lifted his head, to tell her, to explain what had only begun.

'Reynold…' Aliette whispered, her voice a warning.

He ignored her. Only what they'd become mattered. His ache utter agony, he reached for his breeches to release his laces. To free himself and complete what was between them.

Chapter Nineteen

'Open up!' Louve shouted, pounding on the door.

The double-metal latches rattled.

Doors. Metal.

Reynold's fingers shook.

One lace undone, Aliette's delicate hand was frantically tapping against his.

'We need to get up,' she said.

Her hair was partly fanned, partly tucked beneath her shoulder. Her skin flushed, a light to her blue eyes he never wanted to see dimmed again. If he thought she was an angel he'd flown too close to, there was no doubt now.

'Reynold.' She pressed down as if to sit up. Mimicking her, he straightened.

His arms and legs shaking, a coolness to his body from the air where he wasn't pressed against her. One lace unhooked in his breeches. At his sudden movement, he pulsed once, readying for her tight sheath laid bare and plump before him, while Louve hammered on the door, trying to break in.

Reynold made the doors to his sanctuary thick for privacy, and as a last bastion of defence. The fact they reverberated at all meant they had been beaten on for some time.

He was a madman. A monster. Lost in himself, in her, in everything that she was, starving, he...devoured her. Had she protested, pushed him away? Her gripping fingers could have been anything, but he'd ignored the pinch, the rendering.

Her ephemeral words unheard, the part of her thighs, the flat of her feet against the ground. In the end, had she been shoving away from him, his strength too strong to overpower? His need for her had overpowered him.

'Did I hurt you?' he said. 'Aliette, are you in pain? Did I—?'

She gripped his wrist. 'No, only surprised me. That wasn't the kiss I thought I'd receive.'

She hated it. Untried, untouched and he flipped her around like a practised whore.

'I scared you, then.'

She brushed his arm, gave a tender smile. 'I don't think I'm capable of fearing Darkness now. I only want more of him.'

Three hard thumps on the door. Louve was slamming it with his body.

'I'm coming!' he yelled.

Louve cursed. 'You could have told me that before I hurt myself!'

Jerking away, Reynold reached inside his breeches, and stopped at Aliette's smirk. 'It won't go away with that satisfied grin on your face.'

'We're in trouble!' Louve called out.

Reynold shoved to his feet, yanked his tunic on and cracked open the door.

'We have to go,' Louve said.

'Has he returned?'

A low murmur... And another.

'We go immediately.' Reynold closed the door. Kept his pressed hand against it and didn't turn. 'Get dressed.'

Aliette sat up. 'Are we leaving? I thought we were waiting for someone.'

Reynold stayed quiet. His back to her, his breaths evening out, but deep as if he was bracing himself against a coming storm.

A fissure of fear blasted any warmth she felt. 'He's not coming, is he? Your messenger. Because he *can't* come.'

Reynold turned around. His eyes darting from her, to his books, to his belt on the floor. He snatched it up. 'Eude's dead.'

Her legs shaking, Aliette scrambled for her chemise. Out there, people died, but they were secure in a fortress. 'Then we'll stay here.'

He tightened the belt, pulling up the tunic, revealing the tightness of his breeches. He had not been as satisfied as she. She whirled to find her gown.

'We go, or we'll all be killed,' he said.

She pulled the gown over her chemise, her entire body shaking. Reynold before her, holding her hands.

'Breathe. There's time,' he said, adjusting her clothing. She couldn't look at him.

'My boots!'

He let her go, grabbed her boots and stockings. Pointed to the padded bench where she sat down.

Grabbing one stocking from his hand, she pulled it up her leg. 'Whoever's after you can't know of Grace and me, of Helewise and Vernon. We'll return to the streets. No one need know we were ever here.'

She reached for the other held stocking. 'We'll—'

He clenched the limp garment. His open expression one of pain. Agony. As if he was *hurt* by what she said.

Cursing, he placed the stocking in her hand and whirled to his desk. Securing the message he started with one hand, he picked up his quill. Stopped. Cursed again.

A message for a messenger who was no longer alive.

She'd never seen Reynold without thought, without control, except for his kiss. She revelled in it. Now there was a vulnerability to him as he bowed over his papers.

It wasn't Louve informing him a mercenary had died that did this to him. It was her…telling him to leave her and her family behind. She hadn't thought how those words could be interpreted. Her entire body shook with what they shared and death stalked their sanctuary. She couldn't think!

'I'm sorry, Reynold—

He swiped a satchel and propped it on his chair. Flipping it open, he slid parchments inside. He kept his thoughts, and his grey gaze, turned away from her.

Aliette sighed. She was only just now learning to trust, of course she'd make mistakes. Of course she'd have doubts. In truth, it wasn't completely unreasonable to leave her behind. 'If there is danger, it is safer for you to leave us.'

He looked then, and his look…his look said she'd taken a knife to him. When she finally blinked, the tide of his grey eyes had ebbed. 'For Grace's sake, I won't risk it. I can't carry a child around if there is no parent. She would be exposed.'

There was no explaining her emotions now. He wasn't listening to her fumbling attempts. If it was true there was danger, then there was a flaw in his plan. She had to say it. 'Even if they believe I'm the mother, you could still be the father. Wouldn't it be best if—?'

Then his lips curved into a smile. One that did not meet his barren eyes. 'They're watching. Always. I've never lain with a servant before and they wouldn't expect it now. They'd never believe it. Why would I demean myself so?'

Demean. Aliette took a step back. All her life she'd been treated as if her worth was lower than the slop thrown at her. Since her family had abandoned her, she'd believed it. The pain of their departure had defined her. She'd told Reynold he could do no worse to her than what her family already did, but she was wrong.

Insults had been flung at her in the past, but his words struck. Slivers, cracks—she had no more defences. Now Darkness was bashing her against the rocks. The happiness she'd felt in his arms just moments before taken by his words, by his cold gaze. The eddying grey gone.

'*Who's* watching?'

'As if I would tell you. As if it matters. On

the way, we travel separately. We'll find other women…for the men, perhaps. Then you can travel with them. What transpired in this room will not happen again.'

She hadn't expected it to happen at all. But she'd fallen asleep on the bench next to him; she'd seen him hold Grace. She thought she could trust him. But he proved he was just like all the others. He might not be physically leaving her as her parents did, but she felt his withdrawal all the same.

But for Vernon, Helewise, Gabriel and Grace, she could endure his disdain.

'So we're to leave without knowing the dangers,' she said, needed anger framing each word. 'Without knowing where we're going.'

'Do I know all of your secrets?' he asked.

No. And now he never would. Her defences reforming, she knew what she had to do.

'That's what I thought.' He flipped the satchel's cover closed, and bound it.

'We'll go,' she said. Eventually he'd tire of them. Maybe outside Paris was where their future lay. 'Not because you order it, but because it's what we decide to do. It's what is best for my family.'

'I don't think you understand,' he said, a gleam of icy amusement in his eyes. 'You'd do well to remember that the day before I took you, I slashed the throat of a servant and raised the bloodied blade to Grace's mother. Then my men buried one corpse in unhallowed ground and the other was left in her derelict home to rot. All so that absolutely no one could trace their deaths to me.'

Bile rose in her throat.

'Understand this, thief, you will travel where I travel. Now and always. When it comes to the protection of my daughter, you don't have a choice.'

Ruined. That's what he was now, destroyed. Reynold slung the satchel over his shoulders and took the stairs two at a time.

He hadn't been long in his Paris location. He could never stay in France for any length of time with his family residence so close. Most of the men had been with him since England. They knew what to do to close his home. He didn't. Not this time. Years travelling undercover from one location to another and this was different.

He'd killed the night he took Grace and… worse…he'd raised his blade to the mother of his child. It didn't matter that he hadn't killed her. It didn't matter if she was in pain and begged him, if his hand trembled and there was a chance he wouldn't have done it. He'd still raised the knife. He was still a monster.

And he had confessed it all to Aliette.

She was a light in the sky that had been forever dark. Warmth when all he felt was cold. Of course he kept flying towards her. When she offered him her kisses despite what was written in blood in his past, despite what he might have done that night, he felt…forgiveness. It was as though she saw him. Truly saw him.

He thought she understood all his toil, his hardships. All the sin he'd committed because he must. Of course, he knelt before her. He would have prayed to her if she'd asked. Crawled however far she desired.

But she hadn't understood at all. She hadn't forgiven or known the sacrifices he made and why. Because the moment Louve appeared to announce Eude's death, the moment when all his warnings of danger were truth, she told him she'd stay behind.

She hadn't accepted him, not if her first reaction was to throw him away. Maudlin. A fool, but he'd given her every bit of his stained soul. And she simply discarded it. Worse, she thought he'd leave her.

He loved her.

All for naught and he could do no other action than keep her. The fact was, she'd been in the household for weeks. She'd been caring for Grace and seen leaving his household. If there were spies, and there were always spies, his enemies would be aware of her and his daughter. For his daughter's safety, he'd keep Aliette and the family she chose over him.

He swept across the courtyard and down the staircase to the hidden exit. Eude was killed near the front of his house. He wouldn't risk anyone knowing they'd left. As for the horses, new ones would have to be purchased and the old left behind.

He was all too aware this was a fool's endeavour and it was already too late. If Eude was dead, then someone knew about him. Which brother had ordered the killing, which parent, or had someone else been added to the game?

There was too much conjecture. Eude had carried no messages. It had been weeks since he'd sent him to Scotland. He knew Malcolm of Clan Colquhoun had the Jewel of Kings. He did not know if he had the dagger with scrollwork and two rubies which was essential for his game.

For now, they needed another place to hide. One that would be near and easy to travel to. There was only one he'd never used because he wanted to call it a true home one day. The town of Troyes was small and there would be no anonymity there, but it was accessible by the Seine.

Travelling by boat was detectable, but also easy to defend.

Unlike his body and soul. Bitterly, he thought of Odysseus. A tale of a man suffering great obstacles to return to his cherished wife who waited for him. Such a fantastical tale of a love that would not die and nothing he'd ever experienced or witnessed. His parents hated each other.

When he first read it, he was engrossed in Odysseus's adventures and dismissed Penelope and the marriage bed. But as he grew older and more isolated, the bed made from a living tree began to plague him. To the point he believed if he had the book made, if he simply *owned* the story, the love between a husband and wife wouldn't taunt him so.

But though the book travelled with him, he never read the copy he'd commissioned. Of course it was the thief who first opened it. All to mock him with because, in these brief weeks, he began to envision Aliette was the wife at the end of his long journey.

False beliefs and feelings if she could believe he could abandon her as her parents did. Because to think that meant she didn't believe in him. She wasn't Penelope waiting years without faltering. He wasn't as significant to her as she was to him.

Yanking off the mattress, he propped it against the far wall. Gripping the bed rail, he pulled the sturdy frame to the opposing corner. The hatch to the secret passageway was almost undetectable, but he knew it was underneath.

The stolen moments reading with Aliette could never be his future. He must rip out whatever hold she had on his body and heart. He must rip apart the wings he kept repairing to reach her.

Prying the lever under the first nail, he worked it free and carefully did the same to the rest of the boards. When most of them escaped this way a few men had to repair the flooring and return the room as it was. Their exit in the open would be a distraction, a target, but necessary. If this Paris location was to be used again, he didn't want his family knowing about the underground passage.

'Hiding more secrets from me, my friend,' Louve said from behind him. 'And an escape route at that? What if I desired to ride away undetected from you?'

'Which is precisely why I didn't tell you,' Reynold replied, unsurprised that Louve had snuck up on him. The man was unnaturally quiet. 'I despise paying my men and them not performing their duties. Now help me with these nails.'

* * *

'Can we trust him, child?' Vernon stated. 'I can't see the man, look him in the eye and tell myself.'

'None of us can,' Helewise said. 'He hasn't been still since we arrived.'

'I like Baldr.' Gabriel sneezed.

The man who had twisted her arm and Gabriel's cold had worsened. This did not bode well. None of this did.

'We can't trust him.' She out of everyone knew this to be true.

'But you do,' Gabriel said. 'Else, why would we be here? And you've been gone a long time with him. We missed you.'

'You know that I missed you all very much.' Aliette bent just a bit, wanting to gather him to her, but knew better. He still shied away from contact, but how to explain something as complex as Reynold to a child?

She had trusted Reynold, or at least was beginning to. Day after day, she kept walking further into the dark with him until she could almost see him clearly. He longed for Grace, read to her. Firm with his men, but never unfair. He truly could abandon them, but didn't. She suspected that he did it to protect them, but... He held to his secrets.

Mercenaries, danger. Eude was killed. She was stolen. Grace was stolen. Now they were to flee in the middle of the day. These occurrences weren't her life, yet now they were. The longer she stayed with Reynold, with Darkness, the longer everything else would be grey. Contradictions, and she couldn't see properly.

When Reynold touched her, kissed her, it felt like…happiness. But she was wrong if he could use such words against her so easily. He displayed a darker side. One full of bitterness, anger. Wrath.

He portrayed Darkness, who was capable of taking parents away. Trust Darkness? It wasn't a question of trust. The question was, should she? No, but she would, temporarily, if it meant safety for her family. An impossible task to explain to a child.

'You know Frederick from the vegetable stall?' At Gabriel's nod, she continued, 'He gives us vegetables sometimes, but he also calls the guards when he's in the mood. Reynold, all these men, Baldr, included, are like that. We can be with them, travel with them, but don't ever forget who they are and don't ever forgot who you are.'

As she had with her captor. She needed to remember she couldn't see in the dark, nor was she supposed to.

'I understand,' Gabriel said.

Chapter Twenty

Aliette couldn't stop trembling as Reynold and his men escorted them through a passage hidden underneath her bed. Not a torch between them, but they shuffled forward with ropes tied around their waists.

With Grace cradled in a sling around her, Aliette clutched the rope that held her to the others. She kept moving only because Gabriel was behind her and depending on each step she took. Because Helewise and Vernon were between mercenaries depending on their strength to keep them moving forward.

It was easier than she thought it would be to step down that staircase into the dark. Maybe because she had already been exposed to so much of it these last days. No torch, no talking. After the pounding of boards against the hatch behind her, everyone was as silent as possible.

Step after step, the passage seemingly unending, the smell of dank earth reminding her of a graveyard. At three tugs on the rope, she stopped and adjusted Grace against her. The child was awake, her head moving though there was nothing to see.

A sound in the front before a shaft of light illuminated Reynold's outstretched hand and upturned face. In his other hand was a drawn dagger. Then, with a nod, the other mercenaries held the hatch while Reynold untied the rope and she did the same.

Louve loomed into her line of sight. 'You and your family stay in here out of the light.'

She glanced at Helewise as Louve disappeared up the hatch along with Reynold.

'She's very quiet,' Helewise said to her left.

Aliette jumped before she calmed herself and patted Grace's back. 'I don't know why she doesn't talk or cry, but maybe she's like her... Maybe she's waiting.'

Brushing Grace's head, Helewise said, 'Do you think she hears?'

'I don't know.' She didn't know much about babies and that worried her the most of all. 'She turns her head at sound, like now. Maybe no one talked to her before I came. Maybe she senses that it isn't safe to cry.'

'It appears us females are the only ones who are wary.' Helewise indicated to Gabriel and Vernon, who were quietly talking to the two mercenaries in the back.

One of the mercenaries was Guarin, whom she had taught to pluck a chicken, but that familiarity provided little comfort. 'I think we're right to be wary, I don't know where we are.'

'Maybe our men are right to not care when things have improved so much,' Helewise said. 'Gabriel... I wouldn't have expected this of him, but perhaps since you have been here weeks and well cared for, he feels that this is where he can be a child again. Safe and protected.'

It was more than safety because in such a short time, Gabriel was smiling. The food she'd stolen since she'd been kidnapped had given him strength, but being here with the men was altogether different.

The change in him was remarkable. She didn't think it was the house, food or clothing that made the difference. They'd hardly been here long enough for that to take effect. It was the men. How they catered and respected the boy. His shoulders were straighter and he stood a little taller. It was all too clear she hadn't provided enough protection or guidance. The fact he had it now, even temporarily, she was grateful for.

'Being well fed and clothed seems to have improved my husband's tongue,' Helewise pointed out.

'I don't know whether Vernon's talking more or

Guarin. Would you believe when I first arrived, the men weren't allowed to speak to me?'

'Why?'

'I suspect the secrecy has something to do with why we travel now.' Aliette reached for Helewise's gnarled hand. 'I never thanked you for travelling with us.'

'Didn't know I had a choice.' Helewise gave a quiet laugh and patted their clasped hands. 'Don't be so surprised, I haven't had much of a choice with you for years. The moment I glanced your way you've been ordering me and Vernon about.'

Was she as bad as her parents? Ordering them about because she thought she knew better? 'I didn't mean—'

'I meant to thank you.'

Aliette's eyes watered. 'I starved you most days. The demands I made. I don't know what I was thinking. And then this. I fear I've made your lives worse.'

Helewise plucked at her new gown. 'Not worse. Interesting. We've had some time to talk before this man of yours arrived and stuffed us in this tunnel. Enough to know that you've had little influence on what's happened since that day in the market.'

Reynold was hardly hers. She didn't know if he belonged to anyone. 'Why are you with me?

You still don't need to be. Reynold captured me to care for Grace, but you, you could possibly have—'

'Don't even think about it. You've spoiled us, we'd be no use in the streets now.'

'I feared you stayed because I pleaded with you,' Aliette said. 'Because I'm selfish.'

'Because you don't want to be alone?'

Aliette nodded.

'Maybe we don't want to be alone either. Maybe you need to accept we're together now. Even if I'm hiding in a tunnel that smells and don't know what's exactly under my feet.'

Knowing she'd cry, Aliette squeezed Helewise's hand and held it as Louve jumped down and approached them. She felt the other mercenaries, Vernon and Gabriel gather around.

'There's transportation above. Your family, including Grace, will be hidden.'

'And me?' Aliette said, reluctantly handing Grace over. Louve turned and gave her to the man behind him.

'Stay here. Let me get them settled.'

Helewise patted her hand again before she took the arm of Guarin. Vernon was on his other side. Gabriel skipped behind them, offering to help.

Then they were all gone and she was alone. Helewise was right. It did stink, but as long as she kept her eyes on that open hatch, she could keep the fear from her. But the moments stretched on, long enough for her to strain her eyes and ears for any scuffling or fighting. There were voices, horses, what sounded like a cart rolling. But down in the tunnel she couldn't tell the distance or direction of the sound. All she knew was that time was passing and it was enough for her to worry.

A shadow, then Louve appeared before her again. This time he did not jump, but leaned in with his arms outstretched.

'Is everything fine?' she asked.

'Everyone is safe. It's only you now.'

Only her. No Reynold, not a glance or a word. He had disappeared through that hatch and she didn't know if he'd be there when she emerged in the day again. But this wasn't about him anymore. It was about keeping her family safe. Taking Louve's hand, she let him hoist her up.

They were outside one of the walls of the city, outside the reach of watch guards. Other mercenaries she thought were behind in the fortress were there with horses supplies...and two women. Their hair in tangles, their clothes loose. She'd seen them before. By their gaze, they were not surprised to see her.

She saw no sign of her family. There were two

small identical carts, so small she wondered how her family fit.

'Ignore the carts. Your family is secure and cannot be seen,' Louve said. 'You'll ride with me.'

Her eyes went to Reynold, but his back was turned as he talked to Baldr. Between the distance and his silence she felt like the strangers he meant them to be. Abandoned again. But she'd been through worse and her family was hidden. She would ensure they remained safe.

Louve mounted, then held out his hand. She'd never ridden a horse before; she'd never done any of this before. She jumped and he hoisted her behind him. Awkward, clumsy, she adjusted with her arms and her legs, but couldn't do so without plastering herself to Louve.

Reynold turned his horse, his calculating gaze resting on each of the parties, but those telling eyes only glanced over her before he yanked the reins and stormed ahead with two mercenaries at his side. She felt that gaze despite its brevity and the riders between them. However, not as many mercenaries as the house had held.

'Where is everyone?'

'You could have told me they weren't yours.' Louve turned his head, his voice almost a whisper.

'Who?' she said.

'The ones you've been feeding. I would have cared for them. You didn't have to risk it yourself.'

'There was no risk. They're my family. One I chose and who chose me.'

'You know you had me under the impression you'd left a husband and a child.'

She gaped.

'You can imagine my relief.' Louve shook his head. 'You want to tell me about them? There are days we must travel.'

Days with Reynold ignoring her. Days with the carts travelling behind. No caring of Grace, no worry for food. Had she ever had this much time and so much to think about…and matters she needed to forget?

'About Gabriel?' she said.

'The couple as well. They are…amusing.'

On that she agreed. 'They have their own humour. That is what made me notice them.'

'Helewise's laugh?' Louve said. 'I think all of France can hear that laugh.'

She had never talked of her family. No one ever asked and for a moment she thought to refuse. Louve's loyalty was to Reynold. But then she'd have to fill the silence with her thoughts, which would inevitably bring her back to Reynold. Her attention should be only on her family, so she told of the day she met Vernon and Helewise. Told of how embarrassed she was when she asked Vernon to recite what made Helewise laugh. It had been a bawdy tale. At the time, she'd been embarrassed—now she laughed along with Louve.

'So truly no husbands or other children around?' Louve asked, wiping the tears of laughter from his eyes. 'No one else we have to worry for?'

A husband, children. Aliette's laughter died. She loved her family, but as close as they were, there was a part of her that longed. She had her family, but there always felt as though something was missing. If she just trusted, or felt safe, maybe she wouldn't be waiting to be left behind again. But she was always left behind. Reynold might be forcing her on this trip, but he had made it clear he wanted nothing to do with her.

'No others,' she said. 'Not that it matters if there were.'

'With certainty, it matters to him. He's always watchful of the landscape. He never trusts. Now, he rides with singular purpose as if he's pursued. What happened in that room?'

Aliette thought she'd hurt Reynold with her panicked words about leaving her. She'd apologised, reasoned with him that her words were a logical choice. But his manners to her became cold, his words turned cruel.

Maybe she was wrong that they had shared something. Maybe Darkness was incapable of caring. Maybe her sleeping when he was near didn't mean she trusted him. Maybe...

'Nothing occurred.'

'He doesn't glare knives if nothing occurred.'

Reynold rode ahead of them, his back straight, shoulders tense. Was it her who he was angry with, or was the situation of leaving Paris as dire as she suspected? Which begged the question.

'Where are the other mercenaries?'

She was tired of talking about Reynold. She made a vow that this trip would be about her family and needed to turn the conversation to them. Could they breathe in the carts? Were they padded with blankets for comfort? Irresponsible not to demand an inspection. Irresponsible to take them on a dangerous journey.

At Louve's silence, she continued, 'Will you not tell me anything? This will be a very long journey if we are to keep all our secrets.'

'I'm not worried about who will outlast whom to talk. You can't get off the horse without my help.' Placing both reins in one hand, Louve rested his other hand on her thigh. Startled at the sudden intimacy, she shifted her leg, but he didn't remove it.

'Take your hand off my leg.'

Louve gave a laugh, but didn't remove it. 'The better demand would be why it's there.'

She grabbed his wrist to lift it off.

'Don't,' he said. 'A few more moments and the perception will be enough.'

'Perception?'

'You are to ride with me for only part of the journey. Soon you'll ride with Guarin, then Baldr, and so on.'

'On his command, no doubt,' she said. Riding from one man to another. Passed around like a—

'Will they be touching me, too?'

'Yes.'

Like one of the women here who were tossed from one mercenary to another. The feeling of friendship with Louve was gone. If she could jump from the horse, she would.

'Easy, Aliette. You need to appear happy to be in our august company. You're supposed to be enjoying my touch and our conversation.'

'Who will notice? There are only a few people on the roads and even those are mostly children and chickens.'

'Anyone passing is a spy for the right amount of coin.'

And so she was touched against her will. 'Why does he think he can dictate how we travel or who is to maul me?'

Louve returned his hand to the reins. 'He has never explained his deeds. He simply gives orders and they are obeyed.'

That wasn't the whole truth. 'But you know why he does it.'

Louve shook his head. 'I guessed only because I have been with him the longest, but we do not share confidences.'

It wasn't what Louve said, but the tone that made her believe him. He sounded almost remorseful that he wasn't closer to Reynold. If they'd been together for years, if Louve was the closest Reynold ever got to a friend, what did that say for her?

'So we're both in the dark.' Because they were purposefully kept there. At a cost to Louve, to her and her family. One she'd pay for Gabriel's sake, Grace's as well. But she'd do it for them, not because Darkness ordered it.

She eyed the other women riding, caught the eye of one and tried to smile. The other woman just looked surprised. Was she not supposed to be friendly? Did they know she wasn't like them? If they knew, then Reynold's enemies would. 'Maybe I should ride between your legs like the others.'

'Never, I couldn't defend myself. I'm sore from

him pounding me into the ground at training,' Louve said. 'What are you doing?'

'Unbinding my hair like the other women.'

Louve exhaled roughly. 'You're doing more than that.'

'I'm loosening my laces. I don't have breasts, though, so I think this is only going to bare my—'

'Stop!' Louve said. 'He won't approve.'

'I don't need his approval. I'm doing this to protect—'

'I know why you're doing it, but the result will be the same. With his sword through my stomach.' Louve looked her up and down. 'That's too loose.'

'I don't have as much as the others. I thought it'd help if I—'

'It does *not* help. Just riding with us is enough.'

She had had enough. 'For what? You have to know more than me. He can't kidnap me and expect me to simply follow him.'

'You're angry with him.' Louve rode and she let him while he mulled his words. She *waited*. What had her life come to?

'He's complicated.' Louve exhaled. 'Have you watched his deeds or have you only listened to his words? Has he said words against the poor, or that you're not worthy?' He turned his head and she avoided his eyes. 'I can see he did. *Watch* his deeds. He gives the extra food to the poor and all the men here need him far worse than he needs our swords. He's helped more than you.'

He hadn't helped her at all. Food, clothing, shelter. Things she wished for all her life, but the price was… The price was wanting love. Belonging. Safety. Trust. She was beginning to believe those were obtainable until she said a few words and he turned cruel once again.

There was a moment when she thought she'd… wounded him somehow, but since then he'd ignored her so completely. Now she didn't know if he could be hurt by anything.

'I don't intend to wait around for any more of his help,' she said.

Louve gave some sound. 'The two of you are quite alike, you know. It's rather amusing.'

'I don't know what you're talking about.'

'Neither does he. But you will. By the time you understand, I won't have to explain.'

Chapter Twenty-One

They stopped at midday to rest. Aliette knew they followed the Seine. She could see it in the distance. It seemed too obvious of a road and destination, but what did she know of travelling to avoid enemies?

Reynold had also dismounted, but stayed in the front. Arms crossed, he talked to the mercenaries who flanked him. Ignoring him, she turned to concentrate on the carts and their cargo. For now she wanted to ensure Vernon and Helewise travelled well. To change Grace's linens, to feed Gabriel. She didn't like that the carts travelled close to the back.

Baldr grabbed her arm. 'We ride next.'

'I need to see the child,' she said.

'Make no acknowledgement with the carts.'

'But the boy—' His expression and hold tightened. She yanked back. 'We need to talk on how you handle me.'

He loosened his grip, but not enough to free her. 'I'm not used to your kind of female.'

'*Any* female you need to stop hurting, not just me.'

Baldr's pale face flushed with colour.

Her ire at him eased. Maybe he didn't know how large or intimidating he was. 'The passengers haven't relieved themselves. They'll need help, please.'

'Let her go.'

An even, controlled voice behind them. When Baldr released her, she turned. Reynold stood as still as the trees behind him.

'I want to help with Grace,' she said. 'They can't stay in the carts like this.'

'Baldr's correct. Ignore the carts, there are spies.'

'We're out of the city, and near the woods. They can't stay in there.'

'They need to.'

A sound of carts rolling. Aliette whirled around. 'They're leaving!'

Baldr stepped in her way. She stepped around him.

'Thief. Stay put.'

'Like the other women?' She turned to Reynold. He was staring at Baldr, having some silent conversation that she didn't care to see. 'Where are they going?'

'We travel south via horses. The carts will now travel via boat.'

'South as well?'

A gleam in his eyes at her question. 'South and they will arrive at our same destination. We don't have far to go. Another day, maybe less.'

'And they're safe on the boat?'

Reynold looked to Baldr again, who stepped closer. 'The boat is secure.'

Reynold at her front. Baldr at her back. This wasn't right. Being separated from her family made her apprehensive. Being kept from Grace frightened her.

Everything in her wanted to run towards the carts, but she knew this wasn't wholly about her. Eude had proved that point. 'Is that where the other mercenaries are? On that boat?'

Reynold held that eerie stillness. 'My men are at the dock. It's how we secured the boat for the cargo.'

He wasn't answering her questions and there was time to run. 'Are they safe?' she said.

'Do you think I would risk them?'

There was a risk. She watched the carts slowly travelling towards the river. Two men attached to the carts. One man, Guarin, riding alone. Only three mercenaries and much too precious a cargo.

Unable to stand by, she took steps towards them, willing them to know she was just there. They couldn't travel faster than she could run.

Baldr moved to stop her again. 'Don't you dare,' she said.

'That's enough,' Reynold said. 'We must go.'

'Can we talk privately?'

'No.'

Did she trust Reynold wouldn't put her family, put his daughter, in danger? 'Tell me truly.'

'They are as safe as we can make them,' Reynold said, walking away.

That wasn't an answer either.

Riding with Baldr was nothing like riding with Louve. He was larger, thicker, and there wasn't enough space on the saddle for them both. At her suggestion that she ride in the front of him, like the other women, in a place that presumably would be more comfortable and have more room, Baldr looked alarmed.

She was left with clutching the back of his tunic with each sway of the horse and fearing she'd fall off any moment. 'I could ride with another.'

'He wanted you to ride with me.'

To give the illusion to spies that she was a whore. But if she was a whore, Baldr acted as though he was raised in a nunnery. His back was stiff, his arm rigid on the reins. His head kept craning forward as if looking for trouble from Reynold.

There would be trouble, but it would come from her. She'd agreed to travel, but for her family's sake. Her family who weren't near, but on some boat in the middle of the Seine.

The fact she could see the boat through the trees was no comfort. It was travelling slower than them and with each breath was becoming smaller and smaller.

Feeling the panic to be near them, needing a distraction from her all-too-frequent thoughts of Reynold, she asked, 'Tell me of yourself, Baldr.'

He jerked. She clenched his tunic, pinching his skin underneath, and he jerked again. By luck she stayed in her seat.

'You don't want to know,' he said.

They wouldn't discuss his past then, though she was curious. He spoke French, but wasn't. What lands did he come from, why was he here now? 'Do you like being a…mercenary?'

Baldr shifted again, his great weight shifting her as well. She'd plunge to her death trying to talk. That left watching the trees around them and the other men who were quiet. She guessed Reynold still rode at the front, but Baldr's great width blocked any view forward. She'd known only Paris her entire life. This area was rural, quiet, beautiful, and her family were missing it. Reynold travelled as if he knew where he was going. Did he prefer it here as she was beginning to? Exhaling roughly, catching herself, she needed to not think of Reynold. She needed to remember he wanted—

'I hate being a mercenary,' Baldr said.

Aliette straightened. Finally, someone would talk directly to her. Louve with his riddles wasn't helping her understand Darkness. Except Baldr didn't elaborate, didn't say anything more.

'Is it the guarding, the waiting in the dark or...?' She couldn't say the word killing.

Baldr made a funny sound. 'I have my family. I—'

The pounding of hooves stopped their conversation. Reynold had pulled his horse around and to their side. She never saw him coming. 'You'll ride with me.'

Aliette ignored the rough exhale from Baldr as if he was relieved. She also ignored the other men as Reynold dismounted and came to her side.

She could not ignore the way her heart hammered as his hands wrapped around her waist and he eased her down. Hands that felt familiar, the very scent of him almost as overwhelming as his sudden touch.

She was upon his horse behind him within an instant. There was more space in his saddle, but he urged the horse at a faster pace, which forced her to grip his clothing as tightly as she had Baldr's. She concentrated on that as he wove the horse through his men and the trees until he rode closer to the front again. Closer, but still a bit apart. Enough to talk, though he had told her he didn't want to.

'What am I doing here?'

'You were going to fall off that horse. Baldr had trouble keeping you within my men's protection.'

Is that why she rode where she did and not because he kept her far away from him? 'Then let me ride with someone else.'

'What were you talking about with him?' he said.

Her first instinct was to tell him nothing. But she wanted to avoid thinking of Reynold and that included talking to Reynold for distraction. 'He hates being a mercenary and he can barely ride. Was he meant for this occupation?'

Reynold grunted. 'No. He dislikes every bit of it, except for the food.'

'Then why are you forcing him to do it? Why are you keeping him away from family?'

Reynold shifted in his seat. 'His family was starving and in debt. I gave his mother a year's wages before I left the house.'

'So he's a servant.'

Reynold turned his head. She saw the myriad

of grey in his eyes. The sharp criticism before he spouted his words. 'Is that what you want to think? You took in Vernon, Helewise and Gabriel. Why can't I take in family as well?'

Family. He had his own, but where were they? Reynold never seemed as though he needed anyone. Except when he held Grace. She ignored the image of him cradling his daughter. 'How did you meet him?'

'I was travelling through his village. My men at the time are not the same as you know today. They were cruder and damaged some fields. Baldr's father was unwise and confronted me. His mother offered us food. I accepted and she ladled every drop of her dinner into bowls she borrowed from the other villagers. It was…good. So I took him in.'

'Why?'

He shrugged. The brush of his shoulders, the pull of his wool tunic she clenched in her palm. She released her grip. Eased her hand more flatly again his sides. He breathed deeply as if he could feel that small touch.

'That soup couldn't have been that good to take in her son. You took him in because they needed you to. To save their pride you paid wages in advance. Did he know how to hold a sword?'

'His father was a tenant farmer, his father before that tilled the land as well.'

It would explain Baldr's brute strength. He was more used to shoving a plough through a rocky field than escorting a woman.

'What were the terms?'

Reynold huffed. 'It doesn't matter. You heard him. He hates being a mercenary and I am a cruel master keeping him from his family.'

She deserved his ire. 'Is this how it will be between us?'

'There is no us.'

Cruel words with a bite to them, but it was safer to talk of Baldr then them. 'Tell me.'

'I offered it to both her elder sons. A pouch of silver for one year. Baldr was not quite the youngest in the family, there was a babe, but he was least useful to farming, so he volunteered. The year is not up yet.'

Cruel words, generous deeds, and another example of Darkness's contradictions. But why did he do what he did?

'Tell me something of your past now, Aliette,' he said.

Why ask. He didn't care. 'You've heard enough of mine. Why don't you tell me yours?'

Silence as she expected from him.

'That's what I thought,' she repeated his words.

Though there was a part of her that did trust him. She'd offered herself to him, she slept soundly though he should be an enemy, but she couldn't fully…freely…trust someone who hid themselves so completely.

They were followed. Reynold never saw them. His scouts never heard them, but everything in him felt the eyes upon him.

They were more inland from the Seine now and the boat was far in the distance. He knew by nightfall the boat would catch up and dock on the other bank. Then they'd start the journey again tomorrow. But with every warning in him clamouring, he thought to abandon camp earlier than planned. This night wasn't to be trusted.

Signalling for rest, he dismounted and helped Aliette to her feet. When he could bear to hold her hand no longer, he walked into the woods to wait, to watch, to listen. His men, Louve, would know what to do.

For now, he needed to focus on who followed them, what danger surrounded them. Where they could escape, but in the quiet of the trees with the commotion of his men behind him, he could only think of her.

Her in the dark tunnel with wide blue eyes. Her conversing with Louve, with Baldr. The seething jealousy he felt as she kept gripping the gentle giant. The way she felt against his back. Her fascination with the countryside. He watched and was aware of everything she did. He wondered how she'd react when they arrived in Troyes. When she saw the bed he'd had custom-made to resemble a tree, like in the story of *The Odyssey*. Why had he—?

'The boat is turning the last curve. You can see it now if you want,' Louve said.

'I thought you'd be too busy to irritate me.'

'I thought this time around I'd let the others set their own camp. They know where you want your tent by now.'

'And the horses?' Reynold asked.

'You don't care about the horses,' Louve said.

'Do the men need anything?'

'You don't care about them either.' Louve crossed his arms. 'We both know who you want to talk about. And I know you want to know what was said between us. How it felt to ride—'

'No more.'

'You all didn't talk much.'

'We talked of Baldr. It was enough.'

Louve laughed. 'Was that her choice or yours?'

Reynold ignored him.

'And there's the truth in your mutinous silence.' Louve's mirth died. 'She shared her past with me.'

And he was all kinds of fool. Reynold would take the bait this time. 'Tell me.'

'You should tell her the truth. She's worthy of it.'

'I can't. If the worst scenario occurs, then there might be protection for her.'

'Or for your daughter,' Louve replied.

Reynold reached for his dagger before he realised what he was doing. Louve caught it and raised his brow. Willing himself to calm, Reynold said, 'I won't sacrifice either one of them.'

'No, it's apparent to all despite your distance you'd sacrifice yourself first.'

He never sacrificed himself. That was the point of living the way he did and hiring the men he surrounded himself with. All of them would make the sacrifice.

But the mere image of Louve protecting Grace or Aliette flooded him with protective jealousy. 'Says the man who talks of loyalty as if the rest of us have any of it,' he scoffed.

Louve looked to the Seine, then back to him. 'I think you're learning it despite yourself.'

'Tell your story and be done with it, then send Baldr here as well.'

The sparse moonlight didn't allow her to see across the water and, despite the freezing weather, no fire behind her on the other side lit the way. If Aliette hadn't seen the boat dock when the sunlight was dying, she wouldn't know where to look.

The crunch of the icy ground behind her told her someone approached. The way her body felt told her who.

'You need to get some sleep.'

Her body was stiff from standing, from staring out across the water, but it didn't demand rest. 'I'm not tired.'

'It's cold.'

She was past feeling the weather and still there was no movement from the other side. At twilight, she'd seen a few people milling around the boat, but she couldn't decipher whom. All she knew was that her family and Grace were on the other side and she was too far away.

Why this mattered she couldn't rightly say. But it was made clear she didn't have a say…in any of it. Kidnapped, kept captive to care for a child who wasn't with her. Her family kidnapped and kept away as well.

No matter her loose hair and clothing, she wasn't like the other women and Reynold had made it clear he had no purpose for her.

'It doesn't matter if it's cold or that I stand here, does it?' she said. 'I have no purpose being with you and the men. I thought you wanted me for Grace. Who is taking care of her?'

'My men.'

'Your men! Didn't you rage at me when they held her in the courtyard? And my family isn't your responsibility.'

'Your family is part of you and you are essential for my purposes. Are we truly back to arguing this? Grace is important to me. Gabriel…'

He looked away, then back to her, his almost-open expression closing again. Waiting for her reaction? She'd give him one.

'Gabriel, what?' she said. 'What do you want to say about him!'

'Why was Gabriel's punishment the loss of his ear?'

Aliette stilled. 'This is the conversation you want to have with me? And how do you know it was a punishment?'

His jaw tightened.

'They told you, didn't they? All those conversations I've had with your men and I thought it was their own questions, but it was you ordering them to ask.'

'I didn't order them to.'

'But you demanded the answers. You *are* a coward.' She relished his flinch. 'These *ques-*

tions could have been asked before you took them from their home!'

'That wasn't their home. They have no home.'

'Finally the truth! Will you acknowledge your fortress in Paris wasn't their home and certainly not that boat they are trapped on?' At his closed expression, she added, 'Are they even on that boat?'

'They are protected.'

'But we're not.' The boat was isolated, covered on three sides by water, protected by mercenaries via land. While she travelled with Reynold and could be surrounded by murderers. 'Why are you talking to me?'

'Why did you think I'd lea—' He jerked his gaze away, exhaled roughly, before continuing, 'We're in the middle of the forest. There is no one else about.'

Aliette's heart beat unevenly. She didn't know what to say. Too many contradictions with this man, and not enough truth.

'Who are you?' she said.

'I think you know, but are refusing to see. I… hope you are refusing to see.' He continued to look across the water. His expression a pained reflection. 'I am curious about them. Will you tell me?'

She wanted to tell him to leave, but knew he

wouldn't, and she wouldn't leave, not when she could watch over her family from here. Her family that he wanted to know of.

Of them, but not of her. Watch his deeds, but even his deeds to her weren't kind. He was just like all the rest. It was how her life had been, why it hurt more than any other she didn't want to examine.

But if something happened to her, would their stories endear them to him? 'Gabriel doesn't know, or maybe can't comprehend why they harmed his ear,' she said. 'From what he did tell me, it was the first time he was caught. It should have been a flogging or a branding. I suspect, since his parents were hung, there was some… rage that spilled over onto their son.'

'And his hearing?'

'I don't know what he was like before. It could have been why he was caught.'

'He seems sick.'

'In summer he'll be better.'

'He'll be better with shelter, food.'

Too true. 'When I found him, his hands hadn't one callous—his cries broke my heart. The guards completely ignored him.'

Reynold nodded his head as if in agreement. 'You never stole those loaves that day.'

What did it matter? 'Why else would I be returning them?'

His eyes narrowed as if she disappointed him again. She didn't care. 'You were protecting the boy. You're too cunning to steal from Ido. With that many loaves, *you* would have been flogged or branded.'

Did he want the truth? 'It wouldn't have been my first offence. If they had taken me—'

He clenched his burned hand. '*You* would have lost a hand with no coin to pay off the burgher. What were you thinking!'

'You would have done the same.'

'Sacrifice myself for others. Think again.'

Disdainful words, yet…he *was* sacrificing himself. Danger around them, but he was ensuring her family was kept hidden and safe.

Who was this man? It was as if Darkness was slowly revealing himself, but she didn't know if she could trust him enough to wait.

Looking away as if discomfited by her staring, he said, 'When you were caught before…were you harmed?'

When she was caught… Not so long ago, there were many days of starvation; days she was so hungry, she only slept. But the first time she was caught stealing, that fear and pain was etched forever in her memory. Now that she was older, she could look at it differently. Remember that the guard hadn't been as cruel as he could have been. Gabriel was proof of true cruelty. 'I don't remember.'

'You do and you're protecting him!' He paced to the side. 'Is there no one you wouldn't protect? Blind, crooked, deaf. Are there more I should worry about along the way?'

Darkness was pacing. Did thoughts of her cause such worry?

'I'll defend those who deserve defence. Anyone. Even those who feel they don't need or deserve it.'

Would she defend him?

Reynold tried to keep his attention on his surroundings. Attempted to hear the conversations behind him, but his entire existence was on the thief. He shouldn't be obsessed with her thoughts. Shouldn't be standing here. They were exposed to the mercenaries, the women, to whoever followed them. They could be seen across the river. But after talking with Baldr and Louve, he needed to know more of her.

And talking of her family instead of what was between them was safer. He *was* a coward.

Even so he could not hide from everything because the more she revealed of Gabriel, the more he compared his own life to that boy. The more he realised how remarkable and compassionate this woman was. He needed to stay distant, to keep her away with his words, his deeds, and yet…once again he donned his wings trying to be near her. Close enough to ask a question he already knew the answer to. 'Did he see the hanging of his parents?'

Surprise. Pain. She crossed her arms and took a step back. 'He did.'

'Did they see him?'

A quick nod was all Reynold needed to understand what had happened, but he couldn't comprehend the depth of courage it took. 'You took him. Why? You cannot even speak of it. There were horrors he no doubt witnessed. Slurs made— waste thrown.'

'All of that, but he had to see them.'

Aliette wasn't cruel like his mother. Why did she do it? 'Does any child need to see their parents hung?'

She wiped her tears. 'I… I only let him see when they reached the platform. I turned him before the deed.'

'Into your arms.' At her nod, he said, 'You took him so his parents could see him and see you.'

'My hands were on his shoulders.'

'You protected him. You went, though you never did before, because you wanted them to know he would be taken care of. You did it for them.'

'You act as though that is a fault,' she said.

'To put yourself up like that, to scar him to ease the conscience of two people who would soon be dead. What care have they whether their issue is taken?'

She shook her head. 'You don't understand. I did it for him, too. When Gabriel is older, he'll know he comforted his parents at that moment. That he was brave enough, displayed the courage to face that horror, so that he could provide two people who loved him love in return. It's how he can learn to love again. Don't you see?'

Never could he have guessed this fathomless selflessness. But love? He thought he understood it with Aliette, but he was wrong. He had to be wrong because she thought he'd leave her behind to be found by his enemies.

'Love?' he said. 'What do you know of it? You were abandoned just as Gabriel's parents left him.'

She flinched. 'They didn't abandon him.'

'Gabriel's parents both stole. They both got caught. If they had had any intention of providing care, only one of them would have taken the risk. They were fools.'

Disbelief flashed across her pleading features,

then her eyes grew wide. A curve to her lips, as though she knew something he didn't. 'You don't believe that.'

He felt a hard thump in his heart. 'I said it.'

'You did say it, but what would you have done? If you were your parents and your child was starving, would you risk your life?'

'Don't mention my family.'

'Why? You mention mine. Is the reason you find abundance in your stories because you have no one?'

'What if I have my books and stories, thief? All the better than to surround myself with people and yet still not find a home.' Aliette paled as if he had struck her. 'I didn't mean—'

'You did. All this time I kept thinking you used words to keep people away, that you couldn't possibly be that cruel. But I'm wrong, aren't I? You don't care about people. Just those stories. After all, you have a home, wealth, parents, yet they aren't surrounding you with love and affection, with warmth. Where are your parents, Reynold?'

Safely ensconced in a castle plotting revenge on their son.

She couldn't know that when he talked of enemies he talked of his parents. His family. Everyone assumed it was someone outside the united Warstone clan. No father should try to drown his son. No mother burns her babies to test their loyalty. Aliette couldn't know, but it was a mistake to fly so close to her because despite his words to keep her away, she saw him.

'Goodnight, thief, get some sleep.'

Chapter Twenty-Two

Horses' hooves pounding against mud and snow woke Aliette before Reynold ripped open the blanket that covered the tent's entrance.

'Get out of here!'

Long hours and she had fallen asleep mere moments before. Reynold was blurred through half-open eyes. 'What is happening?'

'There are fools who announce their presence. As if we would camp and not be protected.'

A bellow. The high-pitched whinny of a felled horse.

'They have met our guards,' Reynold said, his voice full of fierce satisfaction.

Aliette sat up. There were cries… 'Guards?'

'My men are in the trees.'

'Reynold! They've got fire,' Louve shouted.

Darkness changed in an instant. 'Follow Louve,' he said. 'Get out of the tent and go to the trees near our horses. There are men there who will protect you.'

Then he was gone and she was fully awake.

To hear urgency. Raw. Visceral. A clang of

metal, the slam of blunt force. To feel the barrage of vibrations and pounding. Horses? Men falling? Loud and incessant.

Aliette scrambled out of the tent, tore the blanket from the rope.

'Leave that,' Louve commanded.

Aliette dropped the blanket. At one point she'd have begged for a blanket such as this. The sounds were unmuted now, close, becoming closer. Trees blocked the way to see clearly, but the light of torches cast long shadows towards her.

'The women?'

'Safe.' Louve pointed over the clash of men. 'On the other side. We need to get you there.'

Glancing at the blanket as if he knew the importance to her, Louve pulled her close. A few steps away and the trees no longer blocked the fighting.

Mercenaries. Men, illuminated by raging torches. The arc of swords above their heads. Some thrusting, holding the hilt with two hands. Others swooping and caving their bodies to avoid death. And Reynold in the thick of it, a macabre spectre. The swift swirl of Darkness.

Except—

'What is he doing?' Louve said.

She felt the same. Reynold's sword was sheathed,

he needed help! Louve had the only weapon, but he stepped right to avoid her hand.

'You'll get him killed if you take my knife. You'll get *me* killed if we stay here. Let's go!'

Another glance, the melee closer. Reynold still standing. She could feel the heat of the torches. Some fallen, some thrown. A tree was ablaze, the smoke hazing the men. Were there fewer standing? They swerved left, she lost sight.

She followed Louve, ran and crouched as he did, grabbed a thick branch. Another turn. Swiped a sturdy rock, dropped the branch and grabbed some more rocks. With Louve in front of her, she tore left to get closer and hid behind a tree.

The reverberations of men and scattered horses thumped through her chest, but now she could see. Reynold downing men, but not killing them. His clashes were raw prolonged brutality. Why he didn't pull a sword, why the others fighting against him didn't pull theirs she couldn't fathom.

The other mercenaries leapt around as though they'd been part of this strange battle before. In the corner of her eye, she caught Louve entering the fray with a shout of words towards Reynold, who jerked, allowing his foe to gain a punch. She pressed further against the tree.

Then she saw him. A man, an enemy, behind

the fighting and to her left. Hiding among the trees, but creeping closer, his eyes trained on Reynold's back. His hand locked around a dagger's handle for an easy strike.

She palmed the rocks she'd gathered in her gown. She'd get one, maybe two chances to take him down, the trees a barrier, the mercenaries fighting another.

The first fit her hand perfectly, but wouldn't take him down. The next heavier and too cumbersome to throw. She glanced at Reynold, his back exposed, the man he engaged noting his friend who was creeping steadily closer.

Aliette heard no sounds or vibrations except for her heart and breath. Saw nothing except the man and Reynold's vulnerability.

She threw, the rock knocking against his temple. He crumpled down, but was not out, so she clenched the larger rock and leapt upon him.

The man fighting Reynold dodged towards her and she struck the side of her captive's head. He went limp under her. Reynold whipped around. His grey gaze like fire locked on her.

'You fool.' With a snarl, he released his sword at his side and plunged it into the man charging her. Reynold's sword slashed out again. 'Fools, all of you!'

Aliette was exposed, the cover of trees blocked.

She was helpless as one, two men were felled under Reynold's sword. He was swarmed now.

She'd done nothing more than she always did to protect herself, and her family. To grab objects and knock out her attacker so she could run. But she'd released something here. Something different. This wasn't the battle as before. The men no longer fighting as if they'd seen it all before.

Crouching low against the enemy she'd felled, his chest rising and lowering, she felt all the fool if she were to die here like this, so steadfast on saving Reynold when her own—

Aliette scrambled away from the man until she broke free and ran to the shore.

No!

The boat was engulfed in flames.

Chest heaving, his fists raw, Reynold strained to sense any movement at all. He recognised none of the trained men who attacked, but most carried heavy purses. It could only be his family who sent them. Splashing in the river, the sound of grief. Rage rising again, he sprinted.

Not fast enough. Aliette flailed her arms and body in the Seine. Remnants of the flaming boat protruded above the water.

The boat! Storming over her gown and chemise

strewn on the pebbles, he tore off his chainmail, the hauberk, his boots. No time for the rest.

Aliette, who'd saved him. And now, flinging himself in the water, he cried out, 'Stop!'

Abject terror. Cries of pain. Her heart broken. Reynold felt each sputtering gasp of air like a gash against him. She'd drown before she reached the opposite bank and was too far gone to swim back. Another stroke, a stronger kick, he wrapped an arm around her chest.

'No!' She fought him. A fist against his nose, a jab to his eye. The water was too deep to plant his feet and shove back. He could get no leverage on her. And all too aware that they were both vulnerable, exposed. He'd be unable to avoid arrows, fire. A thrown dagger.

'It's over,' he shouted. 'They're safe. We must swim back!

'No! Grace, Gabriel. My family.' Clawing at him, she screamed, 'The boat, the boat!'

Cursing himself, he squeezed her to him. Her hand uselessly slapped at the water's uneven surface as she struggled against his might.

'They're not there,' he called out. 'They're *not* there.'

'Where?' she whimpered, her eyes focused on the remnants of the boat, on the groan of splintering wood crashing into the water.

Damn his pride. She was worthy of the truth, but not like this. 'We're swimming back.'

This time she helped him. Small at first, her attention on the boat, on her family, but her legs kicked along with his until they reached the shore, and he dragged her on to the bank and rested her on her strewn clothing.

'Reynold,' Louve said, coming from the trees.

He covered her body with his own. Aliette clung to him.

'Did you get them all?' he bit out.

Louve stopped, threw two blankets their way. 'Yes. I heard the splashing—how deep did you go? I'll build the fire.'

The fire, warmth, could wait. Not the danger. 'All are dead?'

'None survived.'

No survivors gave them time to reach the house in Troyes. No time to waste, but Aliette's trembles were increasing. His focus was wholly on her.

'Leave. Take care of the others, keep all away from this shore.'

'We need to—'

Aliette's tiny hands gripped his tunic as if she was drowning. 'Now!'

Watching Louve retreat, he whispered. 'Are you well? Have you been hurt?'

'Where are they? If not on the boat, then where?' she sobbed. 'And why?'

He pushed up. She didn't release her hold on his tunic and their legs were tangled. This close, the moonlight showed little, her soaked hair darker than the clothes they laid on, the brightness of her skin dimmed by shadows and night.

But her eyes— Her questions were not soft this time, her gaze did not beckon. Sheened with despair and a growing awareness of betrayal, Aliette's eyes beseeched and demanded that he tell the truth.

'They were never in the carts. When we took them from the tunnel, we settled them in a carriage with blankets and food. One that was sent ahead of us, along a different path that will purposefully keep them a day behind.'

Releasing her grip, he felt her fingers spasm as if to strike. He braced for it, deserved whatever pain she deemed necessary.

'You hid them from me?' She scrambled out from under him, clenched her chemise which was locked under their knees. 'Where are they now?'

'Still a day behind and safe.'

She yanked on the chemise. 'How do you know?'

'Because the men who were on that boat, which is now gone, gave the signal.'

'What men?' She pointed. 'What boat! How far do the lies go? Did *you* burn it?'

When he shook his head, she continued, 'So your enemy did.' She threw the corner of her chemise down and stood. Naked. Glorious. The moonlight glistening off her skin, pebbled from the cold.

He stood with her. Gathered her clothes to drape around her and she shoved them away, shoved him away.

'I can't help them! I can't keep them safe if you hide them from me! How dare you direct my life, their lives? How—?'

'I'm the target.' He pounded his chest. 'Do you understand? The bulk of my hired swords are there protecting the carriage. I ensured *they* were the safe ones.'

'They're safe,' she repeated. Her sodden hair wrapped around her shoulders, a thick tendril around her neck. The flash of her blue eyes showing wariness, showing anger. The white of her skin darkening, chafing from the cold. The end of winter, but the air was sharp.

He took a step forward, holding out her clothes like an offering. Relief swept through him as she took them, though she only clutched them to her.

'But you aren't. You're travelling by this road, in front of many. Those men who attacked—'

'I knew they would come. I was prepared.' He took a step back, and another. 'But you—Louve had you.'

'You didn't draw your sword or a dagger. He was approaching your back.'

'And you just leapt upon him?'

She shook her head, her expression one of determination. 'Tell me. What was in those carts… that boat? What were your mercenaries carrying? And stop lying! Why would they target that boat if you were not on it? I want answers.'

He wanted to argue; he didn't understand why she was there watching his back. But she did need answers. 'Because it would hurt me, because it would send a message that they could get to me.'

Her brows drew up, her body shuddering, her voice scathing. 'A boat without your daughter would hurt you?'

'My *books* were on that boat.'

Shock and disbelief wiped out her anger, but not the outrage or the betrayal. Damn him for having this conversation here. His men far enough away so they were private, but at what cost?

He wanted to draw her close to him, to comfort her, to explain, to ask questions, to make her warm again. But his own clothes were saturated with icy water as well. He ripped off his tunic, tore at the belt that held his breeches.

All the while Aliette stood glaring at him. Cautiously, he took the chemise from her hands. When she didn't step away, he dressed her. First the chemise, then the gown. They were unlaced, but provided some protection.

'Your books,' she whispered. 'You knew they'd attack that boat and you put your books on it.'

'Yes.' The cost was heavy, but not if he lost Grace or Aliette. '*The Odyssey*, and the ones I've read with you, are in the satchels with my men. Do you understand now? I knew they would attack. I knew that boat was a target. I made it one. I made it…interesting—worthwhile—for them to attack that and not Gabriel or Grace. Not you.'

She clenched her clothes to her. 'I don't understand. How would they know that would hurt you?'

A small comfort to know she understood the sacrifice he had made by placing those small bundles on there. All the hours reading to her, she understood what his books meant to him. The stories had been his sole company for years. But then his enemies knew that. 'Because they know me. Know me like you do,' he said.

'*Who* is trying to hurt you?'

He needed to tell her. But it was cold, they were wet, Louve said the attackers were dead, but the shock that raced through them was easing. When it was gone, all that would be left was standing in the cold.

'They're not just trying to hurt me. They intend to kill me.'

He threw one blanket over his shoulders, unfurled the other and wrapped it around her. She grabbed the blanket, but shook him off. Again.

'Swear to me they're safe,' she said. 'That Grace, that Helewise, Vernon and Gabriel are well.'

He placed his hands on her shoulders. 'I won't let them harm those you love.'

'I know you're a Warstone.' She yanked at her hair. Pulled free a few trapped tendrils. 'I know the king has enemies. But who, who would be after you like this? Why the fortress? Why the subterfuge and the lying to me? Who is trying to kill you?'

He released his hands from her shoulders, and straightened his own. 'My family. And if they hadn't trained me into the unfeeling, cold-hearted monster I am, they would have succeeded in my death long before now.'

Aliette swayed. Her fear for herself, for the men who protected her, for her family, for Grace, plummeted away. Her terror brought by the burning boat, her helpless rage as Reynold dragged her to the sand instead of the opposite shore, disappeared.

Suddenly, as if the ground had vanished beneath her. Like knowing with certainty that Darkness could never be known, that Reynold would remain in the shadows forever. Only to be told in two words that everything she thought true... wasn't.

His family. Reynold's family were his enemies. They were trying to kill him and, from the men, the fortress, from his wariness with her, they'd been trying to do so for a very long time.

And then she knew, saw, everything. Every question she had about the man in front of her answered. Darkness—which expanded past her surroundings and imagination, which blanketed and bound every living thing in the world. Who could see far and make the rest of them blind. Who had the power to wrench everything she ever loved away from her—suffered.

Unbearable, utter suffering. A loneliness as vast and dark as an abandoned soul.

Like her own. Both of them harmed; neither of them wanted. Both unwilling to trust. This was the connection she'd felt between them that kept pulling her towards him despite the cruelty of his words, despite the danger to him. She felt this loneliness with him.

'Your family,' she repeated. 'Why?'

'We need to get you to a fire,' he said. 'You're trembling.'

So was he. But something told her he didn't feel the cold as he should though his breeches were wet, the melting snow was under their feet and every breath they exhaled was visible.

It wasn't the weather affecting her. It was *him*. This lethal man, with wealth and power. Who could make kings beg and had done terrible things to others, to her, merely writhed and endured through life and she *recognised* him.

'Do you mean anything you say to me?'

His gaze snapped to hers.

He said his words to push her away. Watch his deeds; she did. She was beginning to understand, but some things still didn't make sense. 'You didn't want to kill the servant, did you?'

He swallowed once, twice. 'My hand trembled. I was tying her up to dispose of her later when she threatened Grace's life. I reacted immediately.'

'You kept your sword sheathed tonight as well, until I was attacked. How did Grace's mother die? Tell me.'

Reynold's eyes looked everywhere but into her own.

Despite caution and survival, despite her certain doom, she took the one step between them and slapped him brutally across the cheek.

Relishing the sting in her palm, she snapped, 'Never again will you hide facts from me. I can't learn to trust you if—'

Eyes narrowing, his nostrils flared. Clenching her arm, he yanked her against him and slammed his lips against hers.

The kiss was nothing but raw need, infinite longing. His hips shunting fast, hard as his tongue tangled with hers. She cried out between dangerous kisses. Warning kisses. They called to her own threats, her own need to punish him. Because he hid in the dark from her. Because he lied to hurt himself, to hurt her. No more!

Tugging back, clenching his arms, hooking a leg around his hip. He cared for her family, for Grace, her. He did so reluctantly, angrily, but he didn't harm or abandon. He gave warnings and protected them. So many more questions, so much more she couldn't fully comprehend. But for the first time in her life, she could see in the dark.

He pulled his lips away. 'You have every right to be furious with me, but you're in my arms again. I could barely let you go before.'

Her fingers twined with his hair, flitted across his ear, along his stubbled jaw. 'I know. I know.'

'I didn't mean what I said in the study. I hid the truth because you need to be hid from it. There truly is danger.'

He was apologising because she had hurt him and he hurt her back. Apologising because his family wanted everything he cared for dead. The things he must have done over the years. The heinous acts to survive. But so had she, so had she.

'I don't want you to let me go. No more waiting.'

Adjusting his grip, he cradled and lifted her thighs until both her legs straddled his hips. He groaned low, feral. His fingers kneading, caressing. Dipping his head, grazing his lips below her jaw, he nipped along the cords of her neck. Hot breaths. Icy winter air. But she wanted more. She would *take* more.

She wrapped her hand around his neck, tried to return his lips to hers, but he kept firm. To wait? She tugged harder.

Growling, his breath fast and hard against her lips. His eyes unwavering as she pleaded, demanded. Then as if he was helpless, defeated, he pressed his forehead to her shoulder, and held on.

Just held on.

Fingers flexing against her hips, clawing his way into her. His body flushed and pressed against her. It was as if he was falling and he held on to stop himself.

Could Darkness fall? Expansive, swirling, forever... She knew with certainty that if she fell it would be there in that blind, boundless, dark endlessness.

If she fell it would be with him.

'Don't stop,' she whispered. 'Don't end this. Please, Reynold. Please. I want you.'

'Why did you attack that man, Aliette? When you were safe, why did you come to rescue me?'

She brushed through his hair. So many things she could say to him, but knew only one truth. 'Because you needed me to.'

He made a sound like a wound. 'Tell me something about this is true. That I'm not dreaming, that I'm not beating my wings towards a shore where you aren't there. Tell me that—'

'No.' She clasped his face in her hands.

He gripped her hands to pull them away. She wouldn't let go. 'All of this is true. Don't lie or hide from me again. I want to trust you. I need to.'

Grey eyes. Endless. Forever. 'My God. I—'

Darkness unleashed. Shuddering, clasping her closer, knees buckling to the ground. He arranged her beneath him. The sand and pebbles muted by the blanket bunched underneath, by her gown, by her chemise.

Nothing buffeted her from him. His kisses, his hands that drew up her gown, that caressed her legs, widen them so she could cradle him between them.

She wanted it all. Now. Here. They weren't safely ensconced in a study. Her skin was tight with the cold, with desire, with need. Her breaths painful because of the icy air, because she couldn't catch it and didn't want to.

The blanket he drew over his shoulders draped across his lower back, as he released his breeches, freed himself.

She laid her hand upon his cheek and his eyes flew to hers. Held.

'Whatever this is, it's true,' she vowed. 'All of it.'

He clenched his eyes. 'I hardly dare hope. I need you so badly.'

'Don't wait.'

Releasing his breath, a reverent caress against her cheek. A moment poised. Then in one stroke, he took her maidenhead. Pain searing, but he did not stop. Thrusting his hips again, he took, he gave. His head lowering, teasing her gown open, pressing kisses against her breasts, laving her nipples with his tongue. Her own hands gripping his shoulders, sliding under the blanket along his back, anything to find purchase as he dragged himself out and slammed back again.

And again.

Pain morphing to pleasure, as her bodied tightened to an unbearable degree. Needing release, she curled her body into him, pounded her fists. He curved his hands underneath to lift her towards him.

Bowing his head to her shoulders, his harsh breath, his prayers matching hers. Swivelling his hips, gentling his thrusts until her breaths grew jagged, until his own stopped. Until he gentled even more, she broke apart, and he drove his hips forward, holding them there. Just holding them there.

Her breaths eased before her heart did. Every limb shook as she slowly unravelled from him. He pulled away, gathered the blanket and drew it over them.

She petted him, laughed, and he lifted his head. 'You laugh and I'm undone.' Groaning, he flipped to the side. 'I hurt you. I couldn't stop, I wanted to, but—'

'You didn't hurt me…just surprised me,' she said, repeating her words she gave him before. She brushed away the darkest of hair that covered his eyes. Traced with her thumb the barest of marks in the tender part of his cheek. 'I may have hurt you, however.'

A smile softened his lips. 'Ah, yes, I'll watch for your elbows next time we swim.'

He came after her and kept her family safe. If she was broken before, it was only because she hadn't met this man who filled up the jagged pieces inside her with his own. If he hadn't snatched her from the streets, how much more of her life would she have lived longing to belong?

'Reynold,' she said.

'Hmmm,' He gathered her close, surrounded her with his warmth. With comfort.

'Thank you for not waiting,' she whispered.

Chapter Twenty-Three

'Tell me about them,' Aliette said. They were a sombre group who travelled the next day. The sun was full up by the time all the arrangements were made. Matters that never in her life could she have dreamed of.

Reynold attempted to hide most of it from her. Such as the bodies of the fallen men that the mercenaries had taken care of in the middle of the night. Louve explained there were pits and the Seine. Facts she'd remember next time she dove headlong into the river again.

Reynold waited as well until a rider waved on the opposite bank. An obvious signal that the carriage was intact and her family was well. She was happy they were no longer a full day behind, though she was still uneasy that they were separated. Her family would understand, but how was Grace faring? Mere weeks taking care of Reynold's daughter and her arms ached to hold her again.

For now, she rode with Reynold, her back to his front, his legs supporting hers. Everything today different than yesterday because he had held her the night long, because they had left the beach, warmed themselves by the fire, stayed in his tent. She was fed, held, cherished.

She trusted him.

He lifted a tendril of her hair. 'I detested this brown gown the moment I was forced to purchase it for you. When we arrive in Troyes, we'll order bolts of new fabric. Your hair, your eyes. To clothe you in green...you'd make every man beg for your favour.'

The brown gown would serve her well. Reynold avoiding his family, wouldn't. 'Tell me,' she repeated.

'There's a baker there, too, who is far superior to—'

'Reynold.'

He unwound the lock and let it drop. 'You ask me about my family after last night, after I told you their intentions.'

'There must have been something good in your life. Something—' She'd dreamed of a family her entire life—never did she dream of one that was cruel.

Exhaling, he rested his head on her shoulder. 'There was nothing, Aliette. Nothing until you.'

'Please don't tell me that.'

He splayed his left hand so she could fully see

the concentrated scarring in his palm, the fissures like veins that flared out around his fingers. 'This wound was given to me by my mother. From the age of four, she made us hold our left hand over a candle. Year after year until we could hold it long enough to satisfy her. She ordered it to burn out our weaknesses. So we would know what true pain was.'

'No more.' Clasping that hand, she pressed it to her heart, kissed it, and he let her, so she didn't let go.

'Once my father thought my brothers were taking it easy on me in training. They weren't. They were teasing and toying with me, but he was impatient for the pain to begin,' he continued. 'So he faced me himself. I was ten and every scar you see along my stomach, against my back, my legs, my arms were all made by his sword, his blade, his dagger. After I healed enough, I trained harder. Years went on with running, swimming, and, if it wasn't good enough, my father forced me under the water to hold my breath.'

Anger scraped at his words, but underneath, she heard only loss.

'That was the last time he touched me. I left that night.'

Now they were trying to kill him. Held by him,

rocked with the sway of the horse, and her tears wouldn't stop. Not for him, not for her.

'Anything else, Reynold, tell me something else.'

At his sound of bemusement she shifted in her seat to see him more clearly.

'You do this,' he said brushing her tears. 'Make demands, order me about. You don't seem to understand that no one else would dare do it.'

'When have I ordered you about?'

'When I first met you, you demanded food for Grace. And now you want to know aspects of my life I've shared with no one.'

All true, but how to tell him it wasn't for her, but for him. Because when her family left her, she remembered her brother and she found Helewise and Vernon… Gabriel. He couldn't, shouldn't, have had only cruelty and death.

'Will you tell me of Grace's mother?'

'I'm not a good man, Aliette. I did raise my blade to her, but she died before I could harm her.'

He had raised his blade and had been punishing himself for it ever since. 'I want to understand.'

'You understand so much more than anyone. You always seemed to, even before I told you.'

Because he recognised her as well. 'Then maybe I want something better for you.'

He trailed his fingers down her shoulder and

along her arm. 'Touching you is better. Your wanting something better for me is…better. You have no idea just the way you are with me—' He flashed a smile. 'I recognise that look.'

'You're stalling, waiting and thinking to distract me. I have no patience for such things. If I did, I would have starved to death.'

'So not knowing about me equates to your survival as an orphan? Hmm, that is something better as well. If you must know something good, there are my books,' he said as if talking of anything this personal made him uncomfortable. 'They've been my companions. And once, when my brother Balthus was an infant, he smiled at me. Those were good moments in my life. Good, but not like you. Nowhere near as much as you.'

Books. A smile. These are what carried him through? What kind of life had he had before he kidnapped her? Cruel, selfish. No wonder he pushed people away with his words. She thought she couldn't trust. She now knew he couldn't either. And yet… Reynold had somehow retained his humanity. A weakness that he hid because of survival. Because his mother had burned his hand.

'I had a brother,' she said, turning back around, settling into the strength of him. 'He is, was, older than I. I remember little about my family now.

Mostly they are just emotions to me. I like to remember that he was kind.'

Reynold did not hold her more tightly to him, but in the confines of the horse, and the way he gently grasped the reins, she felt as if he surrounded her. As if the storm that was him engulfed her. Except this time Darkness did not feel...dark.

'Why did they leave you?' he said, the words spilling out. His voice, for once uneven, broke on his words. '*How* could they leave you? You who come to anyone's defence, who won't leave anyone behind?'

A question she'd asked herself many times, though she always knew the answer.

She clenched his hand, her fingers digging into his palm before she released them. 'My family had grand aspirations. Always mimicking those in the higher classes. I remember my mother or maybe it was my brother teaching me to speak properly. To make it easier to be the expert thieves they thought they were. I was useless to them. Too clumsy to pick from purses, too honest to tell a sad tale.'

The irony of it all was she felt true pain the next day and every day afterwards. She knew how to plead for bread, for her life. And she had been broken until one day she was kidnapped by the man she should have feared the most and—

'Aliette, I wouldn't—couldn't—despite everything against us, despite my better judgement—leave you behind.'

She didn't know everything and there was so much more to say, but in this she knew. Linking her hand with his hurt one, she said, 'I know.'

Reynold knew, while still a fair distance from his home, that his enemy was waiting for him there. At any moment, he knew he could turn around. That despite his so-called burdens, there was time and distance on his side to stay safe and keep running. Except… Reynold brushed the top of Aliette's hand, ducked his head to the crook of her neck to breathe her in.

He wouldn't do it. His parents and his brothers would never stop pursuing him. If nothing changed, their children would be at war as well. After she gave him just a glimpse of her childhood, he realised they shared so much in common. His parents hadn't abandoned him, but them wanting him to be something he was not was as true for him as Aliette.

If he continued to hide, the reign of their hatred would continue. No more. Raising his fist, he called for his men to stop.

'What is it?' Aliette turned in her seat, her large blue eyes taking in everything he showed her. 'They're here, aren't they?'

He nodded. 'Up ahead, they wait for me.' Because he had set traps in the landscape and had ridden past them, noting they'd been triggered. Only a battalion on horses could have disturbed them all.

Because Eude had been killed in Paris and his death was merely a message. A message that they knew his location, who was with him, where he would travel next because there was no other possibility when he had the burdens of a family he chose. Because of Aliette and the future he wanted.

He'd been reading the story of his life for a very long time—the time for adventures and plot changes was over. He'd turn to this chapter of his life earlier than he ever dreamed and, because he loved Aliette, he would see it through.

Dismounting, he tossed the reins to Louve. 'I'll need your horse.'

'Reynold, what are you doing?' Aliette said.

Holding Aliette's horse firm, Louve dismounted. 'Are you certain?'

'You question me on my knowledge, mercenary?' Reynold said.

Louve snorted. 'If you know there are enemies

ahead, then there are enemies ahead. I question whether this is wise.'

To meet one of his brothers or his father at his home, to attempt to stop this, was the wisest decision of his life. 'What do you think?'

Louve smiled. 'I think when you get your head chopped off, I'll inherit some coin and be in charge.'

'Have you been reading my papers?'

Louve indicated to Aliette. 'No, I think you're learning about who's important…like me.'

'You'll know what to do.'

Louve's grin changed and he wrapped the horse's reins tighter around his fist. 'You never need to ask.'

'Reynold, don't. Whatever you do,' Aliette said, 'you can't go, not and leave me here.'

'Stay on the horse, thief. Stay safe. Stay alive.' He looked at her stomach and back into her terror-filled eyes. He had lain with her in all ways. It was possible she carried his child. He knew she carried his heart. 'The carriage with your family will catch up with you soon. I need you to do this. Do you understand?'

'I don't agree.'

'I wouldn't want you to.'

With a subtle kick, Reynold rode away from the life he led and the game he played very well.

Rode it towards another fate he knew nothing about, with no control or power to stop whatever force waited to kill him.

And because he couldn't stop wishing to be closer to her he turned to catch one last glimpse. He saw his future wife clasping her arms around herself, rocking on the horse he'd left her on, staring at the setting sun, at the light dimming from twilight into night.

Chapter Twenty-Four

The torches surrounding his favoured home were ablaze, which made it all the easier to see the armed men surrounding it and his brother Balthus at the top of the gate.

One swift arrow and he'd be dead. Instead, the gate swung open and he rode into the courtyard. Balthus ran down the stairs as he dismounted.

It had been years since he'd seen his youngest brother. Gone was the flush of youth, he was a man now, a warrior in his own right. His death would come down to a true fight.

So be it. For once his hand was steady.

'Sheathe your sword, Brother, you can see mine is not drawn,' Balthus said. 'You've had a long journey and I've prepared food for you.'

Reynold did not take his hand from the pommel while there were men with their bows on shoulders. He had no place for cover, but he could draw fast enough for one strike...which was all he needed.

Balthus looked around him. 'Although I have

to admit, I had food enough prepared for more than you. The others won't be coming?'

'Never.'

'Pity, I ordered the slaughter of your fattest pigs. Now, it seems, I should have spared one or two of them for another time.'

This wasn't the Balthus he'd talked to those years before, the one who stood next to Guy, who spewed his vitriol hate. At that time, Balthus's eyes were filled with judgement. Now there was almost amusement, as if he were pleased with the surprise of his visit.

Reynold wasn't pleased at all.

'Let's get this over with, shall we?' Reynold said, knowing the comment wasn't as he would usually proceed. It seemed he was learning Aliette's impatience. Or maybe... 'I need peace in my life.'

'I agree and your wine is excellent.' Balthus waved his hand towards the home. 'Come, let's sit. It's cold enough in daylight, at night, it's uncomfortable.'

Reynold wasn't going anywhere, not until he understood what was happening. He had expected to defeat whichever family member dared take over his home. To threaten them so terribly, they'd leave him alone. If that didn't work, to bribe, to beg.

Balthus raised a brow. 'You think I poisoned our supper? It's *your* food.'

'It's my house.'

'You've lived in some fine homes over the years,' Balthus said, pointing to the house. 'I like this one best.'

He did, too. It was why— No, it couldn't be.

Balthus noticed where his gaze strayed and raised his left, heavily bandaged hand palm up. 'I visited Mother again. She questioned my loyalty at Ian's brilliant plan to flush you out of Paris. You had only two directions to go: he chose one way—I chose this way.'

Reynold left nothing to chance. 'No one knew of this home.'

'True. The rest of them don't. Ian believes I travelled east, but I discovered this place on my own years ago and enquired about purchasing it. You can imagine my surprise.'

For years, his brother kept this house a secret from his family. There was no possibility for Balthus to divide his loyalty, so the only conclusion was: 'You have more patience than I gave you credit for. Setting this trap and waiting to spring it.'

Balthus sighed. 'Ian's intentions to kill you depended on me doing my familial duty should you flee towards me. Mother doubted my loyalty. I should boast and tell that I held my hand to the flame the longest of any as I renewed my vow to her. Of course, there is the fact that I might never be able to use it again.'

'So she doubts your loyalty and this is why you're here. Preparing food, inviting me into my own damn house. You want to align with me. You think I'm going to harbour you? Draw your sword and let's be done with this. One less Warstone brother to contend for the top.'

Balthus tilted his head. 'I didn't think you'd do it.'

'Kill you? You murdered Eude!'

'Ian's doing, that's how close he got to you. And those men you killed by the river were mine. I think we're even.'

'Raise your sword. My books are ash. They're worth more than any Warstone.'

'Better the books than the woman.'

Reynold knew not to reveal that Aliette meant anything to him. But a growl began before he could contain it and he warned Balthus anyway, 'You couldn't get near her.'

'That's what it is, isn't it? Your threatening death to your younger brother because the woman is making you protective.' Balthus lost his smirk, a flash of wistfulness crossed his features. It was gone before Reynold could decipher it properly.

'Can't imagine our sire ever raising his sword to protect our dame.'

No. If his mother got close to a cliff, his father would find a way to make her fall look like an accident.

Balthus shook himself. 'Needless to say, Mother doesn't doubt my loyalty and, despite what gnarled mess my hand will be when it heals, she continues to love me more than any of you. Or she will, until she discovers that I didn't kill you. Nor do I intend to.'

Reynold swayed. 'We're going inside. Now.'

The house was as Reynold remembered it. The reds and creams, the tall windows. They were covered with oiled cloth for the winter, but soon that would be taken down and the hall would be flooded with light.

The whole house was designed for light. He loved the sun, but it was more than that. When he imagined himself in this home, it was after a very long war. When he finally defeated his family. When that day came, he wanted light surrounding him and to never hide again. To end the war, he never imagined dining with them.

'Why are you here? Why are you acting as if we can simply converse like brothers?' Reynold asked the moment the wine was poured and they had privacy. So much change because of Aliette. He never would have felt the need to demand the truth. He would have waited for Balthus to drink, to loosen his tongue and reveal everything.

But Reynold wanted the answer before the drink. Wanted the truth to be told without influence, because his brother wanted to tell him.

'We are brothers,' Balthus said.

'We were raised as enemies.'

'True. Which explains why Ian tried to kill me after Guy's death.' Balthus chuckled. 'I can see you are surprised. I was, too, because it makes no sense to play his card early. But maybe he thought with you already on our parents' death list, and Guy murdered, everything would fall to him.'

He needed to ask, without asking. 'Everything?'

Balthus gave a knowing look. 'We don't have the Jewel of Kings. Which is why it surprised me that Ian took the chance. I always thought he'd take us all down once the jewel was secure.'

Ian was an excellent swordsman and cunning as well. If Balthus had escaped, then his younger brother had acquired great skill. 'How'd you survive?'

'Because Ian, instead of ruining the perfect parting of his hair, ordered an Englishman named Howe to kill me. It wasn't facing each other, but with an archer. A damn fine one, too. If it wasn't for the fact I know how to ride a horse into the woods, I wouldn't be here now.'

There were too many possibilities. 'If Ian tried to kill you, then how did he trust you with this plan to trap me? How do I not know he's not riding through the gates while we talk?'

'Because he doesn't know I know. I was hunting and pretended to make chase on game.'

Reynold knew better than to trust this, but the answers were coming fast and assured. Could his brother be that good of a liar? 'How did Mother take his deeds? She couldn't have been pleased because she loves you best.'

'Since Ian failed, he won't be able to surprise me again. I like that power of knowledge I have over him, so I haven't told her. Just as I haven't told her of this house. Because I like the power I have over you.'

No, this wasn't about power, it was something else. Something Reynold couldn't quite comprehend. Not yet. 'Or you're conflicted and loyal to us both.'

'He tried to kill me—you agreed to sit and have wine with me.'

Did his brother just differentiate between them? Could Balthus decipher that there was a difference between brothers? 'And so now there's trust between us? Do you think me a fool?'

'Then what is this?' Balthus said. 'We are talking, sitting, dining.'

'I'm merely extracting information from you before I kill you,' Reynold replied.

'You could since you are the better swordsman. But my men would kill you directly after.' Balthus tilted his head to the side. 'I remember you. I remember you…protecting me.'

He had loved his sibling and had incurred numerous punishments trying to protect him. 'You were too young when I left.'

'Your screams made an impression on me. They hurt you far worse than the rest of us because of it. Encouraged our brothers to lay waste to you as well. Ian and Guy bragged about it long after you left. They thought you weak to leave.'

'I came out the better for it by leaving.' And Balthus had come to harm with his parents' manipulations. He'd abandoned his brother to a cruel fate.

'And I, left behind, didn't,' Bathus said. 'Or is it, I shouldn't forgive you for leaving me with them?'

Uneasy with how quickly his brother understood him, Reynold stood. 'Warstones never ask for forgiveness. What is the point of this misguided conversation? There are many years since then and there can be no true trust between us. There's been too many harms done.'

Balthus frowned. 'Maybe so, but I want to know why you protected me when they hurt you for it. I couldn't have done anything to earn it.'

And in that, Reynold understood what Balthus hadn't. He knew because of Aliette. That sometimes compassion didn't have to be earned. It was simply there.

He wanted to deny he'd done it because he cared for the infant Balthus was, but answering with a lie wouldn't solve anything…if there was something to solve. 'I didn't want you to turn out like the rest of us.'

Balthus's eyes widened and Reynold knew he revealed too much of his remorse. A mistake.

A weakness. A word his mother used. But Aliette knew the truth of him—did he feel weak with her?

Reynold held out his left hand, the one badly scarred, the one Aliette had shed tears over. That moment had only given him strength…and the beginning of something else. The ability to trust. Though, for now, caution when it came to his brother was necessary. Still… 'I don't deserve your forgiveness for leaving you with them.'

Balthus's eyes gleamed with something like

awe and wonder. 'You don't, but you want to ask me for it anyway. You're as tired of all this as I am. Just as I hop—'

A booming voice hailed a greeting, two called out in warning. A creak and neighing of horses underscored by the uneven rumble of carriage wheels. Above it all a child was wailing broken sobs that cut across the night air and made Reynold break into a cold sweat.

Heart stopping, Reynold drew his sword. 'You'll stay here.'

Balthus looked to Reynold, to his sword and shrugged. 'The wine may be gone upon your return.'

Sword out, Reynold rushed outside. The gate was open and the courtyard was littered with Balthus's men, his own, Louve, the carriage that had carried his daughter.

Everyone he had told to stay away were here with his enemy, with his family. Every emotion flooded him as well. Frustration, anger, joy and overwhelming fear. He couldn't move as it overtook him.

Aliette, holding Grace, walked up to him. A litany of sounds from her lips, a song. 'There he is. There he is. I told you he was here and that we'd all be together again. See, we are!'

She never stopped until she was within his

reach. Until his daughter was within his reach. His daughter. 'She's… I can *hear* her.'

At his words, Grace whipped her head towards him. Her cries stopped. Her wet, reddened eyes widened. She hiccupped, once, twice. Aliette patted her back.

'All of France can hear her.' Helewise hobbled up. 'Hasn't stopped since the moment the carts were drawn away. Days of her crying. I could hardly get food down her and, when I did, she mostly spit it up or choked. When we joined Aliette, she started babbling.'

'She was trying to ask for you, Reynold.' Aliette said, her eyes tender.

Reynold felt his hand slip on his sword as he took in his daughter, his future wife. Vernon and Gabriel were standing next to Baldr and Guarin. Louve looked as though he would burst with laughter.

Sheathing his sword, he held open his arms. 'Give her to me.'

'Here you go.' Her tone was half-amusement, half-warning, and Reynold caught Aliette's narrowed gaze above his daughter's head. The thief was not pleased about something.

'What is wro—?'

'I'm glad I had the food prepared,' Balthus

said behind him. 'It seems we'll need every bit of it now.'

Swiftly, Reynold stepped between Balthus and Aliette.

'I'm his younger brother, Balthus.'

Reynold watched the silent interplay between his brother and Aliette. Both wary, both with their chins determined. Then Aliette smiled and Balthus just looked flummoxed. He knew that feeling well.

Everything about her demeanour was warm and friendly, but he felt her ire directed towards him all the same.

'It's nice to meet you, Balthus.' She rubbed a hand against his daughter's back to ease the hiccups. 'I'm Aliette and this is Grace. Behind us are Vernon, Helewise, Gabriel. Oh, and I'm sure you'll meet the men.'

Reynold looked to a man he shouldn't trust, to a woman he'd lay his life down for. For once, he felt as if the wings he made, which had failed him over and over, were finally and completely perfectly formed. Because within his reach was more than he ever dreamed of—his wings could withstand any upcoming storm.

He turned to Balthus. 'Well, my Brother, it appears we have much to catch up on.'

His brother's eyes sheened with understanding. 'So simple.'

'Not simple,' Reynold said with echoes of a recent conversation in his mind. 'Extremely complicated. But I should let you know I've become rather fond of complications.'

Chapter Twenty-Five

'You're starving,' Reynold said behind her.

'I couldn't eat,' Aliette replied, knowing she'd never said those words before in her life. But so many things had changed since she'd met this man who wasn't as dark as the night sky she now stared out at for answers.

Unlike the windows downstairs, these windows were only shuttered, and she threw them open while Grace slowly fell asleep in her basket.

The private rooms were more spacious than the fortress in Paris. It felt like home though she could see the strength of the gates and walls surrounding, and the land outside had been maintained for optimal protection.

'You're—angry with me,' Reynold said.

'Furious,' she said refusing to turn around to acknowledge him in any way. She'd been hurt when he rode off without her. She thought she'd made it clear he wasn't to take the road alone again.

She wanted to follow him immediately, but they had to wait for the arrival of her family and the rest of the mercenaries. What Aliette hadn't expected was an inconsolable Grace and a worn-out Helewise and Vernon who had been caring for the child. The cries had broken her heart. But when Grace placed her hand on Aliette's cheek and started wording sounds in a voice so pitiful, she cried. This child could speak—she could talk and hear. She just needed her father.

'Why?'

'So many books from great thinkers and you cannot guess?'

'You weren't angry when I left,' he said. 'So I can only surmise you're angry because I did.'

'Aren't you clever?'

Utter silence except the sounds of the great banquet in the Hall below which were muffled through the thick oak doors. What could be heard was much laughter as the flagons of wine that Reynold authorised were poured.

'Turn around and face me,' he said.

'No.'

He gave some growl of displeasure. She ignored that as well. He had done plenty of deeds she wasn't pleased with.

'Is it because I left and you think I abandoned you like your parents?' he said. 'You compare me to them? Why am I not surprised! It was my duty to face him. Not you, not anyone else.'

They had already talked of this and he truly didn't understand. 'There's a part of me that was hurt terribly when my parents rejected me and there is a part of me that feels unworthy. But it goes further than that. It's not up to you to decide what's best for me. I am no child. You don't own me, you never will. I had hoped that we could be partners, but you are not prepared to do the hard thing. To take the leap of faith.'

'Please turn, Aliette.'

She shook her head. Face Darkness and his eddying gaze? She had no strength against it and she needed to bend him to her this time. She'd argued with him, faced him, struck him. She'd shared her body and her trust, and he still rode away from her.

'I'm trying to protect you. That man could have killed you.'

'He could have killed you,' she said.

'Then you would have been well cared for... and safe.'

At that she turned and faced Darkness. It was all there before her. Tall. Arrogant. The swathe of his dark hair, the long lashes that shaded his very knowing eyes.

But this time, he didn't know.

'No, Reynold, if something happened to you, I would not have been well cared for or safe. You would have left me in the worst possible way. I could never recover if I had an ounce of changing your deeds and you took that ability away. You left me behind...for you so that you can do some duty, fulfil some vow you made. I can't trust you if you think you know what's better. If you don't trust me.'

A flexing of his burned hand. 'It's a game. That's all. One I intend to finish.'

'But if you don't stop this, your deeds will get you killed.'

'I'm not dead, I don't intend to be killed. So nothing is wrong.'

'All those books and opinions and you can't see how false that statement is. I won't be dictated to again. You can't force me on to whatever path you're on.'

'I can't stop this game. It began long before I was born—I can only win it.'

'Then let me and my family go.'

He paled, took a step back, another. His steady gaze suddenly tremulous. His shoulders slumped, his stomach curved in as if she swiped a blade at him and he dodged it. As if she was on the attack and she was.

'Balthus already knows she's your child. He heard you ask to hold her. You don't need me for your ruse anymore. And it'll be safer for me and my family to leave. You and Grace are the target. I have no consequence to your family at all.'

'Of course.' Reynold swallowed hard, another step back until his hand was on the latch. 'It is for the best that you leave. You can…go. Perhaps partake of some food tonight and I'll arrange matters for you to leave in the morning.'

Aliette stared at the man who had once frightened her. Who had manipulated, deceived and hadn't placed his trust in her. She looked at Darkness, who was now giving her the freedom to choose.

'What are you doing?' he said.

'I'm sitting.'

'I agreed that you are no longer captive.'

'I'm not going to be dictated to by you, Reynold. Balthus doesn't act like your enemy.'

His eyes darted to her, to another chair and he walked slowly to it. All the aspects of his elegance were there, but the arrogance was gone, humbled. It was that vulnerability which gave her hope.

'He doesn't,' he said. 'But we haven't had time to talk. He isn't safe—I cannot trust him. It was his men who attacked our camp.'

'And now he eats at your table.'

Entering the courtyard, seeing Reynold, then a

man approach behind him. Younger, but so similar. Aliette knew who he was.

But he wasn't who she expected, not after Reynold's depiction of his family. Because the man who stood just behind Darkness was as torn and conflicted a man as she'd ever seen. In that she wanted to forgive him, to give him and Reynold a chance.

'I don't understand this,' he said. 'Why are you not leaving?'

'I'm listening to you, Reynold. That is all.'

'I don't explain my deeds to anyone, Aliette.'

She crossed her arms.

'You want my feelings?' he said. 'I don't acknowledge my feelings even to myself. But I can tell you of my helplessness, knowing you rode into that courtyard full of my enemies. That you exposed yourself to someone I hid from all my life because it is right to fear them!'

'I won't let you do this alone. I'm not going anywhere.'

'And so that is it? You're staying?'

'That depends on you and what you're not telling me.'

'Why are you demanding this of me?'

'It's my choice to listen to you, just as it's your choice to tell me what happened between you and your family,' she said. 'No one demanding or dictating what they think is best for the other. I think this is how we can trust each other.'

He curled his fist. 'This is not simple. This is far more gruelling than you can guess. Once you know what I do, there is no going back to anything simple.'

'Perhaps so. But that should be my choice, too.' Gone was the superiority—Reynold looked wrecked. So close and they could have what she thought was there. Their connection from the pain in the past could only strengthen with what they must face in the future. She didn't doubt Reynold's family was his enemy. She just needed him to understand she'd be there beside him for it. He needed to tell her.

'Tell me, Darkness. Make the choice to trust me. To choose…us.'

He bowed his head, clenched his eyes tight. She waited. This time she knew she'd wait as long as it took because if there were slivers and cracks in her defences, he had them, too. She simply needed to wait until he could show her what was behind them.

'My parents are motivated by wealth, by power.' His words spilled out as if torn from him. 'Far more than I know certain monarchs are. I can't explain their cruelty any more than you can explain your parents abandoning you. But entire towns have been massacred because they whispered in the king's ear. I wouldn't be surprised if his unnatural hatred towards the Scots was because they want to divide England's attention. To make France stronger.

'As many books as I've read, as many years I've survived, the answer why they do the things they do continues to elude me. I only can explain the outcomes.

'That to gain the wealth and power they require it goes beyond mere chests of sequestered gold—it goes to something called the Jewel of Kings.'

He paused then as if expecting a reaction. She couldn't give it. Nothing of what he said was familiar.

'You don't know it.' She shook her head, and he continued, 'It exists as an oblong gem the size of a duck's egg, but it's hidden inside the hollow handle of an ornate dagger with scrollwork and gems.'

She shrugged. 'Don't they have enough treasures?'

'It's not the gems or the silver. It's what the gem represents. It's a legend that whoever—'

'Holds the gem, holds the power of Scotland.'

'You do know it.'

'Like people know of King Arthur and Camelot. The Jewel is Excalibur. But it's a symbol and doesn't exist.' She remembered this now. 'Vernon, Helewise's husband, likes stories.'

Reynold's lips curved. 'The Jewel of Kings is real and my parents want that power.'

'It's real…then for what purpose?'

'To rule over England and Scotland at the very least. They have resources. An Englishman with some cunning and a great network of hired thieves. A Scottish clan who accidentally got hold of it, but only have the gem now and not the dagger. Both are needed to win the game.'

'I thought it was the gem that was the Jewel of Kings.'

'It is, but combine it with the dagger and…'

'Tell me.'

'I have told no one. This is not easy.'

'It's not supposed to be,' she said as gently as she could.

'It's my love of books, cartularies, my curiosity. I've scavenged the deepest bowels of churches, stolen fragments of parchment. Over the years, I've pieced it all together. Combined, I believe the dagger and gem point to a treasure great enough to buy countries. I believe that's where the legend of Scotland came about.'

'Do your parents know this?'

'No. And as far as I know, neither does Balthus.'

'But he will,' she said. 'Because you'll tell him.'

'I can't trust him. Not after all these years. And I won't trust him because it wouldn't be right by you, Grace, the others. I wouldn't be protecting you the way I should if I turned my back on a Warstone.'

And yet… 'But it would be right by you to do it. If you gave him trust. If he was treated as you were, you'll both be wary of each other. But that doesn't mean you can't try.'

He shook his head. 'The power and wealth the jewel represents would turn a priest into a murderer. Warstones are already murderers. It's in our blood.'

'No, it's not. I know the man you are.'

His brows drew in. 'Don't trust me. You know some, but not all. The plots I've done, the lives I've meddled in. Some were good people, too.'

'You've lied to me, kidnapped me, but—'

'I raised a blade to Grace's mother intent on killing her though I'm her father.'

'I know. We all know. It's not because of your hair or eyes. It's how you look at Grace. As if she's every sunrise and sunset. You look at your daughter, as I wished, as every child wishes, her father looked at her. We all know the truth.'

He closed his eyes. 'I was cruel telling you

about Grace's mother.' In truth, he'd displayed a callousness he didn't feel. Could she sense it?

'Cruel…but you didn't lie to me how you killed that night or that you left her body.'

He shook his head. 'If I had done any different, the guards could have asked questions, tried to find a murderer. I couldn't allow anyone to find us.'

She gazed at the child asleep in the basket. Knew she wouldn't fit in there forever, but would always fit in her arms. Whatever was in Grace's past, Aliette vowed she'd face as well. For her and Reynold's sake.

'Who was her mother?'

'You and your important questions. Does it matter? I did not honour her as I should. My daughter will never forgive me.'

'What was she like?'

'She was a handmaiden from court.'

His eyes still closed, his expression telling her his thoughts were far away.

'Is this part of your game? Did you want to kill her because she intended to tell someone?'

He opened his eyes and pinned her with his gaze. 'Why are you asking these questions? What does it matter? I've killed hundreds in my games and I've killed hundreds more just because.'

'You taught me to read.'

'I don't see—'

'Then you taught me to *question* what I read. It is only natural for me to question you as well. I think you had a reason to kill her and it wasn't for your games.'

'Believe what you want.'

'Oh, I will. Because you tried not killing the servant, or Grace's mother. Their deaths meant something to you. Why? Was Grace in the room? I've seen how you hold her, Reynold. I know you love her.'

'I do.'

'Then why did you raise your weapon to her mother?'

As if he was helpless to, he took the steps necessary to crouch at his daughter's basket. To feather her dark hair away from her cheek. She moved restlessly and he stopped, gripped the basket's edge.

'She asked me to,' he whispered. 'She was dying. No healer, not even God, could save her.'

'You were there and she looked on you for mercy.'

'She asked for mercy, but my hand, it trembled. Grace was in the room, I tried to kill the servant, but couldn't. I was going to fail Grace's mother as well...'

'No silence now, please,' she said.

'She died before I could strike. I couldn't even give her that final mercy. I needed to—'

She couldn't hear any more of his words. 'Protect Grace. And you have. You kidnapped me. You've done everything you could.'

'Look what further destruction I brought.'

She pointed to the child sleeping. 'Look what joy you brought. You told me once your life wasn't abundant, that the stories were all you had. I want more for you.'

'The stories saved me because they showed me there could be something else. When I'm with you, I hope for our own story, but... Ian or my parents are out there. Grace will ask questions.'

'You can't keep thinking you know best and protect me or her. And you shouldn't bear the brunt of all the pain and misery of this game.'

'I deserve to.'

'No one deserves to. No one deserves punishment, or judgement or guilt. What we do deserve is love.'

'What would you know of it?' Reynold stood, stepped away from the basket and walked to the opened window.

He was hurting. That was why his words stung. How often must he have talked this way to others to protect and hide. She wouldn't let him anymore because she had seen his deeds.

'You're not the only one who observes,' she said. 'I watched Vernon and Helewise. I recognised what they had.'

'And now you feel love with them. With Gabriel.'

'I care for them. But… I never belonged. I always felt I forced myself on them. Like a piece of a game that tried to fit to another puzzle. But my jagged bits inside me never fit with them. I'm lucky that they let me take care of them. And we all care for each other very much. But if it came to Vernon saving my life over Helewise, I know whom he would choose.'

'What of Gabriel? He needs you. He comes to you when he's hurt. He goes to Helewise when he's hurt.'

'He comes to me for necessary things. I don't know if Gabriel is capable of love anymore… though I hope he can. His parents' death wounded him. And as much care as Helewise and I have lavished on him, I wonder if there's a stitch or a patch that can ever heal him. I think he has to find his own puzzle someday.'

She looked over at Reynold. Watched him watching the night sky. His back was to her, his stance wide. A ruler looking over his domain.

She knew otherwise. He stood this way to avoid showing her more of himself. He asked questions and pricked and prodded to quit the conversation. He said talking of the Jewel was difficult, but for that he had sat and kept his gaze upon her. He told her the tale of his parents and their greed.

But this he wanted to avoid. No. He *waited*. She wouldn't let him. Standing very slowly, she walked behind him.

Saw the tenseness in his shoulders, felt the heat of his back against her front. But she did not touch him. Instead, 'I know what love is,' she said, 'but I haven't felt it until you. I haven't felt as though I belonged until you shoved me into that fortress of yours in Paris.'

He leaned forward, placed his hand on the sill and bowed his head.

'I haven't felt safe or protected until you gave all your warnings that I wasn't safe and yet every action you've done since I arrived was to guard me. Even my virtue, something that should have meant nothing to a man of your nobility, wealth and station, you protected until I undressed for you.

'That's why I demand things, ask questions of you. Why I want more though it isn't safe.'

He pushed himself off the sill and turned around. Ruthless. Savage. Arrogance still drawn in every feature of his countenance. But his eyes...his eyes beckoned her to continue, so she did.

'You love me. That's why you've fought me, because you want to protect me. I didn't recognise it because I wasn't expecting love. But you fell for me.'

'Immediately,' he answered, in that even voice of his. It wasn't cold this time, but warm, tender. Telling her in one word that she was right about everything.

'Why then?'

'Because of my family, because of who I am, because you deserve so much more than me. But I couldn't let you go…just as I couldn't let her go.'

He shook her head. 'I didn't remember her mother's name if I even learned it. What will I tell Grace about her?' He looked at her apologetically. 'I'm sorry.'

'I want to know.'

'Why would you want to know my cruelty?'

'Because you did it to protect yourself and I suspect you've protected others over the years. You pretend this is all some game that you're manipulating and you've taken risks as difficult as Orpheus and Odysseus.'

'I will take more—it's not over.'

'I hope for your sake, it's not. I can't imagine how cruel your parents are. Massacres, wars? And I know your brothers are not innocent. But whatever it is, I can't imagine you killing them and what that would do to your soul.'

'It would be no more or less than they deserve.'

'Maybe, but is that for you to judge?'

'I'm no judge. I'm their executioner. I've killed hundreds, Aliette. I could not have done otherwise.'

'To survive. But…you've been different since you've taken in Grace. Louve and I both noticed. Underneath it all, you're trying to be better.'

He clenched his jaw. 'If it comes down to it, I will protect you by any means. I did unsheathe my sword today.'

'Only when it became necessary,' she said.

He shook his head as if wanting to deny her words. 'I will win my game. I won't give it up.'

'I understand that now. I'm not asking you to. Your parents don't deserve this legend. And it terrifies me that someone of their calibre would want it. But when you get this Jewel of Kings, what will happen to it then?'

He looked at her so long, she thought he wouldn't answer. They'd been talking for so long she almost forgot he could do this.

'It will disappear.'

Not the words, but his gravity of his voice was what gave him away. 'And you intended to disappear with it.'

He nodded. 'But not now. The Jewel, the task of it all, will go to someone else.'

'Balthus?'

He shook his head. 'There's no trust between us, but I will tell him what no one else knows as I will tell others. If only because one person isn't enough. I know that now. Even if there was honour and stalwartness...priorities change...or are changed for them.'

'For the better.'

'For the better,' he agreed. 'There are others who are aware of it and are already forming alliances. I'll send messages out. There will need to be a meeting.'

'With people you've considered enemies.'

'With good people who will consider me one. Just as you did. Why do you call me Darkness? Is it my hair?'

She shook her head.

'My eyes?'

'They're grey!'

He frowned. 'My clothing?'

She grinned. 'You don't like it when I have secrets. What if I tell you about Orpheus and Eurydice now?'

'Now when I've failed every vow I've given. To keep my secrets, to not let anyone close. You want to talk about loss and doubts and faltering.

Orpheus failed to save his wife from the Underworld because he doubted she was behind him!'

This had to stop. 'You think this journey we've been on is all about you failing? If you're Orpheus or Odysseus, I've been every bit Eurydice and Penelope!'

She pointed to her chest. 'I was an abandoned child, that is nothing new in Paris. But they left in the middle of the night…in the dark. I've hated the night and being kept in the dark ever since. I imagine that's how Eurydice felt, buried under the earth in hell. Hidden from warmth, from light and love. But her husband Orpheus showed it all to her again. That's what the story is about: longing and happiness and risking everything for it. He looked back. Maybe he did it because he was happy and overcome. Maybe he was worried she wasn't there and wanted to ensure she needed no help. But he risked everything for her. Orpheus showed love was worth that risk. Orpheus's trials showed Eurydice his love. That is what he gave her.

'You may think you're failing me, but you aren't. You said cruel words to shove me away and, because of my past, I believed them, until I saw you. And I realised all this time you've been protecting me, showing me you care, showing your love with your deeds.'

'But—'

Shaking her head to stop him, she wouldn't let him talk. These words needed to be heard. '*The Odyssey* isn't only about the trials of Odysseus. In all those years, Penelope had them, too. Other suitors, family that demanded she give up on the man she loved for the sake of her duties. She waited because her love for him endured through those trials.

'I, too, have had trials with what I've faced. My fear of the dark. My lack of trust in people. Then you put me in a dark tunnel and made me walk it.'

'I never wanted you to feel that fear.'

'It...didn't last. Knowing we were all tied together down there, I realised there was something stronger than the dark. My feelings for my family, for you. As for my trust, I think Grace had something to do with that.'

His gaze softened. 'She affected me the moment I realised she existed.'

'If it was just me fighting you, I would have found a way to escape. But I couldn't simply abandon Grace.'

'Because you found an infant swaddled in blankets in the dead winter. When you took one look at a starving child whom I didn't know how to hold properly, you demanded I fetch food.'

Aliette nodded. 'Then it became a matter of my

family versus her. And you made this fortress I couldn't leave. But, by staying, it forced me to look at the world a different way. You with your contradictions and secrets. With your reluctant kindness.' She placed her hand on his cheek. He leaned into her touch. 'You're not perfect, but you've been worth the risk...worth the wait. Because as different as we are, we're so much the same. I recognise you in the dark and would follow you anywhere.'

He kissed her palm, a curve to his lips that she felt. 'I am perfect. It's my family trying to kill us that makes our marriage less than ideal.'

'Marriage?'

'You don't believe I want to marry you?'

'I don't completely trust this either. This is new for me as well. I'm not used to being loved when I didn't demand it.'

'Oh, you demanded it.'

'How?'

'Informing me that I love you. Not waiting for me to tell you the depth of that love.'

'If I waited for a scrap of bread to ensure I wouldn't get caught, someone else would get it.'

'So I'm a scrap of bread.' He took her wrist. 'This is why I fell in love with you...this ordinariness. You do things around me as if they have no consequence.'

'Things,' she said, though she couldn't keep her thoughts. Not when he brushed his thumb against her inner wrist.

'Like comparing me to a bread scrap. Like taking in Vernon and Helewise. You were a starving orphan and you volunteered to help others. Like the bravery and compassion you showed Gabriel when you took him to see his parents.'

'They needed me. I…needed them.'

He shook his head as if he couldn't comprehend such recklessness. 'Like taking care of Grace and making room for me on the bench. Like singing and flitting from one room to another to gather items. *Everyone* asks permission from me. And you just took.'

'My gathering items made you fall in love with me?'

'Your backside is just as perfect to me as your front.'

Reynold was teasing her. She grinned. 'I'll have to gather more items in front of you more often. Maybe bend down to pick them up.'

'I'll be a dead man in a year if you torture me any further. Of course there was also the time when you encouraged my men to disobey me. To mutiny and talk to you instead of the silence I ordered.'

So long ago. 'I made you angry that day.'

'All the more reason to love you, but none more than when you wiggled your toes. If I hadn't already given my heart to you, that would have been the moment.'

'They are nice toes.'

'They are.' She loved every word he was saying. Her whole life she'd been starved of compliments and praise and his were all the better because it wasn't about the curl of her hair, or her unblemished skin. But about them together, sharing, yet she still didn't understand. 'Why, Reynold? Why these moments?'

'You don't know how extraordinary you are to me. There was nothing usual or typical in my life until you. Everything I did as a child had consequences. The way I walk, talk. Eat. All of it was regulated.'

His even voice, the elegant way he moved. It broke her heart a little, knowing this was beaten into him.

'After I severed ties from the family, I was even more rigorous to make sure I could take them down. So I could stay alive. And you—'

'I just do things.'

He linked his fingers with hers, the eddying grey of his eyes now steady. 'There is something I need to show you.'

With a glance at his sleeping daughter, he led

her to the room's other door and opened it. The adjacent room was expansive—entire regiments could march through because of—

Aliette gripped his hand. 'This bed.'

'It's not alive,' he said. 'It's just meant to look as though it is.'

It was attached to the floor, and spread across the ceiling...like a tree, the posts large like twisted oaks, the tops their canopy.

'It's beautiful! It's *the* bed, isn't it.'

'Odysseus was gone for years from Penelope. When he finally returned, she tested him. She told him she'd bring the bed down to him so he could rest. Only her husband knew it was a living tree that couldn't be moved. When he said so, Penelope recognised him. Accepted him. Loved him again.'

He truly loved that story. Had this bed built in the hopes he could live here with his wife who loved him in return. And Reynold had brought her here. Showed her this bed.

Love.

'Do you want me to test you, Reynold?'

'You're doing it now. Why me, Aliette, when I have done so much wrong?'

'You have done wrong, but you've been trying to make it right, and with Grace and her mother, in time she will understand.'

'I can't believe she will ever love me—I can't believe you do. Even if my soul isn't as black to you as it is to me, how?'

'You read to yourself when a passage in Greek is difficult, you hold Grace as if you never want to let go, you have taken in men who need you and…you're very good at untying boots.'

His brows lowered, his mouth quirked. As if her words made no sense to him, but pleased him at the same time. 'These things you notice?'

Releasing his hand, she walked backward until her legs hit the bed, then she sat. 'I recognise you—I accept you. I love you.'

'What are you doing?'

She slid across the bed and delighted in the way he followed until he loomed over her, his dark hair falling across his forehead, his thick eyelashes casting shadows across his face.

'I'm making room for you,' she answered. 'It's a marriage bed, isn't it? A husband-and-wife bed. A waiting-years-for-happiness-and-enduring-every-hardship bed. You had this made and it has been here waiting for us.'

His eyes lit with a feral need, a longing that he no longer hid in the depths of his eddying grey eyes or in his heart. To everyone else he would always be shadows and nightmares. Darkness.

But she could see him now and would always want him more.

'How do you know these things about me? *How* are you different?' he asked, as if the answer continued to elude him.

Everything in her wanted to comfort the longing in his voice. To tell him a thousand words to express the ways.

Threading her fingers through his raven hair and curling every limb she had around him, she whispered, 'Because I love Darkness.'

Epilogue

'I can't believe you have told me of all this,' Balthus said, looking around the hall, which was empty. 'I'll need a flagon of wine.'

'It's morning and there's much to do.' The air was warming, allowing them to look out in the courtyard should they desire. The mercenaries seemed to be getting along. It was all the encouragement Reynold needed to begin his conversation. He felt some satisfaction in surprising his sibling as he told him all the truth. The facts of their parents, the Jewel of Kings, Grace. At first, he believed he'd merely piecemeal the facts, slowly display his vulnerabilities as Balthus revealed his. But after the evening spent with Aliette in the marriage bed, he wanted it all. Now.

It had been difficult leaving the warmth of her wrapped around him. Her dark hair tangled on the pale linen sheets, one fist curled as if, even in sleep, she fought him leaving. After this morning, he wanted to revel in that warmth that she brought to their bed, he wanted to marry her and never have to think of intrigue or battles again.

He didn't want to place any trust in his family, but in the end, he'd have to place a lot of trust in many people. He might as well start here with Balthus.

'My telling you doesn't mean I wholly trust you,' he continued. 'Perhaps there will be more some day. However, with the dagger separated from the gem, there's limited time and we need to act now.'

His brother stood there. His expression confused, wondering...a little wary. But something else that eased through him. Perhaps through them both. A sense that they were brothers. It was something he hadn't felt for a long, long time.

'I've told you nothing and you've given me everything,' Balthus said.

'Not everything. There's only a smattering of coin at Nicholas's estate, Mei Solis, but it's all yours. And Nicholas, being Louve's friend, will give you shelter until you know where to go next.'

'I should have thought about my wealth. Leaving it all in our parents' coffers while I betrayed them wasn't intelligent.'

'If you would have taken your coin, they wouldn't have trusted you despite damaging your hand.'

'Mere moments in your company and I owe you a debt.'

'No debt—I shouldn't have left you.'

'I wasn't ready to go then. It took Ian's deeds to want something else. We may need that flagon for everything I want you to know. I've been privy not only to our parents' secrets, but to our brothers'.'

Years Reynold had toiled to acquire information, now it was being offered freely. 'You have to go. It's not safe for my family.'

'Just like that?'

'If we're brothers, then you know why it's necessary. If we're not, and I'm right in being cautionary with our dialogue, Ian will be expecting you. Either way you have to leave.'

'If you should ever need me—'

'I won't,' Reynold said.

'But if there's a chance—'

'I won't give you one.' Brothers they might be, but newly made brothers. For Aliette's sake, he would continue to be careful. For her sake as well, he would try to trust. In the end, Reynold proved that he could survive without any help, but more that he was the strongest of all his family. Stronger still for the love of Aliette and her found family. That made him stronger than both his brothers.

'Some day I'll prove you can trust me,' Balthus said.

Then they'd be brothers. Too much to hope for, but Aliette had shown him he could. 'That would be welcome.'

Balthus's eyes gleamed before he looked away and exhaled. When he gained his breath, he said, 'So you told me all this to gain my help. Take down Ian, gather the Jewel.'

'Don't pretend this doesn't align with your game. You get your revenge.'

'It must be done. Ian will keep with his plans until more countries are weakened, until he has more power.'

Ian didn't concern Reynold. Not as he once had because he had more important matters to attend to. Like lying in with his new wife, holding his daughter in his arms as he read to her. Teaching Gabriel numbers and swordsmanship.

'You won't need me, but I know he deserves to die,' Balthus said.

'So be it.'

A curve to Balthus's lips and a quick shake of his head. 'God, how wrong Ian is to think you're weak! Though I didn't intend it, I think aligning myself with you was the better decision.'

'Though I didn't intend it, I think placing my trust, sharing my food and coin with you has made me poorer.'

'In time, my Brother, I'll prove my worth to you.' Laughing, Balthus took a step forward as if he was going to clasp Reynold.

Reynold held still. Not encouraging, but certainly not stepping away. After a moment and more than a bit of surprise, Balthus completed his movement. Clamping his outstretched hand on Reynold's shoulder, squeezing it briefly before releasing.

It wasn't a familial embrace, or a handshake between alliances. But it was so much more than he had before.

Balthus looked over his shoulder. 'It appears another needs to talk to you, so I'll take my leave. But know this: we drink again tonight!'

Reynold kept his eye on Balthus, for there was only one person who could sneak up on him. 'What do you need, Louve?'

'Why can't you ever hear me?'

Reynold had asked himself that question many times. 'Maybe I don't want to—remember, I reluctantly took you into my employ.'

Louve walked to his side and they watched Balthus enter the courtyard to announce to his men that they were leaving.

'I'm surprised to see you this morning,' Louve said.

'You think me tamed.'

'I think you have found love and I can't wait to attend the wedding.'

'It will be this morning, for tomorrow you will travel with Balthus,' Reynold said.

'So I'm to be passed from one bastard to another,' Louve grunted.

'You volunteered to be my hired sword,' Reynold said. 'Moreover, you won't want to stay in Troyes.'

'Stay?' Louve quirked a brow. 'You never stay at one residence.'

'I can hardly be mobile now.'

'Ah, yes, your burdens.' Louve looked to the right, his mind far in his thoughts. Reynold gave him this, though everything in him urged to negotiate, to threaten. But this had to be Louve's decision. It was his life after all.

'I'll go,' Louve said. 'Last night Balthus and I had an enlightening discussion about your family history. I thought you were immoral.'

'I am. They trained me well.'

'So though you don't trust him, you expect Balthus to take down your family.'

'Ian first.'

Louve glowered. 'You can't ask one brother to kill another.'

'I'm not asking him.'

Louve smirked. 'You are a bastard. All those late-night chats, the extra training, and you were setting me up. Should have known your friendship came at price.'

'Will you do it?'

'I never liked you. From what I heard, Ian's worse, so should be easy.'

Reynold pointed to a corner. 'That chest is yours.'

'Looks heavy. I'm not taking coin to ensure your vengeance is complete.'

'I know you don't work for my coin, but it's Guy's wealth. I'll keep his land, but since Nicholas—'

Louve held up his hand. 'Since he earned it by helping kill Guy, I'll be happy to cheat him and gloat about it when I see him next.'

'There might be a bit of bastard in you as well,' Reynold said.

'You're only now realising this?'

Friendship. It was here all along. He simply needed Aliette to show him. Now that he had it, though...

'Only take out Ian if it's necessary. Only if it comes to it and you have the opportunity.'

Louve lifted a brow. 'It sounds as though you care what happens to me.'

'Of course I care. I promised Balthus you'd get him to Mei Solis. He's my brother, I wouldn't want him lost.'

Louve laughed low. 'You've learned about promises and loyalty.'

'Perhaps I have.' Reynold went to one side of the chest. 'Take the other handle and I'll help you out with it.'

'We could leave it here.'

'You'll need to put it in a hiding spot. In fact, split it up and find many hiding places.'

'You could tell me yours.'

Reynold stayed silent.

Louve shook his head. 'So we all get our own safeholds and we're taking down your family... who has the backing of the King of England.'

'France as well, although there's difficulty in Gascony.'

'All for this Jewel of Kings.'

'And the dagger. They must be together.'

'And a Colquhoun Highlander has them.'

'He has the Jewel. I fear the dagger may be lost.'

'You want me to help this Scot?'

'I want you and my brother to get it first. Then we'll keep them together and put them in hiding. We'll protect it from getting in the hands of countries and those with ill intent. It's too valuable and with its legend too dangerous.'

'So we form…a society of mercenaries and spies to protect a treasure and a legend.'

'It won't be as difficult as you believe.'

'I've been with you for years. Getting three men to agree on something this important is impossible.'

'Not this time around,' Reynold said, 'because the players who would agree with me to hide the jewel have already been playing the game.'

'You'll be sending out your messages again.'

Reynold gave a knowing smile. 'I already have.'

Louve shook his head. 'All this intrigue and marrying Aliette this very morn. How will you get the church to agree?'

'I am still a Warstone. I can do anything I like.'

'And you're in love,' Louve added.

'I am at that.'

Reynold hurried his steps to return to his sleeping thief.

* * * * *